ADDITIONSE FOR
We Were Angry

Jennifer Davis's stories explore with gentle understanding the lives . . . left behind after the land speculators and the lawyers and doctors and their kids who come for the summer go home to Birmingham and Atlanta, off-seasons as teenagers stretching into lifetimes waiting for someone or something to give them a good reason to leave. . . . [Davis] examines deftly why we choose to stay when we know it would be better to go, how even the subtle pull of a home to which we feel little connection can make escape feel impossible—examinations that have the vivid clarity of a William Christenberry photograph. *We Were Angry* is something special.

—Josh Russell, author of *King of the Animals: Stories*

Telescoping and telescopic, deep, depth-defying stories . . . *We Were Angry* has done all that. Davis has put a new New Southern nuance into her own special, gothically etched, canceled postage stamp of peopled place. This book is the next *Love Medicine,* cast with characters erratically ecstatic, gravely grave, and articulate in their own inarticulateness. They are all graced with a fiery grace and even as we watch their burned-off, burned-over, ever exhausted virtues and vices dissipate into spectacularly occluded skies, everything (every goddamn thing) stings and sings.

—Michael Martone, author of *Plain Air: Sketches from Winesburg, Indiana*

We Were Angry

we were angry

To Katherine
What a joy it's
been to navigate
this writing world
with you!
I am so
excited for
all your
future
successes!

Jennifer S. Davis
10-10-2022

A NOVELLA & STORIES

JENNIFER S. DAVIS

Press 53
Winston-Salem

Press 53, LLC
PO Box 30314
Winston-Salem, NC 27130

First Edition

Cover design by Claire V. Foxx

Author photo by Dotty McCaughey

Cover art, "A stop sign that was obviously ignored" (no.
44306491) by PensiveDragon. Licensed with permission
through Shutterstock.

Library of Congress Control Number
2022906556

ISBN 978-1-950413-49-2 (softcover)
ISBN 978-1-950413-50-8 (hardcover)

For Eric, Jubal, Silas, Tobias, and Elias

The author gratefully acknowledges the editors of the following publications, where these stories were originally published, often in slightly different form:

American Scholar: "We Were Angry"

Epoch: "The Lives of Diamonds"

Greensboro Review: "Orbital Debris"

Southern Indiana Review: "Lessons"

Tin House: "Those Less Fortunate"

Zoetrope: All-Story: "A Face Devoid of Love or Grace"

CONTENTS

we were angry

At our town, with its shuttered strip malls, its buckled porches, its peeling paint, its overgrown parks, where we spent idle nights screaming "Bohemian Rhapsody" and puking up Boone's Farm behind the broken playground equipment. At our teachers, with their beefy hips and feathered bangs and perky calendar-tracking sweaters: jack-o-lanterns, grinning turkeys, ho-ho-ing Santas, heel-clicking leprechauns. At how they made us kneel on the cool tile in front of the class during homeroom to press a yardstick against our knees to measure the length of our skirts. At our guidance counselor, with his lopsided mustache and shiny tie, his wall of books on ACT exam prep and colleges, books he never opened while he talked to us about exciting career opportunities in cosmetology or medical billing, the practical virtues of a vo-tech track. At the monotony of our days, their promise to unfurl one after the other with a bruising consistency as far as we girls could imagine.

Most of our fathers had left us years ago, some for women other than our mothers, some for booze or pills, some in foolish, selfish deaths: a truck wrapped around a telephone pole, a drunken dive in too-shallow water. Our mothers had us young, some of them younger than we were then. Our mothers were tired. Our mothers were angrier than us. They'd been fooled. They'd been cheated. They worked two jobs, sometimes three, spending their rare nights off at the Rodeo Club—their faces purling into their sun-freckled chests—bitching to some wannabe cowboy about the men who had done them wrong, the bosses who underpaid them, the daughters who were hell-bent on becoming everything other than what they'd hoped. In their absence, we experimented with different shades of eyeliner in the small bedrooms of the cramped homes we all lived in, the fans perched on our thrift-store dressers swirling clouds of our cigarette smoke, the music loud and thumping, or we drank PBR down by the boat landing in skimpy outfits we'd lifted from the sad selection in the Auburn mall, some dumbass boy strumming Zeppelin on his guitar, hoping to sing his way into our low-slung skirts.

We'd attended kindergarten in the church basement, the same church our mothers dragged us to each Sunday to prove to the rest of the town they were the kind of mothers who worried about such things as their daughters' souls, the gleam of their patent leather Mary Janes. We exchanged friendship bracelets, folded notebook paper into hand-held magic contraptions that foretold our futures: who we'd marry, how many children we'd have, how much money our husbands would make. We traded make-out partners at church sleep-ins, writhed to "Purple Rain," spent an hour each morning plastering our bangs with Aqua Net, sneaked cigarettes from our mothers' purses, shotgunned beers on rundown pontoon boats sidled up to the expensive MasterCrafts of cute-enough out-of-town boys. And even though most of us had boyfriends, boys we'd known our whole lives, we always hoped someone new would notice us, see that we were meant for something better. So we allowed those other cute-enough boys, vacationing on the lake for the weekend or week from Atlanta or Montgomery or Birmingham, to lay us down on the beer-stained couch in someone's basement. And sometimes we rode in the passenger seats of their Beamers, the thud of the stereos pounding in our chests, out the opened windows, while we worked the zippers at their crotches, their clutched beers resting on our heads as their thighs twitched and tightened. And we saw what we were doing while we were doing it, as if we were watching ourselves in some bad afterschool special, a cautionary tale about young girls heading down the wrong path, the kind of girls who blew nice girls' boyfriends in the school parking lot for a joint.

Because none of this mattered. None of this was real. This was the early '90s, before girls like us could spend their nights constructing better, public versions of themselves on social media. Our true lives were spelled out in private, in our journals, our scrapbooks, the covers of our school notebooks: our names intertwined with those of movie stars; lists of our top ten places to live; magazine cut-outs of wedding gowns pasted onto snapshots our mothers took of us before dances or proms, our hair fluffed, our lips stained and puckered in the self-conscious way of girls still young enough to hope someone might actually be watching.

Mandy Miles was not us. Mandy was tall and blonde and blue-eyed, with a zippy little Miata her father bought her because Mandy was the kind of girl whose father stayed, a father who bought his daughter a brand-new, apple-red car for her sweet sixteen, a father who named his boat after her, a father who owned a pharmacy a town over, a better town. He scooped tiny pills into tiny bottles for old people and anxious women and men with back injuries from the textile mill, and he made so much money doing a job that didn't seem nearly as complicated as working a cash register or remembering a ten-top's dinner orders. Mandy's mother didn't look old or sad or dried out. Diana Miles was a prettier, softer version of Mandy. The same blonde hair. The same blue eyes. She wore a heart pendant encrusted with sparkling diamonds, and she was in the habit of poking one delicate finger through the heart of that heart when talking, and Mrs. Miles was always talking. She was the kind of woman who assumed people wanted to hear what she had to say. She was the kind of woman men listened to. The Mileses lived in a sprawling house on the side of the hill overlooking the lake, and we imagined them there, sitting on their porch in the late afternoon in matching chaise lounges, their iced teas sweating in the circle of their hands, the sun fading like a shutting eye into a thin seam of light as they admired all that lay before them.

Once, when we were in grade school, we went to a sleepover birthday party at Mandy's sprawling house on the side of the hill by the lake. Our mothers dropped us off with our Strawberry Shortcake sleeping bags, our stashes of drugstore makeup we'd swiped from their purses, our presents for Mandy, cheap gifts—puzzles and marbles and plastic, marble-eating hippos—that embarrassed us the minute we stepped into that house with its matching appliances, sleek hardwood floors, and artwork lit by separate little lights. Mandy had recently moved to our town from Atlanta, her parents in search of a slower pace, a rural life—fishing off the pier, golfing in the middle of the week, small-town values—and we assumed this party was her mother's idea, her mother's want for Mandy to make new friends in a new place. Mandy's father brought Pizza Hut from the next town over, where he worked, the better town that had a Pizza Hut, a Quincy's Steakhouse, a Red Lobster, but did not have the beautiful lake with the more affordable lakefront property that was still too expensive for our mothers to own. We ate pizza, a birthday cake shaped like a Barbie, ice cream hardened by Magic Shell. And Mandy, who was plump then, her middle round against her acid-washed jeans, sat silently each time her mother placed a new treat before us, cramming bite after bite of food into her mouth.

Afterward, Mrs. Miles drank red wine while we sipped sparkling cider from champagne flutes. Mandy, who'd ignored us most of the night, finally said to her mother, "Why are you doing this to me?" Then she sat in a corner and read a book while an apologetic Mrs. Miles, who called us *beautiful young ladies*, who called us *darlings*, who called us *sweet things*, sat cross-legged on the floor in a black satin negligee—which astonished and thrilled us, her assumption we were accustomed to sharing such sophisticated intimacy—and dealt us our fates from her tarot cards. She kept them wrapped in red velvet tied with blue ribbon, like our fates were something worth protecting.

When it was time to go to bed, a tipsy Mrs. Miles herded us into Mandy's room, with its soft pink carpeting and a light fixture engraved with floating rose petals, and a canopy bed netted in miles of butter-yellow lace, and we unrolled our sleeping bags on the floor in a tight clot in the middle of the room, a room as big as all the bedrooms in our homes put together. And after Mrs. Miles kissed us all good night, her lips hot on our foreheads, we pulled out our school pencil bags, where we hid the cheap makeup we'd stolen from our mothers, and plastered our eyes in silvery blue, our cheeks in too-bright red. Mandy sat at the fringe of our circle, a silent lump. We forgot she was there until she snatched a lipstick, a deep coral that made our mothers' teeth look like the color of weak coffee, and circled her mouth again and again, the lipstick spreading in concentric rings, like water rippling from a thrown pebble. "Pretty?" she said, and then she laughed for the first time that night.

Our mothers, with purple-smudged eyes and morning hair and our younger siblings chittering in the backseat, picked us up the next day before their early shifts, and when Mrs. Miles escorted us to our cars with only a short robe wrapped around her lovely negligee, they said, "What kind of respectable mother walks down her driveway in broad daylight in her nightgown?" They frowned suspiciously as Mr. Miles stopped washing his Mercedes long enough to offer them a sudsy wave, said, "That husband of hers sure has an eye for expensive things." And we knew—like us—our mothers had a long list of things they wished for: a sprawling house on the hill right by the lake, a boat named after them, matching appliances in a brightly lit kitchen, a silk negligee so soft and finely woven it felt like a second, better skin.

In Sunday school that morning we sang:
   He's still working on me,
   To make me what I ought to be,
   It took Him just a week to make the moon and the stars,
   The Sun and the Earth and Mercury and Mars,
   How loving and patient He must be,
   Because He's still working on me.

Before big church, the men, dressed in their sport jackets and khakis, sat in folding metal chairs in the church kitchen and sipped coffee from Styrofoam cups. They talked about factories moving to Mexico and the disintegration of the traditional family and the misguidedness of atheists and feminists and the removal of Christ from schools and the moral downfall of the country in general, and they strategized a game plan to right the world again, speaking in the language of sports: discipline, comeback, rebuilding, an eye on the ball, step up to the plate, not much time on the clock, offense, send in the heavy hitters, total dominance.

What we girls saw when we lay shoulder to shoulder on our backs on the merry-go-round in the church playground: drooping power lines threading one house to another, a cloudless sky with no beginning or end, the dark shadow of the old church steeple spinning in and out of sight.

We decided we hated Mandy after that sleepover. What choice did we have, really? And when she grew tall and impossibly thin, a book reader, a smart-girl darling of all the teachers, maybe we gossiped about her—about what she didn't eat, about what she was probably doing with the college boys we imagined she hung out with. And maybe we huddled in the halls at school when she passed, all blonde light and blue eyes, giggling at her skinny butt, her skeletal fingers. And maybe we rolled the trees in the front yard of that sprawling house on the hill right on the lake when we were bored on Friday nights, scrawling shaving cream obscenities on the hood of Mr. Miles's Mercedes. And maybe we drew cadaver-like cartoons of her and let them slip to the floor after class for her to see, calling her a *stuck-up cunt* when she stepped over them without looking down or at us. Or even once, after a long night of shotgunning beers on the boat landing, maybe we all snuck over to her house in the back of a pickup and shoved one of our boyfriends' hunting knives into the tires of that apple-red Miata, laughing riotously on the drive back home, our hair whipping in the moist wind. And maybe we should have felt bad about these things. Maybe we shouldn't have blamed Mandy for the names that replaced our own in the mouths of some of the cute-enough out-of-town boys: white trash, redneck, slut. Maybe we should have considered we might be part of the reason why Mandy rarely ate, why during fifth period when the halls were empty and she didn't think anyone would hear that awful, guttural hacking, Mandy threw up in the girl's bathroom what little she did eat. We saw her compulsion as yet another sign she didn't deserve what she had, didn't see how good she had it. Believe this: we felt righteous.

None of us would admit it, but sometimes late at night, lying alone in our twin beds in the bedrooms of the small homes we all lived in, the fans perched on our thrift-store dressers failing to stir the leaden air, we imagined we were Mandy lying in her bed in that sprawling house on the hill, the mattress so plush that we felt we were floating, like we'd laid ourselves into the late summer lake, the temperature the exact warmth of our skin, so there was nothing separating us from water and water from us, just a fluid softness. The evening sounds of our cramped homes became something else, something other than the tired, solitary workings of our mothers: the late-night murmurs of a father laughing at a talk-show comedian's antics; the soothing hum of the dinner dishes in a stainless-steel washer; the swooshing pendulum on a grandfather clock that bore our family name. And in this way we tricked ourselves into a gentle, comforting sleep, the pulse of the crickets outside of Mandy's imagined bedroom overwhelming the anxious whisper of our own hearts.

Some of us had a tender spot for Mrs. Miles, even though we were never invited back for a sleepover or a BBQ or a swim party. So when we heard that Mrs. Miles went missing that summer before our senior year, that she'd left home after breakfast to get groceries and never returned, that a scarf she might have been wearing was found on the side of a red dirt road a few miles from her home, some of us, most of us, were genuinely concerned. "Holy shit," we said, thinking of what we would feel if some horrible thing happened to our own mothers, women who lived hard lives many thought invited such trouble, although the only danger we'd ever really feared in our town was an inability to leave it. And maybe, just maybe, some of us felt a small, unsettling satisfaction, thinking of Mandy, of how scared she must be now that her life in the sprawling house on the hill right on the lake wouldn't be her life anymore, because we were angry, but we still believed in God then, and if he loved all of us equally, why did she have a father who stayed, an apple-red Miata, her own jet ski, a future that promised escape? Perhaps it seemed stunningly fair she should lose a mother who said things like *darlings*, like *sweet things*, who saw something more in us girls than her own loss.

We'd heard about Mrs. Miles's disappearance through one of
the boys who had a scanner, heard about it as the police were
hearing about it, and that night, when we were shotgunning
beers on the boat landing, our boyfriends' hands tucked firmly
in our back pockets, their chins tucked in the flesh of our
necks, we thought, *What kind of fucked-up world is this?* We
girls had all agreed that Mrs. Miles was dead, that no woman
in her right mind would willingly abandon the life the Mileses
lived, but we were surprised when the boys announced, "If
she's dead, Mr. Miles did it. You saw the way she dressed, the
way she carried on with other men. I bet he dumped her in the
creek that runs back where they found the scarf. Ditched her
car in the lake. It ain't right, but who could blame him, really?
You don't know what a woman can drive a man to do." Their
confidence pissed us off because we thought we were women,
and we thought we knew exactly what a woman could drive a
man to do, and we spent most of our energy trying to do just
that. "There's going to be a search tomorrow morning," the
boys said, animated in a way we'd never seen them before.
They talked about which guns they would bring, what they
would do if they found Mrs. Miles's body, because surely it
was out there somewhere, discarded for them to find, and
their photos would be on the front page of the *Lakeview
Record*, and they would look respectful, their rifles propped
beside them, their caps held in their hands, their mussed
hair pushed from their earnest eyes. For the first time we
girls began to wonder what our boys wanted in life, if they
dreamed of places other than this, of girls other than us, what
they thought of when holding our bared bodies against their
slight, trembling chests, and we were angry that yet again we
were not enough.

Our mothers said, "Wouldn't it be nice to get in the car and
start driving and never stop? I couldn't even imagine it. Starting
over. Everything new. A new name. A new life." They looked
at us in a way that let us know they'd imagined it often, said,
"I mean, I would miss you kids like crazy, but I can't help but
wonder. When is it my turn?"

Of course, the next morning we were all there standing along
that red dirt road where they'd found the scarf just as the sun

slid into the bluing sky. The boys with their trucks, their worn boots, their baseball caps pulled low to hide bloodshot eyes. The sheriff, his broad stomach swelling in his tan uniform. The sloped-backed men—the lobes of their nostrils fern-veined from too much booze—with their rifles, their hunting dogs, their fingers twitching against coffee mugs as they barked clipped instructions: Keep an eye out for piles of brush, earth recently moved, clothing, personal items. Stay in groups. Watch for moccasins.

We didn't even notice Mandy at first, sitting quietly with Mr. Miles on the tailgate of someone's pickup, clutching a stack of fliers. "Thank you for coming," she said, offering a flier to anyone who passed nearby, subdued for once, not like she was in class, always ass-kissing the teachers, always raising her hand to answer questions we didn't think needed asking, talking about internships and scholarships and sororities and travel-abroad programs while we worried if our mothers would be able to save enough money to send us on the school trip to Panama City or pay for senior pictures. Her father said nothing. We tried not to stare at him. Tried not to think of how Mandy could sit there and hold the hand that might have killed her mother, although, of course, there was no hard evidence that he'd done it, or that she'd even been killed, not yet anyway. And if he didn't show up and sit quietly holding his daughter's hand, that would be a kind of evidence in itself, we reasoned.

But he looked so lost, so stricken, we began to think that maybe he didn't murder his wife and throw her body in a creek, that maybe he loved Mrs. Miles, who, everyone agreed, was a wonderful lady, a kind mother. "Mrs. Miles is a fighter," we all murmured. "God will watch over her," we all said, not knowing how these statements made sense, or if they were appropriate, or what was appropriate when searching for the body of a mother lost in the woods. But everyone nodded gravely, said, "Yes indeed, God will watch over her," and we couldn't help but ask ourselves where God was when Mrs. Miles had been snatched from the grocery store parking lot, or when she looked at the groceries sitting on the backseat of her car, decided she didn't want to be a wife and mother anymore, and turned away from home, or when our mothers were knocked up just out of high school, some even earlier, or when our fathers disappeared into their own misery.

The flier read:
   MISSING
   Diana Miles
   Age: 39
   Hair: Blonde
   Height: 5'6"
   Weight: 120
   Last seen at the Piggly Wiggly in Lakeview on July 1st at 10 AM wearing a pink sundress. Bring our wife and mother home.

Beneath the print was a smudged photo of a smiling Mrs. Miles in a dark, low-cut swimsuit, sitting in a lounge chair on a pier, Mandy in oversized jeans and a baggy T-shirt standing behind her, Mandy's eyes wide and clear even in print, her blonde hair so light it bled into the white of the page. "It's my mother's favorite picture of us," Mandy explained when some of us stared wordlessly at the image because who puts a photo of their mother in a swimsuit on a missing persons flier? "She looks real happy," we all agreed. "Real pretty."

Mr. Miles and Mandy searched with the lead group, their orange vests flashing bright against the deep green of the woods. We girls stayed close together as we wove through the maze of trees, the forest ground thick with leaves and vines and mud from summer rains, our matching white Keds ruined by the iron-red dirt. Of course, we all wanted Mrs. Miles to be found, but unlike the boys, who were plummeting through the woods ahead of us, breaking branches, leaping over felled logs, barely containing their enthusiasm, none of us wanted to be the one to find her. We still had hope then of tidy lives filled with beauty, of rich boyfriends and romantic proposals, of fantastic careers as interior decorators and makeup artists, of blissful days lazing on balconies and poolsides with stunning views of beaches and bronzed bodies far from our old town. None of us wanted to be touched by a deliberate act of savagery, which somehow seemed so much more profound than the careless acts of savagery we'd encountered in our young lives: boys accidentally shooting each other while hunting, drunken classmates hurtling their cars into trees, men getting caught in the machinery at the mill. We couldn't help but wonder what witnessing Mrs. Miles's body would mean to the future us we still believed would tumble out of our town the day after graduation, taking nothing more with us than beer-hazed memories of sweet boys promising sweet things we expected to find somewhere else.

So when the dogs started barking in the near distance, a frenzied howling, we stilled for a moment, all together, as one breathing organism. "I don't want to see," someone said, but we were already moving toward the commotion, the mud from the rains sucking us into the earth and releasing us reluctantly. And then we were in a small clearing, a campground of sorts on the edge of the creek, the sun high now in the blazing blue sky, a perfect summer day for laying out at the lake, squeezing Sun-In and lemons in our hair, shotgunning beers pulled from scuff-scabbed coolers. The dogs were circling something at the silt-rimmed water, the men shaking their heads and talking on their radios, gesturing at the clamoring boys to stay back. Mr. Miles stood under a tree, his thin face pressed into his thin hands. Mandy was squatting next to a leaf-covered mound, stroking what looked like matted hair. We all stopped breathing for a moment, our hearts raging in our chests.

And although we were standing right there, seeing everything, we felt like we often felt, as if all of this was happening to some other girls, and the lives we were destined to be living were already in motion, waiting for us to step in, to catch up with ourselves. "It's an old dog," Mandy said quietly, not lifting her head, her pale hair curtaining her face. "Looks like somebody shot it. Who would do a thing like that?" And suddenly, we were embarrassed, by the boys' disappointed faces, by the time we took that morning to line our eyes and roll our hair in case the newspaper took pictures, by Mandy's tenderness toward an old dog put down by his owner in a way as familiar to us as mothers who worked the late shift and left TV dinners for us in the freezer, as fathers who failed to call on our birthdays. And we were angry. Angry that girls like Mandy were allowed such ignorance.

Mr. Miles sold his sprawling house on the hill right on the lake and moved Mandy back to Atlanta at the end of the summer. As the weeks passed and Mrs. Miles remained missing, we wondered less and less about what had happened to her. What did it matter? We girls understood that people leave or are taken or die in a hundred different ways, and in the end, they are still just gone. And we'd almost forgotten about Mandy, who headed off to Tuscaloosa for college the summer after graduation, where we heard she'd painted her dorm room and fingernails black, shaved her head, spiked her nose with a fat silver bar, and tattooed some saying about the purpose of life in Latin on her bony back, her professors awed by the spectacular suffering she detailed in her heartbreaking essays, her grief-stricken poetry, which only made her angrier.

And most of us had forgotten our silly dreams of fantastic careers as interior decorators and makeup artists, of blissful days lazing on balconies and poolsides with stunning views of beaches and bronzed bodies far from our town. Girls like us were expected to forget so others could get on with the business of living by forgetting us. But we would never forget seeing Mandy standing in the stark light of her bedroom window the night we thrust that hunting knife in the tire of her apple-red Miata, the way she lifted her nightgown over her head and tossed it aside, the accusatory way she stood nude and silent, watching us, the big bones of her joints pressing against her skin like clenched fists, how shocked we were to see our own anguish staring, unblinking, back at us.

orbital debris

I

Something about him was unsettling. Not only the way the boy looked—the cavernous cheeks, the perpetual scowl, the tenebrous owl eyes—but how he moved as he worked through the field behind their neighborhood, his gait angry, the stick he whipped through the brush convulsing like a dowsing rod. Every morning this summer Addie had watched the boy wander in the knee-high grass of the field while she sipped coffee on her rear patio, designed in the "New Orleans Courtyard" style she'd chosen from the builder's options when she and Hal bought the place.

It had sounded so delicious then—*a French-inspired hideaway to soothe the soul under the wide expanse of stars, your own secret garden.* But then the market crashed and the money and buyers dried up before the remaining phases of the residential development could be implemented. More than a few of the faux-Craftsman homes were empty, some never occupied, others foreclosed. The cleared field behind Addie's home, which was intended to boast the pool, community center, and playground, had *gone to seed*, as Hal used to say, fond of using farmers' colloquialisms, although as a concession to her the closest he'd come to farming in the ten years prior to Addie putting him in the ground had been to thumb morosely through *Progressive Farmer* at the kitchen table, and God forgive her, Addie was grateful for that.

The boy was there now, in the field, the dark gloom of clouds gathering in the east hulking over his form like a re-atomizing supervillain, the kind of alarming illustration found in the comic books Addie remembered schoolmates wedging in their textbooks so many decades ago. The grass writhed around the boy's branch-thin thighs, the storm coming in fast as they tended to do every afternoon, the year's El Niño slamming their corner of Alabama with record levels of rain.

But the boy did not seem to notice the threat above him. He stomped through the field, jamming his stick at this and that. Occasionally, he would squat to study the ground, and in those moments, he was completely consumed by the roil of grass; it was as if he'd vanished.

Addie often wondered if the boy's mother knew how her son, who looked to be no more than twelve or so, passed the day. Addie had seen the woman only at a distance, hauling her trash bin down the driveway or gazing at the newsletter on the community bulletin board staked at the junction of three quaintly named streets: Cottage Lane, Dogwood Trace, Magnolia Pass. If the boy's mother had a husband, Addie had never laid eyes on him. Given the boy's brooding posture, his sullen stare when he caught Addie observing him, she suspected the father was not around. At the very least, *something* was not right. Something drove that boy to the field, compelled him to foolishness, to giving himself over to a field gone wild, to standing, at this very moment, under the glare of a fierce storm with no intentions of escaping it.

The rabbits were starting to stir, and they leapt en masse past Addie's patio. The rabbits were another silly idea from the builder, a bizarre bucolic touch for a few dozen houses wedged between a Costco and an aging mall on the outskirts of Montgomery. With few natural predators other than the restless house cats who escaped their foyers on occasion, the rabbits did what rabbits do: multiplied. Their pebbly shit studded the sidewalks; it was impossible to take a stroll without soiling one's shoes. Mounds of rabbit quivered on too-green lawns, their expressions stunned. Hal, who had been unable to parse the purpose of decorative animals, once struck one across the head with a potting shovel for habitually shitting on their patio. Addie had watched from the kitchen window. The rabbit did not even think of moving when Hal raised the shovel, could not seem to comprehend that the world might be bent toward unnecessary violence.

It wasn't right, Addie thought, to breed the wild out of the wild. But even the tremor-eyed rabbits knew what was coming now. They stormed the lawn, hopping into bushes, under the latticework of porches. Addie stood, her knees protesting the abrupt movement. "Get out of the field!" she yelled at the boy, the volume of her voice swelling against her cheeks. "You're going to get yourself killed." She waved her hands, beckoning him to her patio.

He must have heard her. His head pitched up. His ears cocked. He stared straight at her, his big eyes moons. The black was on him now, the sky preparing to cleave, lightning severing the clouds. The boy hesitated, gripped his stick as if he intended to ignore her, jabbed at something at his feet. And then the sky ruptured, the winds tearing Addie's coffee cup right off the table, her newspaper scudding to the ground, the brightly colored pages levitating around her calves. A finger of light reached out toward the boy, a perfect spear of lightning. Like a shock cord, it retracted before it touched him, lassoing back up into the clouds.

Addie had never seen him move quickly before, not like the other kids who played basketball in the alley or scootered around on their wheeled contraptions. No, the boy generally maneuvered like an octogenarian, his skinny legs buckling beneath him, the joints of his body bending in curious angles like a little Pinocchio.

But the boy was *running* toward her. Fast. The wind whipped his longish hair into a ducktail; his wet T-shirt stuck to his body like a caul. Even from a distance, Addie could see the boy's ribs beneath the fabric, each slash of bone. Then he was standing not three feet away, waiting hesitantly at the patio step, just outside the protection of the awning. His thin chest heaved. The veins of his neck jerked. His owl eyes ballooned. He seemed slightly inhuman, otherworldly even, a haint conjured by the storm.

II

When Daniel returned home from the old lady's house, his own was silent; it smelled of rain and a medley of essential oils, his mother's latest obsession. Barely past four, the house was pitch black, the drapes drawn against the soupy light. He found his mother in the living room that hinged the kitchen. She still wore her scrubs, bright teal and freckled with kicking bears in top hats. A fashion magazine draped her lap, unopened. Her profile, his same profile, cut a dark, shadowy void. Her thumb and middle finger noosed the stem of a half-empty wine glass.

She stared at the covered window, the last breath of the storm pelting its panes. Daniel knew she hated it here, the rain, the constant moistness, the promiscuous green growth of the landscape, the way everything seemed to ooze and seep. But for some reason, she refused to leave, refused to return to Southern California where she'd grown up, where she met Daniel's father, where they'd lived pre-children—if the family photo albums told any truth—a happy life before his father uprooted her for a job as head of surgery in the regional hospital where Daniel's mother now worked as a nurse.

He pulled back the drapes to let in what little light the day offered, then eased onto the sofa beside her. His mud-stained hands twitched against his knees. She studied them for a moment, then looked away, blinked, her lashes, as long as spider legs, pinching together, then fanning open. Her eyelashes and eyebrows were untouched by the gray that shot through her hair, as if they belonged to an earlier version of herself.

"I lost a patient," she said.

"I'm sorry." Daniel considered holding his mother's hand, but even as young as he was, he understood the gesture would be too jarring in its strangeness, what little language of touch they'd known lost to them since his father's death the year before. They both stared out the window at the neat line of spindly young oaks bordering the sidewalk in front of their house. They'd moved after his father died, his mother in search of unsullied newness, a blank slate, the soothing homogeny of the architecture part of the neighborhood's appeal.

"A girl," his mother continued. "She was talking—about playing with her cat when she felt better—and then she wasn't. She closed her eyes, and that was it." His mother turned to him when she said this, her face so stricken he could barely look at her without feeling the familiar fury punch from his gut to his throat.

"Rice and steamed vegetables OK for dinner?" Daniel asked, unfolding off the couch.

"Sounds lovely," his mother said, although he knew she would not eat more than a child-sized bite or two. And then, after she thought he was asleep, she'd sip wine in the dark silence and scroll through new-age internet forums until she passed out on the couch.

He could not understand it, his mother's willingness to work with terminal children, other than she found comfort in knowing with certainty the outcome of things. There'd been hope for his father, torturous hope for months, and still the end had been like all endings. There'd been no hope for the older brother Daniel never met, the teenager who'd died in a car wreck on some backwoods dirt road, a case of empty beer cans scattered around his body in a loose constellation, the fancy BMW their parents had bought him as a graduation gift accordioned against a tree, his girlfriend slung over a branch of the same tree, her auburn hair draping like Spanish Moss. Or at least, this was what Daniel saw when he tried to imagine the scenario, which he did often enough to scare himself.

No, there had been no hope for Brett. Not until Daniel, a consolation baby—no one made a secret about his purpose—entered the world on the first anniversary of Brett's death sixteen years ago. Brett reborn, their mother insisted on the rare occasions she drunkenly collided with her living son in the small hours of the night, into Daniel's own body. In the years after Brett's death, their once unreligious mother had tried on a variety of faiths—Hinduism, Buddhism, Mormonism, Taoism—never settling with one for more than a year or two before whatever relief it provided waned. But this concept, the possibility of Brett's rebirth, she'd held to stubbornly, and who could blame her, his father had said gently when Daniel had complained as a small boy, terrified a dead brother might erupt from his belly horror-film style. What mother wouldn't want to feel her son in the world?

If true, Daniel often thought, other than being a stupid teenager, what horrible things had Brett done to be punished with such a body in his new life?

"What's that?" his mother asked now, pointing at the metal detector he'd propped against the coat closet. It looked like a weed whacker.

"That old lady two streets over gave it to me. I ran into her house for a minute when the rain started."

"Why would a stranger give you a metal detector?"

Daniel shrugged. "She said she didn't need it anymore. Didn't want things to clutter up her house."

His mother studied the contraption thoughtfully. "Be careful," she cautioned. "Very few people give away things without an expectation of something in return."

Daniel clamped the rice steamer closed. He'd become the lone cook in the house after his father died, and although he'd discovered no secret culinary talent, he liked the ritual of preparing food. In the kitchen he felt a certain superiority over the other boys at school, boys who were obsessed with sneaker brands and sports and flippable bangs. He'd always been different—he went to a school populated by students whose last names dominated most of Montgomery's street signs, and he could barely run a lap during gym without tripping over his own feet—but this distinction, cooking for his mother, seemed noble.

"What would an old lady want from me?" Daniel asked, but even as he said it, he knew that in general, his mother was right. No one had ever given him a thing without an expectation of something in return. An unexpected gift of a Snickers at school from one of the shaggy-bang boys had eventually cost him his Trig homework, an unsolicited kiss on the cheek from one of the prettier girls a peek at his Physics exam. Even the gift of his body, the sight of which seemed to repulse so many, required that he share it with Brett when his mother so desired.

The old lady's house had looked as if she was just moving in or about to move out. Packed boxes towered in the dining room. A wide-screen TV rested on the floor. The only furniture was a table in the kitchen with a few chairs ringing it, and a small couch in the living room facing a blank wall where the TV would have been in a normal person's house.

He'd paused upon entering her home, eyeing the boxes, the bare dining room to the right.

"You moving?" he asked, his voice sounding strange in the naked room.

"Sooner or later."

"If you haven't moved yet, where's the rest of your stuff?"

The woman shrugged, said, "I didn't need it anymore. Probably never did."

After she ushered Daniel into the kitchen, she fetched a towel and wrapped it around his shoulders, seating him at the table. She poured him some lemonade from a carton she pulled from the side of the refrigerator, then sat across from him, her chin perched on her scrawny hands. She was tiny and birdlike, her blotched skin loosening behind the ears, her nose so long the fleshy tip touched her top lip. She stared at him for a minute, runny green eyes narrowed. "I'm Miss Addie," she said. Her accent, a muddied, old-fashioned drawl, was so thick it would have required subtitles if she were on one of those redneck reality shows.

"Daniel," he said.

She nodded approvingly. "That's a fine name. People give kids all kinds of ridiculous names these days."

"I didn't have anything to do with it," Daniel said.

She surprised him by laughing, a quick, guttural snort that seemed to originate deep in her throat. When she quieted, they sat there in silence, each staring past the other.

"I ain't so good with kids," Miss Addie said apologetically, though Daniel had no idea why she felt the need to apologize. Adults were always apologizing to him. Daniel suspected they felt sorry for him, that he made them uncomfortable. "Never had any of my own," she added. Then she stood and limped over to a utility closet and fished around before retrieving a bright green metal detector and shoving it toward him.

"This was my husband's. He intended to hunt for Civil War nonsense—artillery shells and belt buckles and whatnot. Swore there was a skirmish fought right in that field you've been poking in. But he didn't get around to using it. Maybe it will help you find whatever you're looking for."

"Maybe," Daniel said uncertainly, but he could not resist reaching for the gift.

She cocked her head, nostrils shuddering. "What are you looking for, anyway?"

This was what Daniel was searching for that summer: his brother's class ring, the school mascot, a cartoonish tiger, prowling up the side, the center stone an oversized ruby. One lazy, early June morning it had occurred to Daniel that if what he owned belonged to Brett, then in theory what Brett once owned should belong to him. So he went into his mother's closet where she stored all of Brett's old clothes. They were in remarkably good shape and, though dated, still more stylish than most of Daniel's own clothes. He tried on a casual linen button-up shirt, something Brett might have worn to school or on a date. It smelled of dust and mothballs. The arms hung past his fingertips. He took it anyway, along with a few other shirts and a fancy tan blazer, then carefully closed the boxes and arranged them in the back of the closet like he'd found them.

On his way out of his mother's room he'd noticed her jewelry box sitting on her dresser. Before he knew what he was doing, he opened it. There were his mother's pearls, worn mainly at funerals, and her wedding ring, which she'd only removed a few weeks prior. In the back, tucked in a little velvet pouch, he found Brett's class ring. Before he could talk himself out of it, he shoved it into his pocket, intending to keep it for only a day. At first, he slipped his hand into his pocket every few minutes; the ring felt hot to his touch, like a tiny organ pulsing heat. And then he became distracted by the day's project, a kite he designed and built himself, which he attempted to fly for hours in the grassy field behind his neighborhood, a childish pursuit he suspected would invoke a barrage of taunts from his classmates if anyone saw him. But this was not a problem because, outside of school, Daniel never saw anyone except his mother. By the time he remembered to check for the ring, he found nothing but a wad of kite string.

What he told the old woman, a lie inspired by a television program he'd watched by himself in the middle of the night after waking from another disturbing dream: "Space junk. Orbital debris rocketing around the asteroid belt. Sometimes it breaks through the atmosphere. Bits of rockets and satellites."

"Good Lord," Miss Addie had said. "There's junk in space, too?"

"Orbital debris?" his brother seemed to say now from one of the photo frames that rested on Daniel's dresser, his large blue eyes those of an all-American movie star. Their mother had rewritten Brett's modest achievements into epic feats since his death, but his looks required no exaggeration. He was a rare kind of handsome, overwhelming in its intensity, like staring directly into the sun.

"Poor Daniel," Brett whispered gloomily from his photo, but Daniel caught his brother's faint snigger, and Daniel suspected, not for the first time, his brother had been a bit of an asshole when he felt like it. He actually liked this about Brett. Boys who looked like Daniel—painfully thin, short, bug-eyed—were not permitted the luxury of assholeishness.

The top of the desk, which his mother had decorated, served as a shrine of sorts: pictures of Brett from diapers to graduation gown, a sterling silver rattle with Brett's full name and date of birth engraved on the handle (there was no such rattle for Daniel), seashells Brett had collected from sands of the Gulf on a family vacation as a toddler. And hidden beneath a photo of ten-year-old Brett in a Little League baseball uniform, a picture of the girl Brett had loved, the girl who'd been with him at the end. In the snapshot, she sat on the edge of a bed in purple-polka-dotted panties, her long, reddish hair tousled on her shoulders, her knees pulled to her chest and squeezed under an oversized T-shirt. She squinted hard at the photographer beneath heavily made-up eyelids, her extended hand languidly shooting a bird, Brett's class ring glaring from her middle finger like an angry, bloodshot eye. The look and the gesture seemed somehow intimate, an invitation. Daniel had found several photos of the girl jammed inside his brother's copy of *The Call of the Wild*, but he preferred this one the most. The edges showed the wear from his brother's hands, and it made Daniel feel close to Brett—mysterious, fabulous wonder-boy—to hold Brett's girl in his own.

Bianca Jones. That was the name scrawled on the back of the photo. Her last name was Grayson now. He'd looked her up on online, and it took only a few minutes from there to figure out her current address several one-traffic-light towns over in Lakeview. He'd marveled at the image of her Facebook profile photo, how the tired woman in the picture could also be the glossy-skinned girl who'd once known his brother. Daniel did the math; she would be well over thirty now, almost double the age of the girl tucked into his dead brother's book.

Last week he had taken his father's car, a vintage Mustang convertible his mother was saving for Daniel, though his sixteenth birthday had passed with no mention of when he might get his license, and driven the hour to the town where Bianca Grayson lived, circling the pocked roads for her address.

The town bordered a beautiful, expansive lake Daniel knew his parents often visited before his brother's death, sometimes renting a cabin and boat for the weekend, but the town proper was primarily boarded storefronts and dollar stores, everything not on the water crumbling and old. After an hour of orbiting the same trash-strewn lawns filled with lanky, mud-kneed kids or old men lounging in clusters, cigarettes pinched between their thumbs and forefingers, Daniel finally found Bianca's place, a small tract house with a patchwork of red dirt and dead grass for a front yard. A pack of kids—one girl, the rest boys—ran wild around the house. He parked the car next to the mailbox and watched, waiting, he supposed, for Bianca to emerge through the faded front door. He wondered how her life might have been different if Brett had not died. He liked to think Brett's death changed the course of Bianca's life, too. He liked to think he was not alone navigating a Brett-less world. He waited until he could wait no longer, until his mother's shift was ending and she would soon be home to discover the missing car, and still, Bianca never emerged once to check on her children, never even pulled back a drape.

Daniel caught his own mother studying him often enough with an expression of wistfulness and disappointment to know that she recognized nothing of her first son in her second, that she never once truly believed any remnant of Brett lived in Daniel. But at night, when he finally found sleep, Daniel sometimes saw Bianca, the girl as his brother had loved her, and the details of her face—the scar that rode the rim of her upper lip, the freckles scattered across her slightly crooked nose—were so finely etched, the pressure of her lips on his so palpable, that when he first woke, her image still hovering in his mind's eye, he half believed that what he had witnessed was more memory than dream, that Brett's soul, however briefly, burned within him.

III

Jacob felt like a tool wobbling down the street on his daughter's lavender bike, his soaked clothes clinging to his skin, the plastic basket drooping from handlebars funneling a spout of water straight at his left cheek. The plan had been to take the Civic, but when he finally worked up the nerve to pull out of his driveway a few hours before dawn, the car had refused to start. It took him two hours to bike the ten miles. The rain pushed against him like an invisible wall.

He couldn't remember the exact address of the old lady's house. It had been pouring when he loaded her donations onto the Goodwill truck a couple of weeks ago—another part-time job that had not paid enough to cover even the electric bill— her house sheathed in rain. He'd been pedaling awhile now, circling the neighborhood, the large, red-brick homes so similar in structure and color, particularly in the night, he worried he would never recognize the one where the bird-faced woman lived. The houses were monstrous in size, several so big they required two heating and air units. Some were silent as tombs, the owners probably off at their vacation homes to escape the summer heat. Others had yards littered with trampolines and miniature battery-operated jeeps, the porches crammed with SUV-sized strollers and bike trailers. What kind of work did these people do, Jacob wondered, to own so much stuff?

By the time the rain stopped and the sun began to emerge—a piss-colored smudge in the horizon—he'd decided to cut his losses and go home. And then he saw the planters on the front porch, two massive, ceramic bowls painted with navy fleur-de-lis. He knew the planters were plantless, filled only with dry, caked potting soil, because when the old lady wasn't watching, he'd put out his break smoke in one, embarrassed by the immense pleasure of the juvenile act. Jacob dropped the bike behind a row of sagging azaleas lining the side of the house and crouched in the shadows of the two-story Craftsman, bile seeping up his throat.

Since he'd lost his steady job installing alarm systems during the last round of cuts, he'd cancelled the cable and pawned the TVs, the Xbox, the laptop, and the crappy Wal-Mart pay-as-you-go smartphone. He listed his good tools on Craigslist, even sold his blood plasma. He'd taken any job that came his way. Still, there was not enough, and Sharla had been very clear in her terms the past weekend: *don't come inside this house without rent money.* He'd spent the last four nights sleeping in the car, waking at dawn to drive to the empty lot next to the Home Depot, where he stood around with the other day laborers in hope that some douche in an oversized, tricked-out truck would choose him for the shit job du jour, which never happened. The younger guys and the Mexicans got picked first, more bang for the buck. Jacob felt like an aging hooker, and when he said as much to Sharla when she came out to the car with another stack of bills, she snorted, said, "When an eighty-year-old dude sticks his hand down your G-string, we'll talk." When they were first starting out, before Jacob landed the alarm systems gig, Sharla had danced for a few months at a pretty tame, tops-off-only joint to make rent, and she never let him forget it.

Last night he was awakened in the backseat of the Civic by a persistent drip, the moon roof's seal undone by age and sun exposure. He sat there for a long time, stripped to his boxers, the stringy heat of the old car unbearable. It was like sitting in a cow's mouth. And then he understood—what he needed to do, the only thing he could do.

He chose the old woman because she had seemed so perversely thrilled to get rid of her things. She practically hummed when he hauled off a nice set of leather couches and a recliner to the Goodwill truck, spreading her arms wide in the emptied living room as if she were about to break out into a jig. Frankly, Jacob found her joy offensive to people like himself, people who were too panicked about not being able to put gas in the tank and food on their table to kick up their heels when the repo man came to haul off their shit. What was the difference, he reasoned, if he cut out the middleman and took her things himself? She wanted to donate to those in need, and God knows, Jacob was in need of many things.

But standing here now, his face pressed to the old lady's window, he wasn't so sure. He'd never stolen anything, unless he counted beer from the stash his father used to hide in his johnboat. Or, if he wanted to get philosophical about it—and Jacob did not—Sharla's youth, which, according to her, was being squandered wiping the asses of his two kids in a house without functioning air-conditioning.

He peeked inside the house. The old lady was nowhere to be seen, and he hoped if she was home she was still asleep. A lady that ancient would surely sleep like the dead. He did not allow himself to consider what he might do if she were awake. Jacob spotted a wall of boxes and a large flat-screen TV perched in the foyer, a new collection of items apparently intended for donation. The TV alone would pull in at least three hundred on Craigslist. Then the obvious hit him: how was he going to carry a fifty-five-inch TV on a bike? The panic, the cold clamping of his lungs, nearly knocked him out. He pressed his cheek, raw from the hard rain, against the cool of the brick.

Maybe not all was lost. There might be some small stuff, jewelry or collectibles, in those boxes, things he could carry in the bike basket. He surprised himself by laughing at the thought of a man barreling down a busy street, balancing a big-screen TV on his handlebars, and he wondered when his own laughter began to sound like that of a stranger's.

He figured he would be less likely to be spotted breaking in at the back of the house, which faced an open field, and so he eased around the side, hugging the house as he moved, his wet, sneakered feet tripping over a paver brick, a ceramic butterfly, a garden hose. And then something soft, malleable, warm.

Jacob looked down to find the furry belly of some kind of small creature wedged under his heel; his foot jacked up reflexively, his shoe hovering over the animal in mid-air like a threat. The thing looked to be a rabbit, its eyes glassy and still. It stared straight through him, its narrow mouth agape, the sharp teeth crooked and yellowed. Then it seemed to release a moan, a long, low keening.

Jacob jumped, nearly falling into the hedges, and by the time he regained his footing, he found himself at the back of the house, gripping a poorly molded wrought iron fence that enclosed a brick patio, a wide field of grass in the distance, black clouds pressing down the horizon like a giant fist.

And the moaning—it grew louder, closer, even though the dead or dying rabbit was now a good ten feet away.

Then he saw her, the woman's body sprawled across the bricks, a waterlogged newspaper a few inches from an outstretched hand. He stared at her for at least a minute before he fully recognized her as human, as the source of the hideous sound. It was the old lady, her clothes matted to her skeletal frame, her mouth fish-lipping the air.

At her feet, French doors winged open to the kitchen. The small dinette table that took up most of the eat-in kitchen was covered in what looked like stacks of photo albums and old papers, and next to those, a hand-carved wooden box, the kind of box in which people keep precious things. Jacob's stomach lurched instinctively at his good luck, and this response frightened him because it took only the space of a breath for him to understand what was about to happen.

He would not call 911. Instead, he would step over the woman's body to enter her home. He would avoid looking at the yellowed black-and-white photos spread on the table, snapshots of the old lady when she wasn't so old, when the thinness of her cheeks appeared pixie-ish and coquettish rather than birdlike, when the man he assumed was her husband still found her lovely enough to bury his broad face in the hollow of her neck. He would reach for the carved box instead of the phone that hung from the wall.

And later, back at his house, sitting, finally, at his own kitchen table across from his wife and kids, there would be much doubt and regret and remorse. But in that exact moment—the moment he flipped open the wooden lid to reveal a string of opaque pearls, a diamond engagement ring, and a man's gold pocket watch—he felt only as if he'd been spared.

IV

The kids were fucking animals. *Animals.* Not precocious. Not curious. Not energetic. Feral animals. Bianca had tried to explain this to Trey, tried to tell him that the way things were going she might be dead by the end of the summer, and not metaphorically devoid of life, but straight-up *dead* dead. She'd begged him to hire her some help, even a neighborhood girl for a few hours a week, but he'd told her that they needed to save money if they were ever going to get into a bigger house, that she should put her feet up now and again, take a nap if she could squeeze one in. If Bianca closed her eyes long enough for a nap, she had no doubt that she'd wake to complete destruction. Tsunami-style devastation.

Trey was a good guy. He was decent to her. He treated the kids well. He was handsome enough. Bianca saw women looking his way. And he was a hard worker, moving his way up from collecting balls on the driving range to ground maintenance assistant manager at the golf course at Living Waters Resort in a matter of a few years. Even so, Bianca couldn't find a single remarkable thing to say about her husband. She knew as much when she'd married him. But she'd been assaulted by a restless anger for a long time after the car accident, a resentment that stemmed, in part, from the way the tragedy had defined her.

Everyone had seen Brett as Bianca's great hope, her way out of this town, her chance for an easier life. And then he'd died, and Bianca had been part of his death, and everyone looked at her with pity, as if her future had been irrevocably altered. Trey, an old high school friend, a good ol' boy with a pickup truck and a gun rack and tepid blue-collar aspirations, had seemed a fine way to fulfill everyone's modest expectations of her.

She was a year shy of her associate's degree with no employment in sight when she learned she was pregnant. Being jobless and pregnant and married, even to Trey, seemed a wiser option than being just jobless and pregnant. If there had been other options, she had been too tired to consider them. Then Sean arrived—a squally mass of flesh—and Bianca thought the baby would cement the deal, make her feel like a real wife and mother, fill her days with playdates and onesie shopping and misty baths where she would coo at the baby like the serene-faced mothers on those Johnson & Johnson commercials. None of that happened. Instead, she grew bored, her anger, at least, dulled by exhaustion. And then the others started coming, no matter how much birth control she pumped into her arm or gut, one after another like fucking rabbits, the youngest, twins, almost two.

Their junk multiplied, too. The house was littered with sippy cups and torn books and ride-ons and little honking cars and tooting trains. The yard was even worse: a disemboweled trampoline, a rusted-out swing set, dozens of sun-faded push toys and tire-deflated trikes. Sometimes, Bianca thought she'd be buried alive, slowly sink into the mire of crap, and to tell the truth, she'd be grateful for the escape.

Wine, she recently discovered, helped tremendously. She wished she'd thought of day-drinking years ago. Trey didn't seem to notice her frequent buzz, and she was careful to buy cheap wine at Walmart so he wouldn't notice the expense either. Over the last few weeks, she'd started a little earlier each day, testing the waters. Today she didn't even pour a bowl of cheerios and make a show of taking a few bites; instead, she filled her coffee cup with chardonnay, then kept refilling it, the children's voices blessedly muffled by the fuzziness of her brain. The rain had been ruthless all summer. Anytime the sky cleared, Bianca shoved the kids out the door and locked it behind them. They were out in the rain-soaked yard now, all four of them terrorizing a neighborhood cat they'd treed. Bianca knew she should stop them, but she also knew that there was no stopping them. She sipped her wine and watched out the window for a moment as Sean, almost twelve now with a throwing arm like a rocket launcher, pegged the tabby with pebbles, his sister scrounging the ground for more ammo. Even the twins were scratching in the mud on their hands and knees, yelping in glee each time the cat screeched. She thought to yell at them to leave the cat alone, but instead she closed the drapes.

Bianca settled deeper into the cushions, the mug of wine resting on her belly, her free hand picking at the frayed threads of the floral couch. When she noticed a patch of dried food, most likely jam from the morning's breakfast, she didn't even think of rising to get a washcloth, and she didn't feel guilty for not thinking of doing so either. She shut her eyes, welcoming the stillness.

Lately, when Bianca stole moments like this, her body floating with the buzz of wine, her mind racing in images—the slope of her own mother's cheek, its white, downy hairs gathering the sunlight as she drove Bianca to grade school; her high school friends sweating out their beer at a lake band party, their long, wet hair lacerating their bony shoulders; Brett the night he died, sitting cross-legged in front of a bonfire, etching a cartoonish stick figure of her into the red dirt—she was certain there must be many Biancas, all living their separate lives at once. Sometimes she liked to think if she focused hard enough she could find her way back to one of those other Biancas, could hit the reset button and get a do-over, but she suspected it wouldn't matter much. Eventually, she would find herself right back on this very couch.

When she heard the knock on the door, she figured it was one of the kids, forever wanting something. She hesitated, savoring the velvety darkness of her eyelids, then stood unsteadily, holding her mug to her chest as she moved across the cluttered room so the wine would slosh onto her old T-shirt instead of the carpet. She threw open the door, ready to respond to whatever request with an *it's-time-you-learn-to-do-it-yourself*, and found herself staring at a weird-looking boy in a creased, tan sports coat that came to his knees. His eyes were huge in his gaunt face. A slab of dark hair paneled his forehead. He smelled of dirt and grass. His whole body shook.

She started to slam the door shut, but her kids were out there in the yard, and what kind of mother would she be to consider only her own safety?

So instead she said, as tersely as she could, "What do you want?"

The boy blinked once, twice. "I don't know." He pistoned his wadded hands deep into his pant pockets. Stared at her shyly.

"You selling something?" Bianca peered around him, as if he were hiding a clipboard or a box of candy bars. Behind him, her own children had stilled. Even the twins had paused in their manic loops around the base of the tree. The cat shivered fearfully on the branch. Sean watched her and the stranger with naked curiosity.

"When you didn't answer the door, I was going to leave it on the step." The boy gestured toward the ground, and Bianca spotted a small object close to the toe of his sneakers. It took a few moments for it to register that it was a ring, its wide band a cheap, cloudy gold. She couldn't tell if the boy was making some kind of love offering or trying to sell her his mother's jewelry to buy meth from one of the cook houses on their street. Either way, she wasn't interested. She was about to tell the boy so in no uncertain terms when he unclenched a hand from his pocket and, without hesitation, touched his hot fingertips to her face.

"You look older than yourself," the boy said. Then he jerked his hand away and ran, all knees and elbows, down the grass-cracked walkway toward an old Mustang.

"Asshole," Bianca whispered. She studied the ring he'd left behind at her feet, turning it with one big toe. It was gaudy and poorly made, the red gem only dull glass. The sight of it enraged her. More junk. She swept it with her heel into the overgrown shrub for the kids to scavenge later.

V

First it was Addie's heart—clogged arteries, an irregular rhythm. Then her lungs—reduced capacity, an aftereffect of thirty years of smoking, a habit she regretted abandoning once she realized she would be punished for it anyway. After her knees went and her doctor doled out the assisted living speech, Addie began giving away her things in preparation for the inevitable move: the heirloom china her mother gifted her when she married Hal;

her formal dining room furniture, with the silk-backed chairs she painstakingly protected from Hal's soiled hands for more than thirty years; and as soon as the Goodwill truck showed up again, everything else she could spare, including the TVs, with their incessant chants of economic doom and endless wars.

She had no children to whom she could farm out her things. There'd been a baby the third year of her marriage, a boy the size of her hand who'd never pinked up. The others died within her, a string of miscarriages throughout her fertile years, until her reproductive organs could not even ignite those weak flames. She'd been sad, of course, but not nearly as sad as she felt she ought to be. If Hal blamed her for their inability to have children, he never let on—a mysterious softness for a man who railed at her for allowing the chicken feed to mold or the morning paper to get wet—and with each loss, he brought her flowers, beautiful daffodils he left in a mason jar on the kitchen table. After the initial thrill of marriage wore off, she found herself at twenty only dutifully fond of her husband. But she loved him with a fervor those mornings she woke to the daffodils.

She'd expected to experience some anxiety while watching the men from the Goodwill haul her things onto the truck a couple of weeks ago when she made the first round of purging, perhaps unmoored without the familiar shadows of her household possessions. Instead, she felt freed, untethered to a past she had no recollection of deliberately choosing. She was also intrigued as the two young men tugged Hal's leather recliner down the front steps. What must it be like, she wondered, to spend one's time collecting the detritus of others' lives?

She was dragging a box of dusty paperbacks to the front porch for the second scheduled pickup when she opened the front door to the boy. She'd only seen him from a distance in the week since she took him in during the storm. He'd worked the field for hours with the metal detector, its robotic burping loud enough to reach her patio. *If the whole of America had the work ethic of that boy*, she thought each time she saw him moving through the field, *we wouldn't be in this economic mess*. But there was something disturbing about his dogged obsession as well, a futility and desperation that made her look away.

The boy, dressed in ratty shorts and a linen button-down at least three sizes too large, stood on her butterfly welcome mat balancing a massive platter of cookies. "For you," Daniel said as soon as she opened the door, pushing the platter toward her. There were more than two dozen cookies, all meticulously shaped, a whole almond pressed into each gut. "Now we're even."

"Your mother made these?" Addie said, not reaching for the cookies. How would she ever eat so many by herself? Their presence alone seemed like an overwhelming obligation.

"No," Daniel responded. He did not appear inclined to elaborate.

"Come on in," Addie relented. "I'll need some help eating them."

He lurched inside, his calves devoid of muscle. He slid the plate of cookies on the kitchen counter. The plate appeared homemade, painted a neon green, like some kind of clumpy pottery a kid would bring home from school as a holiday gift for a parent. "The plate's for you. For the metal detector."

I have a plate, Addie almost said, irritated that, no matter how much she gave away, no matter how many boxes she stacked on her porch, things had a way of returning to her: a free can opener from the bank; a sample issue of a cooking magazine appearing, unwanted, in her mailbox; a new pair of silk pajamas left on her doorstep at Christmas, a gift from the Baptist church around the corner she'd been maudlin enough to visit once after Hal's death. But it seemed important to Daniel she accept the plate, and so she did.

"Thank you," Addie said. Daniel shrugged.

Addie poured them each a glass of milk. They stood at the counter nibbling on the sweet, buttery cookies, both silent under the hum of the fluorescent kitchen lights. Addie knew she was not the best at small talk. She'd rarely invited the other farmers' wives over for coffee and dessert when such things were expected of her years ago, and when she did, the weary-eyed women had filed into her tidy parlor in homemade dresses, babies hoisted onto their wide hips, and they'd eaten their pie and sipped their coffee quietly, some of them never sitting down, all of them excusing themselves for one task or another as soon as politeness allowed. Addie always thought her lack of children made the women uncomfortable, reminded them of how precarious their own fortunes were, and she'd hated them for it.

When she said as much to Hal, he'd told her, "That brain of yours is a wild, strange thing," but he quit pestering her to invite the other wives over, and Addie grew to appreciate long, languid days of her own company. She began to deem the presence of others an annoyance, so much so she found herself unnerved by the tender surge of her heart when she heard the boy lapping his milk in timid sips. What kind of boy sipped his milk?

"You know," Addie said cautiously. "It's not so bad being a bit different. You'll see, when you get older. It has its blessings."

Daniel stared at her over his milk, blinked. "That's what people like to say," he said.

"How's that gadget working for you?" Addie asked, relieved to change the subject. "You find some space junk?"

The boy nodded solemnly, pulling a small bag from his pocket. He dumped its contents on the counter: a few barrettes and other hair contraptions, a slew of bolts and nails, two paint-chipped matchbox cars, a fishing lure, a half dozen defunct lighters, and a mound of coins. No space junk as far as Addie could tell.

"Take your pick," Daniel said.

"But I don't want anything," Addie responded, perhaps too quickly. The boy's face clouded. He snaked his hand toward the counter with the intent of sweeping his finds back into the bag. Addie stilled his arm with a gentle palm before he could finish. Wordlessly, she picked through the mound of objects, finally selecting an old-fashioned metal hair comb covered in dirt but otherwise in surprisingly good shape, the kind she used as a young woman to pull her once-heavy hair from her face the way Hal had liked it.

Later, after the boy left, Addie studied that comb for a long time, thinking of the woman who must have worn it, of the man who might have admired the length of the woman's nape with her hair swept up, what she might have been doing when she lost it, if she was still alive, and if so, if she was old now like Addie. She left the comb on the table and fetched the photo albums and her wooden memory box from the cedar chest Hal had made—one of the few furnishings she did not have the heart to give away—and spent the evening poring over the aged photos and keepsakes, studying each picture like a clue, a possible answer to a question she couldn't quite formulate, until she grew too sleepy to sift through the photos any longer.

That was yesterday, and now Addie can see the comb lying a few inches from her face on the patio brick, but she can't make her arm move to reach for it. Early this morning, on a whim, she'd cleaned the comb with dishwashing soap and carefully positioned it in her hair. Then she'd stepped outside on the patio during a gap in the rain to have her coffee and read the paper. The next thing she recalled was opening her eyes to sky the color of gunmetal, her clothes soaked, the comb in her peripheral vision, her body no longer her own.

That was what she had been trying to tell the stranger, the miserable-looking young man who'd been standing over her when she awoke: that she could not feel her arms or legs or anything really, and that it was such an odd feeling, to have one's consciousness liberated from one's body. But the young man disappeared hours ago, and soon after, when the rain stopped for good and the sky finally blued, she'd heard Daniel, the irregular beat of the metal detector throbbing the saturated air, the sound so comforting that when it stopped abruptly, she was certain for a moment her own heart had ceased beating.

She laid there for what seemed like an eternity, thinking of all she needed to tell the boy. She wanted to tell him how delicious his cookies were, how warm and buttery they'd felt against her tongue. She wanted to tell him that she could have been kinder to her husband, that he had been a good man who took great pleasure in small wonders, like artillery shells in a forgotten field and vases of daffodils on grief-shadowed mornings. She wanted to tell him that, if she had the chance to do it again, she would have called him in from the field weeks ago, would have said, *Beautiful, miraculous boy, come, sit beside me in the shade of the patio, let's rest for a spell and set our worries down.* She wanted to tell him how foolish she'd been to think that anything ever truly belonged to anyone.

But she knows that he's long gone, that he finally found what he was looking for all summer. Addie is surprised to feel a pang of disappointment that she missed it, the moment he discovered that bit of metal the universe spat out. How delighted Daniel must have been, holding a piece of the heavens in his hand! She can imagine it now, the boy standing in the tangle of grass, admiring the borrowed treasure nestled in his palm, the way it glints and blazes in the raw morning light, a tiny, salvaged sun.

a face devoid of love or grace

When the boy goes missing, Hannah's giving Luke a hand job in the golfers' restroom off the cart path near what used to be the eighth tee. The emergency sirens are faint at first, a wiggling in the tunnels of her ears.

"Don't stop," Luke says. He double winks his left eye, two boyish, rapid compressions. Sometimes, when Hannah passes Luke and his wife and kids in the parking lot of their townhomes, he'll sneak her one of those winks. Later, he'll ask something like, *Did you see me yesterday? Give you that wink?* It is, she understands, his idea of a grand gesture.

The cinderblock building throbs with heat, the window unit stolen years ago. Droplets of perspiration catch in the crease in Luke's forehead, a tubular-shaped mole at its center, most likely a 458.1, serving as a mini sweat dam. Hannah's been trying to determine if its perimeters have shifted of late, if its shade, the warm brown of a dog's nose, has darkened.

Hannah works as a medical coder, and she's seen things most people don't think possible—cells cannibalizing cells, nipples spewing green puss, toes decomposing on live bone—all afflictions common enough to have their own designated medical coding, any sickness, however unspeakable, easily translatable into a few tidy digits. Our bodies are not unlike loved ones and lovers: they have the capacity to fail us in thousands of ways, and they do.

"What if something's wrong with Pearl or Brady?" Hannah says, a little nastily, because she's tired—they'd bickered for a good half hour before they'd gotten down to business—and Luke's lack of concern for his kids reaffirms what she's known since they were schoolmates: he's selfish, a certifiable prick. But, in his own way, he's sad, too, lost in the malaise of impending middle age, and sometimes Hannah's sadness needs a companion.

"Pearl's at daycare, and Brady's with Lisa's folks," Luke says defensively. Then he sighs, pushes her away, grabs his jeans at his ankles and yanks them up, his thighs as white as moons. He lights a smoke, slumps against the wall. Hannah arranges her skirt. They stand like this for a while, sweating, listening to the sirens getting closer, Hannah studying his face—the rogue mole, the weak line of his jaw, its overall ordinariness—and Luke studying his cigarette, rolling it between thumb and index finger like he hopes to massage some secret from it.

"You should get that mole checked out," Hannah advises. "A kid at work the other day had a tumor on her face this big." She shapes her hand like she's cupping a baseball. "Barnacled onto her forehead. Had to hold her eyes open to watch the cartoons in the waiting room. There's no telling what can sprout up."

"Fuck me, Hannah." Luke ashes his cigarette with a frustrated pump of his thumb. "Why do you say crap like that?"

"I don't know," Hannah says honestly. "I don't want to. I can't help it."

He presses a dry, dreary kiss on her forehead. "You go on. I'm going to finish my smoke." He slaps her crisply on the ass like she's a horse that needs prodding.

Hannah needs no prodding; she dashes out of the building and down the cart path, the weeds knee-high. When she moves like this through the overgrown, long-defunct golf course after leaving a rendezvous with Luke, she imagines she's a character in a Victorian novel, traipsing through the moors, running away from or toward—will the direction really affect the outcome?—the brooding, unknowable lover in her ill-fated love affair.

She'd parked her car in the townhouse lot and walked to meet Luke without going home first, and her work pumps catch on the cracked asphalt of the narrow cart path. Hannah lives in a townhouse she inherited from her parents. It's located in the golf resort community, Living Waters, which has seen, to put it generously, better days. The resort hammocks a lake created in the 1920s when Alabama Power dammed the Tallapoosa River to build a hydroelectric power plant. Whole villages—mainly Black communities—were flooded and are still preserved many feet beneath the party boats zipping around on summer weekends, girls dangling their legs over the pontoons as they wave coozied beers. The citizens promptly renamed their town Lakeview, and if anyone living remembered the original name, Hannah had never heard them speak it.

Hannah's father worked as a floor supervisor at the textile mill. Her parents couldn't afford lakefront living, but, with uncharacteristic optimism, they saved for years for a modest townhouse on the resort golf course. Neither golfed; her father wheezed like a church organ walking to the mailbox. "I like how tidy everything is on a golf course," he'd explained once, shyly, as if embarrassed by the indulgence.

When Hannah was in high school, ambitious international developers bought the resort and built an additional golf course, one they hoped would draw the tournament circuit, fancier condos and townhouses lining its shoulders. Who, Hannah remembers thinking, would want to come here, to the middle of nowhere? As it turns out, no one. Before the seams in the sod fused, the owners filed for bankruptcy, shuttering the original course to save money, the closure creating what Hannah's father liked to call "the golf course ghetto" for those living on its fairways and greens, the good life shifting out of reach again. And then, right after Hannah graduated, her parents—both devoted smokers—died, one dutifully after the other, and none of it mattered anyway.

The large water hazard behind their townhouse transformed into an algae-skinned community pond where retirees now fish for bony crappie, and children toss stale bread to the ducks. Across the street from the pond stretch acres of undeveloped land. A faded FOR SALE sign promises investment opportunities, but everyone knows the land is hilly, full of gullies, none of its perimeters close enough to the lake to provide lake views. The dense forest shivers its greens when Hannah drives past it to and from work, as mysterious as a drawing in a book of fairytales.

Hannah staggers toward the pond, the sirens intensifying
with each step. When she nears the sixth tee, she sees the patrol
cars, the entire Lakeview police fleet, it appears, rimming the
pond's shoreline. Emergency lights pulse a second before
sirens wail, like the tandem dance of lightning and thunder.
A news van with the name of a Montgomery station painted
on its side careens into the parking lot, its roof festooned with
satellites. Officers cluster in a knot. A group of onlookers
hovers a few feet away. Between the uniformed men and the
crowd, a female officer stands with her arm draped around the
sloped back of a brunette woman in a hot pink tracksuit.

Hannah thinks: *Teddy.*

How could she not have thought of him before? She
inventories the crowd, searching for her brother, his gargantuan
mass impossible to overlook. He is nowhere. She yanks off her
shoes and runs through the sea of weeds to her complex, the
gray of its wood siding as dull as bone. Neighbors loiter in a
daze in their doorways, the sirens leaching the curious from
the air-conditioned cool of their homes.

Hannah throws open the townhouse door. Mary, the girl
Hannah has been paying a few bucks an hour to watch Teddy
occasionally this summer, is sprawled on the couch, painting
her toenails, cobalt-blue hair electric against the pale skin of
her face. Her pregnant belly humps from her midsection.

"What the hell?" Mary says, pausing mid-stroke.

"Don't you hear the sirens?"

"Chill," Mary says, fixing the brush over her little toe. "It's
just some missing kid."

"Jesus, Mary," Hannah says. "Where's Teddy?"

Mary shrugs. "He took off a couple of hours ago to hunt
box turtles in the woods. He'll be back. He always comes back."

"Why didn't you stop him? What do I pay you for if you're
not going to watch him?" Hannah says, but she knows it's
impossible to dissuade Teddy once he decides to do something.

The TV bellows, a court show in which the wizened female
judge spends most of her time adjudicating the female plaintiffs'
poor choices in sexual partners. Hannah grabs the remote
control off the coffee table and flips to the channel on the side
of the news van outside. A picture of a little boy—freckled nose
and squinty smile, his milk teeth square and evenly spaced—fills
the screen. He's wearing a bright orange T-shirt with a graphic

of a chomping tyrannosaur. *Bite Me* floats out of the dinosaur's mouth. The boy has a dimple in his cheek so deep it looks as if someone has scooped out a bit of flesh with one of those melon ballers. His name, according to the scrolling text across the bottom of the screen, is Caleb Lexington.

The photo of the boy is followed by live video of his mother in a pink velvet tracksuit with JUICY rhinestoned across her chest. "Are we on?" she asks. She grabs the microphone from the off-screen reporter, looks directly into the camera. "Ray, if you had something to do with this, if you took our boy, I'll kill you." Her eyes go limp. She holds the mic out to the reporter as if she doesn't quite understand how it ended up in her hand. "I only looked away for a few minutes," she whispers.

"Good God, what is that lady wearing?" Mary says.

"I know that boy." The legitimacy of Hannah's statement surprises her. "I see him sometimes at the pond feeding the ducks."

Actually, Caleb likes to hurl bread at the ducks, then yell and chase them around the pond with a ferocity Hannah suspects does not bode well for his future moral character. According to the reporter, that is exactly what three-year-old Caleb was doing, chasing the ducks at the pond, when he vanished. The concern, other than the fear of abduction or drowning, is that he wandered into the densely wooded acreage across the street and got lost.

The last time Hannah had seen Caleb harassing the ducks, she'd been with Teddy, and he'd chucked his own handful of bread at the boy. "How do you like it?" Teddy asked Caleb, who appeared more curious than scared. The topography of Teddy's face tends to mesmerize children. To be fair to her brother, his own moral compass is compromised by a wrecked frontal lobe that values the well-being of animals, from centipedes to bears, above all else, including children.

"A coyote killed little Ansleigh's Shih Tzu from 21C last month right in front of her," Mary reminds her, and Hannah thinks of a tiny Caleb lost in the woods, battling the wild like a redneck Mowgli. A reporter came out for the coyote mauling, too, interviewing the girl, who, from her enthusiastic comments, seemingly forgot the dead pet in her delight to be in the local paper. Hannah didn't blame her; girls learn fast around here that you take your glow where you can get it.

Caleb's mother is not preening for the cameras; she's bawling now, mascara sluicing down her cheeks. When she tries to speak, gasps belch from her throat.

It strikes Hannah as surreal—the mother crying here on the TV screen and there at the pond, a couple of hundred yards away.

"She did it," Mary says. "Every time a mother caterwauls on the news they find the kid rotting in her car trunk. Now they've got those baby boxes for unwanted newborns—all warm and shit, little baby toasters—so teenage skanks don't toss them in dumpsters. But what do you do with an older kid? You bash its head in and leave it in the woods and howl on camera about predators. People are monsters. The world is going to shit."

"What?" Mary says when Hannah raises a sharp brow. "I saw the baby toasters on the news. I'm not researching options or anything." She caps the nail polish, leans over with admirable flexibility and blows on her toes. "Hey," she says, "is that Teddy?"

Hannah glances toward the door, but it's closed, no hulking Teddy shadowing its frame.

"No, not here." Mary aims a big toe at the TV screen. "Look, Teddy's on TV!"

And there he is, where he wasn't before, at the front of the crowd of craning onlookers. His head floats a foot above everyone else's, graying hair rupturing from what's left of his chin. His pitted forehead tics. His nose, a product of a dozen reconstructive surgeries, slants sharply east. The camera settles on his face, as if it serves as an apt image to illustrate the horror of the loss of a boy, the devastation of a mother. Teddy's lone eye fills the screen.

Searchlights materialize on the fairway when night falls, dozens of glowing orbs suspended in the gloaming.

The lights confuse the sea turtles, Teddy signs. He and Hannah are sitting on the bench in his bedroom peering out the open window overlooking the golf course, their evening ritual for the better part of two decades. Teddy's girth takes up most of the bench. Hannah clings to an edge, her wine glass balanced on one thigh. The scent of sewage from the resort sewage facility up the road tinges the night with an earthy, overly fecund smell, as if anything could grow out there.

Throngs of neighbors roam the course below, the spectacle eerily similar to a scene from a doomsday film, the unfortunate misfits left behind to make sense of things in a forsaken world. The children are spasmodic with excitement. They pelt each other with golf balls they find like Easter eggs in the tall grass. They shove handfuls of sand in each other's faces from the bunkers. Their mothers hover nearby, wary. A few men stalk the cart path with shotguns hoisted over their shoulders, jubilant with vigilance. In the distance, resilient Kentucky blue grass shadows the slight indentation of the fifth-hole green. A beer-bellied guy in a bright orange and blue War Eagle T-shirt pokes a stick at the grass, searching, Hannah presumes, for Caleb's body.

"Emily Dickinson liked to sit in her bedroom window and watch the world pass by," Hannah says, which she's said every night they've sat on this bench. Before Teddy became this Teddy, Hannah had been a whimsical eighth grader, a star student, an avid writer and artist, a lover of books, particularly poetry, which mystified her parents, stolid, pragmatic, work-your-fingers-to-the-bone-and-bear-it kind of people realistically pessimistic about the economic possibilities of their world and, after Teddy's accident, the limits of human decency and compassion. Eventually, Hannah learned well enough.

But for some reason the brief author bio of the plain, wan Dickinson in Mrs. Smith's American lit text stuck with Hannah. The tale of Dickinson's self-imposed isolation, her macabre preoccupations, her immutable sorrow, lingered like an ominous prophecy long after Hannah began neglecting her books and sketch pads for the artistry of Teddy's rehabilitation. There were unexpected gifts in the many demands of Teddy's care: a clear sense of purpose, meaningful work, an escape from the local teenage pastime of self-destruction. While Hannah's friends were getting wasted at the boat landing and deflowered in the beds of hand-me-down trucks, Hannah was teaching her adult brother how to say his name intelligibly, how to shape his fingers to sign the alphabet. At fourteen, Hannah could flush his gastro tube and pump it with a handful of crushed pills with spectacular speed, locate a vein in the meaty hinge of his arm with the tip of a pinkie, run two rotations of his physical therapy exercises in the time it took her parents to coax him to sit up in bed. His afternoon sponge baths were her first lessons in existentialism: Is Teddy Teddy? she'd muse while dragging the sponge over each limb. Was the old Teddy the real Teddy or is the new Teddy the real Teddy? If the old Teddy can become a completely new Teddy, is there really any such thing as Teddy?

She was, her parents bragged to family and friends, a natural caretaker.

Usually, Teddy will ask Hannah to read to him old schoolbooks she keeps under the bench, his preference the naturalist poems of Keats and Shelley, but tonight he signs, *Tons of baby sea turtles, Han. Like a city of turtles every year.*

"I think the sea turtles are safe this far away from the gulf," Hannah reassures Teddy. She feels guilty she has not joined the volunteers. But she cannot leave Teddy, who is weary and rattled from the many questions Lieutenant Loomis asked when he showed up at their door not long after Teddy arrived home: *Why were you at the pond by yourself today? Did you see Caleb Lexington at the pond today? Do you like to watch the children feed the ducks at the pond? Do you know Caleb Lexington? At what time did you go to the pond today? Did you talk with Caleb Lexington?*

When Teddy failed to answer Lieutenant Loomis's questions, the lieutenant changed tactics; he asked Hannah to call him J.B., took his hat off, smiled a lot, slapped Teddy on the shoulder, on the thigh, as if they were old buddies, which, it turns out, they sort of were.

"We graduated the same year," Lieutenant Loomis said. "I was kind of a loner and kept to myself, but I liked Teddy. I remember he played a mean guitar." He looked at his shiny uniform shoes when he said it.

Hannah had no memory, no recollection at all, of Teddy ever playing the guitar, but something in Lieutenant Loomis's softer demeanor must have stirred her brother because Teddy perched his hands over the tablet he occasionally uses to speak and furiously typed a long lecture on ducks (did J.B. know ducks defecate every fifteen minutes for flight efficiency?) and their mating rituals, detailing the drake's aggression when copulating, the fact it has a penis—a rarity in the bird population—that is sometimes the length of its body, all of this delivered in the ridiculously jaunty British accent of Teddy's tablet.

Lieutenant Loomis checked his watch. Fidgeted with his shirt buttons. He eyed Hannah pleadingly, as if he expected her to translate Teddy's ramblings into a declaration of guilt. Hannah should have told him not to bother trying to get a straight answer from her brother. Teddy's hippocampus is a wasteland. If you ask him what he did that morning, he might offer a detailed description, down to the color of his bowel movement, or he might rhapsodize about the monarch butterfly's astonishing ability to traverse continents with a wingspan of ten centimeters.

While Teddy typed, Hannah studied her brother. Could he have hurt the boy? Teddy wouldn't *intentionally* hurt Caleb, yet her brother struggles with regulating his anger and frustration, underestimates his own strength. He's bruised Hannah's arms in his overeager grip, blackened her eyes more than once with a fitful elbow. And a fragile little kid? One firm push, one hard blow, and who knows?

Teddy zoned out after he exhausted his duck trivia, his listing face as expressionless as a melon, saying only, right before Lieutenant Loomis left, "I like your handcuffs," which, in Teddy's own voice, sounded perverted even to Hannah, the syllables halting, what remains of his jaw inflexible, his tongue an unruly wad—a tragedy of his own making. When Hannah was thirteen and Teddy almost twenty, her brother drove his truck down an isolated dirt road used by park rangers to access the trails in Horseshoe Bend National Park, sat on his tailgate and drank a fifth of Smirnoff until the sun rose, then propped the barrel of their father's hunting rifle under his chin, tucked his big toe on the trigger, and blew off half his mandible.

By sheer luck, poachers found him and dumped him on the curb at the local hospital, where they transported him by air to UAB. After the sheriff identified the poachers from the hospital's surveillance footage, they discovered Teddy's truck, and in the glove compartment, a suicide letter wild with vague regret and longing. Until he died, Hannah's father kept it in his bedside drawer next to his mother's obituary, a palm-sized painting of a lagoon gifted to his own father by a Solomon Islander during WWII, and the delicate lace cap Hannah's baby sister, stillborn, had worn at the hospital. The last sentence of Teddy's letter read: *I want I want I want.*

Teddy before his suicide attempt had been no different than most of the young men Hannah knew—underemployed, bored, lit with a nameless rage. He made minimum wage cleaning the elementary and high school, spent his nights cruising town at a wrathful speed or scrapping with other hotheads in the parking lot of the Rodeo Club. He was singular only in his size.

"Why? Why? Why?" her parents kept asking while the surgeons salvaged Teddy at the hospital in Birmingham.

In the absence of any explanation, Hannah provided her own. She spent those long hours in the hospital waiting room, crafting a gothic narrative that explained her brother's inexplicable actions. With few clues to guide her, Hannah settled on unrequited love, conjured an unattainable, sensitive beauty with a fondness for sundresses and cowboy boots, the kind of girl who could right Teddy's tilted world if she'd only give him the chance. At the time, Teddy's attempted suicide had seemed to Hannah, a stupidly romantic teen, the one heroic gesture of her brother's otherwise unexceptional life.

It would be years before she heard the rumors—Teddy and a teenage boy caught in the bushes at the park, the parents' threats of criminal charges. The boy had been seventeen, not much younger than Teddy, and certainly older than some of the girls Teddy's friends had been dating at the time, couplings no one ever blinked an eye at. But he'd been a student at the high school Teddy cleaned, and since Teddy was employed by the school district, the parents' threats had teeth in a conservative town like theirs. At the very least Teddy would have lost his job and suffered unspeakable humiliation.

The ducks hate to be chased. It frightens them. Teddy's good eye blinks. It's a splendid color—a blue as light as those pictures of the ocean at exotic locales in the brochures Hannah keeps in her bedside table. The other one is stitched closed like a patched doll.

"I know," Hannah says, "but we all do things we shouldn't do, particularly little boys. Did you see Caleb today, chasing the ducks? Did you ask him to stop?"

Teddy gestures to a few paunchy men in ill-fitting suits passing on the grass. *Why aren't some of the cops wearing uniforms? The uniforms are the best part.* He is sitting so close to the open window, the screen so flimsy that a nudge, a bump of her hip, would send him tumbling into the air conditioning unit below.

Unable to stop herself, Hannah reaches for the backside of Teddy's thigh and pinches the loose flesh there.

"Ouch," Teddy yells. *Something bit me.*

"I'm sorry," Hannah says, and she is—deeply sorry— every time she sneaks a pinch or smacks him on the forehead with his hairbrush or dumps his peach yogurt into the sink or flushes one of his goldfish down the toilet or hides his alligator slippers in the laundry basket or wishes him dead. She strokes Teddy's hair, and he leans into her and sighs. He smells like a baby: the sweet-sour of urine and applesauce. If she had a pouch, like a mother kangaroo, she would tuck him into it, keep him warm and safe—from himself, from the world, from her.

"Did you see anything at the pond today? Something you want to tell me? Something that will help them find Caleb?"

Sam molted today, and I missed it. Teddy points to one of the half dozen aquariums and terrariums that line his wall. They hold a variety of garden snakes, four box turtles, and a moribund iguana Hannah often mistakes for dead. The wall above them is papered in snake skins. It reminds Hannah of a giant human back suffering a peel after a bad burn. Arranged in a decorative circle around the snakeskins are a series of x-rays from work Hannah was supposed to destroy but brought home for Teddy, who studies their intricate patterns—the iodine-lit pathways of veins, the shadowy geography of tissue and bone—as if they are puzzles to be solved. Sometimes, he'll hold one up to his lamp, ask, *What does this look like?* It's a game they play, a kind of biological Rorschach test. Teddy always answers with the name of an animal; Hannah always answers with a name of a place other than here.

Without warning, Teddy jumps from the bench and climbs into his bed. He pulls the quilt over his head, which means he wants to be alone. His enormous feet hang off the end of the mattress. Those too-big tennis shoes peeking out of a comforter patterned in the frogs of South America seem to sum up all the heartache in the world.

Hannah lingers, sipping the last of her wine. Luke's wife and fuzzy-headed daughter, Pearl, are on their back patio two townhouses over taking in the search. His wife, a mousy girl who never spoke in school beyond answering roll, notices Hannah in the window, offers a restrained wave in deference to the occasion. Hannah doesn't like the woman, but not for the obvious reasons. She finds her self-satisfied. Lisa insisted on naming the baby Pearl, as if her body had produced and polished a wondrous gem. There are over seven billion people alive on the earth at this very moment. More than a hundred billion have lived before. Hannah knows, because she looks up statistics like these, and the fact of her insignificance comforts her.

"A mother duck will pluck down from her own breast to line her nest for her chicks," Teddy announces from beneath the comforter.

Hannah walks to Teddy's bed, sits beside the lump of him. Beneath his mattress is an old *Hustler* he must have found while searching for turtles. He thinks he has hidden the magazine from her. Teddy might not be Teddy, but he is still a man, still has his secrets. She leans close to where she estimates his ear might be, whispers, "Did you hurt that boy in the park?"

"Hurt?" he echoes. His breathing beneath the fabric is wet, fibrous.

"How many kinds of hurt are there, Teddy?" Hannah asks.

But of course, the list is endless.

Hannah hears the thuds on her bedroom window around midnight. She thinks it's a bird at first, throwing itself against the glass, which Teddy says they sometimes do when mistaking the reflection of the sky for the real thing. Then she hears the voices, the low murmurs, the nervous laughter. She gets out of bed and walks to the window, slides back the drapes. There, on her patio, is a ring of five boys, a few small preteens, the rest older. Their faces are half hidden in baseball caps—why do boys these days wear baseball caps at night?—and they are clutching the tallboys and old golf balls Hannah uses as decorations in her flower beds. Most of the search volunteers have called it a night, but a few stragglers walk the fairway, their flashlights staggering in the distance.

Hannah lifts the window, says, "Y'all get on out of here before I call the cops."

They have, it appears, freed Teddy's ferrets from their hutches. A couple of the wilier ferrets make for the grass, but most squat and shudder on the patio, overwhelmed by the freedom, the vast shimmering landscape. Poor babies, Hannah thinks. They've been pampered. Chances are, she'll lose most of them to coyotes and cats before she can round them up. It will be a slaughter.

"From what we hear," one boy says in a wavering voice, "the cops already been here." From the sheer size of the kid, who, like Teddy, towers over his peers, she knows it's Sean Grayson, the star quarterback at Lakeview High and the son of the man who maintains the grounds of the still-functioning golf course. Sometimes, to get out of the house, Hannah takes Teddy to the Friday-night games, and he watches the action on the field with the avid focus of a lifelong fan, mesmerized by the talented Sean, who, just a freshmen, already maneuvers the ball with a precision and grace that transcends their small town. Watching Sean sometimes evokes in Hannah a keen sense of loss, as if perhaps Teddy could have had a chance at something like a football career if not for the accident, and she has to remind herself that the old Teddy had no interest in playing football or any other sport. He was the kid smoking dope behind the bleachers.

Sean lifts his face and stares at her beseechingly; it's obvious from his cowed expression he's here because it's expected of him, and he's hoping she'll be humiliated enough by her disfigured brother and his perverted proclivities to retreat into the house so he and his friends can get back to destroying her patio.

"My dad told me what Tard Teddy done to that kid back in the day," pipes up the smallest kid. Red curls flank his jaw. His braces silver in the patio floodlight. "Bet he done it to that little boy, too. They'll take care of him good in prison."

"Is that you, Brady?" She recognizes Luke's son, all bowed up and pissed off, not unlike Luke at that age. She'd never cared for Luke much then, his arrogance, the cruel set of his mouth. It was an appalling thing to admit, but she preferred him now, humbled by age and mediocrity. "I'll do worse than call the cops," Hannah says. She points a finger at Sean. "I'll call Coach Biddescombe." She turns her attention to Brady. "And you—I'll tell your daddy if you don't put that golf ball down."

The other boys snicker, goad Brady with their elbows. "A pervert don't change his ways," Brady says. "And a retarded pervert's still a motherfucking pervert like a slut's always a slut."

He raises his arm and fires the golf ball at the window, the other boys, including Sean, following suit, Hannah too startled to duck. A pane shatters, the glass showering the boys, who howl and scatter in all directions on the fairway, the white of their sneakers spectral in the moonlight.

Hannah stares at the window. The broken glass splinters the night, the moon a patchwork of disjointed parts. The night looks askew, like another world in which anything could happen. A world in which Teddy might have hurt a small boy—a too-tight grip, a frustrated shove—and tucked the broken body in a safe place, perhaps under a fallen log in the woods, a sweet spot for collecting salamanders and ring-neck snakes.

She hasn't attended church since the preacher suggested Teddy's suicide attempt was part of God's masterful plan, a way to coax a wayward Teddy back into the gentle fold. It had been a relief, really, to escape the bullshit platitudes. So much so she eventually exiled her Bible to the bottom drawer of her dresser, replacing it with stacks of travel guides and brochures, Belize and Jamaica and Tuscany their own kind of salvation.

She still prays daily, in part to have someone to talk to other than Teddy. She does so now, kneeling beside her bed, her hands pressed chastely together like she learned as a child. She asks what she always asks: that God remind her of the rich rewards of sacrifice, the grace of sustained faith, the smallness of her suffering, the basic goodness of mankind, including Teddy, including herself. She waits for serenity to settle upon her.

When that doesn't work, she goes downstairs and pours herself a glass of bourbon, and then another, finally falling asleep on the couch, where she dreams of a young Teddy, before the accident. In her dream he is jovial, his face intact, his skin unmarred, almost iridescent. He gives her a present, a large box wrapped cheerily in a pink bow. She peels the paper away to find another layer, another bow, then another layer, another bow, again and again, the reams of paper spiraling her ankles. Finally—eureka!—she's down to the bare cardboard box. The box opens on its own, *open sesame* she says after the fact, and there, inside the box, is a squat duck, its duck face a squall of fury, its wretched breast plucked bald. *Oh, darling,* dream Hannah says. She places a finger on its little duck head, strokes his velvety down. For some reason, she understands this is a sage duck, an all-knowing duck, a duck oracle, and she asks what she must: *Is my verse alive?* The duck unhinges its bill hesitantly, as if it has something to say but is reluctant to say it. She presses its glossy bill to her ear. *Bite me*, the duck booms. Then it licks her. Then it says, *Delicious.* Since when do ducks have tongues? dream Hannah puzzles.

When Hannah wakes, the sun is brilliant, the sky cloudless. It is good weather, she thinks, to hunt a lost boy.

She slips out onto the patio to have her coffee, the air musky from the hutches. A solitary ferret, frozen with fear, vibrates on the concrete patio, which has been spray-painted with obscenities—*pedo, baby killer, perv.* The flowerpots are busted, the webbing in the patio chairs shredded. She tucks the grateful ferret back into the hutch but doesn't bother cleaning up the mess. Instead she watches a pair of divers, suited and masked, waddle on flippers, like mutant seals, into the nuclear green of the pond. A couple of reporters loiter in the parking lot, their crews sprawled in lounge chairs at the edge of the pond, heavy equipment at their feet, everyone gloomy with the boredom of the wait. A helicopter thrashes the sky above them.

Teddy's inside watching—for the third time that week—a documentary on Chantek, the signing, McDonalds-loving Sumatran orangutan raised as a human, then determined to be too human for his own animal good; eventually, he was banished to a zoo to suffer the indignities of feces-smeared cages and forced companions he calls, with no small derision, orange dogs. Hannah doesn't like the orangutans, the intensity of their stares; they look as if they know something about her that she does not know about herself.

Hannah finds the least damaged chair, rights it, and sits to watch the divers slip beneath the water, their flippers stirring the thin crust of the surface. She should be surprised, she guesses, when she spots Luke tiptoeing barefoot through the grass, bare-chested and in his pajama bottoms, but it seems fitting in a world gone mad.

He squats in front of her so he's hidden by the patio hedge, puts his finger to his mouth to indicate the need for secrecy. "I only have a minute. I told Lisa I'm having a smoke." He points to the graffiti on the patio. "This is what I wanted to warn you about. People are talking all kinds of crazy shit about Teddy, what they think he did to that boy, what they're going to do to him. They say Loomis is getting a warrant, and if he doesn't, they'll take care of things themselves."

"Who's 'they'"? Hannah says.

Luke shrugs his freckled shoulders. "People, Hannah. What does it matter? I'm just saying you might want to go ahead and take him in. He'll be safer in custody until this is all sorted out. If nothing else, get him out of the neighborhood."

"Custody?" Hannah says. "Like jail? Teddy can't go to jail. It would kill him."

"That's generally what happens when someone commits a crime." Luke stretches his arm over a broken flowerpot, rubs his calloused thumb across the top of her foot. "Maybe it wouldn't be such a bad thing for you, you know? Maybe you could finally go back to school like you've been talking about."

Hannah snorts. Auburn University is barely a thirty-minute drive from their town, but for Hannah and most of the people she grew up with, it might as well be on another continent.

"I've been wondering," Hannah says. "Do you know anybody that golfs? I mean, I see people golfing, but I don't know them. My dad sure as hell couldn't afford it. Nobody I know can. I can't think of one person I *know* know who has ever, even once, played golf. Who are these people? Why can they golf? Why can't we?"

"Are you OK, Hannah?" Luke asks. He reaches for her knees and palms them. "Because I really need you to focus."

"You're an asshole, Luke."

"What?" Luke says, looking genuinely perplexed.

A crowd of volunteers is gathering at the sixth tee, linking hands to stretch the width of the fairway, unfolding in a human search chain.

"This is a whole lot of fuss for one little boy," Hannah says. "A million babies die on their day of birth in the world each year. You don't see such a ruckus over them."

Luke draws back his hands. "Do you ever actually hear what you say?"

One of the divers pops through the surface of the pond. The gallery of observers rises from their lawn chairs in unison. They sink down in disappointment when the diver shakes his head no.

"What do you think the duck symbolizes?" Hannah asks Teddy because there is no one else to ask. He won't quit fidgeting with the car stereo, even while she shares her dream. He's been searching for the perfect road-trip song since they left the townhouse over an hour ago, and the constant switching of channels makes her feel as if she's suffering some sort of auditory seizure. She'd feared that they might get mauled by a mob in the townhouse parking lot, or stopped by the police, but the big escape was all very anticlimactic. No one seemed to care they were leaving, the lack of concern reassuring.

Ducks have tongues, Teddy signs. "There's a bone in them called the paraglossum," he says aloud. *Paraglossum* comes out like a train wreck of syllables, but Hannah's fluent in Teddy-speak. He grins at her from the passenger seat. His finely boned hands, as big as salad plates, fumble with the radio buttons, the muscles contracting in jerks. Sometimes, Hannah's transfixed by the thought of those hands weighing their father's gun, gripping its butt, the metal cold against Teddy's sensitive fingertips; but today she sees them grasping Caleb's shoulders, noosing Caleb's neck, thrashing Caleb's limp body.

Hannah tries to put Caleb Lexington and Teddy's possible involvement in his disappearance out of her mind. Nothing productive will come of Hannah worrying over it. If Teddy hurt Caleb, the police will figure it out eventually, and if he didn't, things will go on as they always have. Either option is unthinkable.

"Maybe it means you miss Daren. I liked Daren," Teddy says. "Where's Daren?"

She's occasionally startled by her brother's perceptiveness. Daren was Hannah's last real boyfriend, a revisited high school flame who ultimately cited Teddy as the primary reason for ending things the second time—a readily available excuse. "Daren was a dick," she says.

Daren wasn't a dick.

"Dick-ish, then."

I'm hungry, Teddy signs. He's always hungry. He squirms in the seat, his forehead twitching in agitation, an early warning of a low-blood-sugar tantrum. She pulls off at the next exit for a McDonald's drive-through, catching the tail end of breakfast, and orders a sausage biscuit, a yogurt parfait, and two coffees so hot they burn her fingers. She hands one to Teddy anyway, and when he yelps a moment later, Hannah feels both shamed and satisfied.

She steers into a parking spot. They generally eat in the car when on the road; it's easier than dealing with the gawkers. She tosses the parfait into Teddy's lap, and he tries to pry off the top with hands, his tremors particularly bad because she forgot to give him his medicine this morning. His jaw and facial muscles were so impaired by the trauma of the bullet that eating solids is more painful and troublesome than it's worth, and the inability to eat only magnifies the want. He eyes her biscuit resentfully.

I can't open the yogurt, Teddy signs. He thrusts the parfait at Hannah, knocking her scalding coffee into her lap.

"Jesus, Teddy!" she yells, sopping up the coffee with flimsy napkins. When she's as clean as she's going to get, she unwraps her biscuit and takes a bite, chewing slowly and methodically, and Teddy, watching intently, works his mouth in unison.

"I'm hungry, Hannah," he says, contrite now.

"Well, I can't eat and feed you at the same time," Hannah says. "So you'll have to wait."

She thinks of the old Sunday-school parable of the long spoons, how people in hell, compelled to eat with spoons longer than their arms, refused to feed those across the table, and everyone starved.

"You're a pain in the ass," she says through a mouthful of biscuit. She yanks the top from the parfait, unwraps the plastic spoon, and plunges it into the yogurt, then shovels a massive scoop into Teddy's mouth, clumps falling down his shirt. Before he can swallow, she shoves in another, and another, until the cup is empty.

"Better?" she asks.

Teddy nods gratefully. "I love you, Hannah."

"I love you, too, Teddy," she says because she does. That's what makes everything so terrible.

She hands him a few napkins, throws the rest of her biscuit into the bag, and they pull back onto the highway. As they near the airport, the traffic picks up, luggage pressed against windows, children bent over electronics in backseats. Planes rocket overhead, their mechanical bellies exposed.

"I wonder where everyone is going," she says. It's an unfathomable concept—getting in the car and driving to the airport and flying somewhere far away.

Hannah's only plan is to head east, toward Atlanta; she likes the hilly landscape. She thinks they might shop at the underground mall and have a late lunch in Buckhead, but Teddy notices the advertisement for Six Flags Over Georgia on the McDonald's bag, and before she can curb his enthusiasm, he's concocted a plan she knows she cannot escape.

"It'll be fun," Teddy says. "The Acrophobia, the Goliath, the Ninja! What do you want to ride first?" He's too excited to sign. The words tumble from his mouth.

Hannah has no idea how he knows the names of the rides, if Six Flags is a hot topic amongst Teddy and his friends from physical therapy. He goes on in this manner for a solid half hour until he wears himself out, then he dozes, his head cocked back, his twisted nose flaring with each breath, his eye seeping tears. His hairline, she notes, is receding, time granting no mercy to any body. "Poor Teddy," she says. She strokes her brother's knee as if he were a docile, beloved pet.

When they arrive at Six Flags, the main lot is full. They park in overflow and walk to the entrance, which is chaotic and packed with people, very few of whom seem the least bit happy considering they've come willingly to an amusement park. Parents wearing bloated backpacks wilt in the heat. Toddlers stuffed into strollers pull at their straps, kick off their shoes, pitch bottles and pacifiers into the air. Bored teenagers thumb the screens of their phones, forgetting to move with the line. As always, people gape at Teddy. Even grown men and women who know better can't help themselves; his face is a testament to all the bad things mothers tell their children can happen if they aren't diligent.

After an hour of waiting, Hannah surrenders the outrageous admission fee—enough for a week of groceries—and they trip through the gates with all the other fools. The park smells of sweat and frying oil.

Teddy grabs Hannah's hand and guides her through the crowd. For once, she's grateful for his bulk, following in his wake with relative ease. They stop abruptly at a canary-yellow roller coaster rising above them in a twist of bright metal. "The Georgia Scorcher," Teddy says breathlessly, bouncing on the balls of his feet, his thick fingers still cradling Hannah's.

"You go on and ride, Teddy. I'll wait here." She gestures toward a bench tucked under the shade of a tree, where an older woman in an American flag sweatshirt and chalk-colored

Rockport sneakers sits half asleep, her lap full of rhinestone purses and Six Flags shopping bags, a large birthmark on her cheek the shape and shade of spilled wine, a 757.32. It takes the woman a full minute to notice Hannah, and another to shift her rear end to make room. Hannah has a decent view of Teddy, who is already in line. He waves at her, and she waves back.

"Those are my grandbabies there," the woman says proudly, pointing to two preteens in unflattering cutoffs not far behind Teddy. "They've been riding the Scorcher all day. It's the best ride in the park." One of the girls crosses her arms over her chest and tilts her head away from her sister, who's yelling in her face while punching the air with her finger.

"They look like they're having fun."

"Oh yes," the woman says. "They love it here. We have season passes. You waiting on your kids?"

"My brother."

"No kids?" the woman asks.

Hannah thinks of Luke and his wife, of little baby Pearl, who they probably bring to places like this, though she and Luke never talk about such things, or anything really. Mainly they have sex, efficient and unambitious in its scope, then, if it's late at night and Teddy and Luke's wife are asleep, they sip bourbon from Luke's flask and wander the golf course like aimless teenagers, searching for golf balls or breaking into the old, shuttered clubhouse to sit at the bar, feeling like the last two people in a forgotten land.

Hannah tries to imagine Luke here with her now, their own baby padlocked to her chest in one of those baby carriers, a little Pearl-but-not-Pearl, what it might feel like to palm the head of her own child. She wants to conjure a sense of awe, a reverence for a tiny life she shepherded into the world, but a baby just seems like another thing to take care of.

"Not yet. But I am engaged. To the doctor who owns the practice where I work."

"Doctors work long hours," the woman says forebodingly.

"I'm a poet," Hannah explains. "I need a lot of time for my writing, anyway."

"A poet," the woman repeats. "How interesting." She doesn't sound interested at all.

Teddy is climbing onto the ride now, the attendant lowering the restraints over his chest, the smile on his face as broad as his reconstructed mouth will allow. Hannah fishes in her purse for her phone to take a picture, but the car is already staggering forward, then climbing, climbing, climbing—at least ten stories—before diving violently, the screams of its riders trailing behind. Its contortions look torturous, but when the ride grinds to a stop, everyone exits laughing and jubilant, including Teddy, who makes a beeline for Hannah, his face flush, his hair wild and windblown.

The woman looks at Hannah in the way most people do when they meet Teddy. Before she can say something stupid and condescending, her astonishing birthmark inspires Teddy to find his voice. "Wow," he exclaims in wonder, his hand darting out to knead the woman's face.

Hannah allows the mauling to persist for a few seconds before reprimanding her brother. "Teddy!" she warns, and he releases the woman apologetically.

"It's OK, honey," the woman says, though it's clearly not. "The special ones are God's precious gifts."

I want to ride it again, Teddy signs.

"I thought we'd do the Cyclone next," Hannah says, attempting enthusiasm. She stands, collects her purse. "It's right around the corner."

No. This one. Teddy's knees lock.

"We'll come back later."

"No." He points at the line to the Scorcher, and as Hannah turns to leave, he shoves her, hard. She sails toward the bench, her hands slamming the wood slats.

"Oh my," the woman says. "Did he hurt you?" No one else seems to notice. Crowds continue to stream past. Screams of delighted riders swell and fade.

Teddy waits for Hannah to stand. "The line is getting long," he says, his words startlingly lucid.

"You go on. I'll sit this one out. Maybe the next round."

He vanishes before she finishes a sentence. Silently, the woman hands her a tissue.

There's a nasty gash in Hannah's palm. She considers her hand, the blood beading the seam of the cut. The cells of a body completely replace themselves every seven to ten years. Hannah and Teddy's bodies have been replaced, cell by cell, several times in their lifetimes, at least twice since Teddy held their father's rifle in his hands and positioned the barrel beneath his chin. This hand, she thinks as she presses the tissue against the blood, is an entirely new hand, nothing of the fanciful thirteen-year-old girl left beyond her genetic coding. A person, she thinks, could become anyone.

She feels an urgent need to tell someone this, but when she glances up, the woman is gone.

A few minutes later, Teddy stumbles through the exit gate, his face luminous as he bypasses Hannah and rejoins the line. She watches him thread the roped path, board the coaster, spill off, and do it all again, over and over, the sun sinking in the sky. She waits and waits, yet he never tires, never grows bored. She can't recall ever seeing him so happy.

As dusk sets in, she stands, stretching her back and calf muscles, and scans for a bathroom sign, locating one along the path to the entrance. Teddy, she figures, won't even note her absence.

The park is beyond packed now, purses slamming her arms and legs, strollers nipping at her heels. She keeps her head down, trying to find unoccupied space for her feet and counting her steps to calm herself. When she reaches two hundred, she knows she's passed the bathrooms, but she keeps walking. Faster.

She doesn't slow until she's in the car, panting, struggling to fit the key into the ignition, her hands as palsied as Teddy's. Finally, the engine starts, and she backs cautiously out. The car feels unwieldy as she navigates the lot, maneuvering around the shambling bands of battle-worn families, parents holding their children to keep them safe in the evaporating light. Headlights flick on like lightning bugs.

She files in line to merge onto the highway, the sounds of the machinations of her body amplified, each chant of her heart as audible as a clap. It is, she believes, nothing short of miraculous, like hearing the voice of God.

When her breathing and pulse regulate, she turns on the radio, generic pop filling the car—something about shooting stars and big asses, set to the kind of optimistic electronic beat favored by young girls. Hannah sings along, her voice giddy.

She thinks of heading north for a few days, maybe to the Smokies, where she imagines the mountains shrouded in misty clouds. Wherever she goes, she won't hear the news for some time that Caleb Lexington was discovered that afternoon—

very much alive—splashing in a shallow creek a half mile deep in the woods surrounding her neighborhood. He returned with outlandish tales of squirrels in spectacles and a giant, hot dog-bestowing fairy—the magical, nonsensical imaginings of a preschooler after a grand adventure. In the footage the local TV stations play repeatedly, the boy appears to be in good spirits as he's carried from the canopy of trees, a candy bar plugged into his mouth, which he removes to mug for the cameras. He doesn't stop grinning until he's placed into his sobbing mother's arms, and then something in his expression shifts, his smile growing uncertain, quivering at the edges, before finally coming undone. His mother runs her hands over his chest, his back, each limb, then clutches his chin to examine his face, her gaze locking with his. Only then does he cry, as loud as a newborn. And the boy, so very young, will surely remember none of this: the moment he looked into his mother's eyes and saw in them all that has been lost.

acts of restitution

What Mick did to that old lady is unspeakable, but that doesn't stop his mother from bringing it up nearly daily. Her birthday is no exception.

"I'm the same age she was when you did that to her," she says now, the layer of fat on the birthday pot roast between them as hard as an exoskeleton. Mick has been expecting such an observation. He's surprised she didn't mention it earlier.

"It's like it could have been me," she adds, pointing to her aged face. It was scary, seeing his mother in natural light for the first time in more than fifteen years when she picked him up on his mandatory release date five months ago, him waiting on the curb behind Donaldson Correctional Facility like school had let out.

"I would never hurt you," Mick says. "We've talked about this a thousand times. Let's try to enjoy your birthday." He reaches for the key lime pie, his mother's favorite, sitting there untouched, sweating out its cool sweetness. His mother slaps his hand, no differently than when he was a boy.

"But you did. It's all I can think about sometimes, trying to figure what I did wrong."

"I'm sorry, Mama," he says, and his mother slumps a few additional inches toward the table. She stopped drinking the day Mick was arraigned, but she's the worst kind of dry drunk, one shitty day away from taking a drink, the threat to her sobriety an additional item to tack on to the list of MICK'S CRIMES AGAINST HUMANITY.

"You were such a good boy, Mick. So gentle and soft spoken. You had that stuffed duck with the little green felt fedora that you slept with until you were twelve. Twelve! Do you remember that duck?"

"I remember the duck." He makes another attempt at the pie, and his mother, lightning quick for her age, pops him good.

She gestures to Mick's inked arms, which he does his best to keep covered in public. His skin looks like the tormented pages of some trench-coat kid's notebook. "This Mick's a monster." She sniffles, dabs the corners of her eyes with her napkin.

"Why'd you make the pie if you aren't going to let me eat it?"

Outside the dining room window, Mick can see Mr. Wheeler, their neighbor since Mick was a baby, settle into an Adirondack chair and light a cigar, his evening ritual for as long as Mick can remember. The man used to be a brute, vein-thronged biceps the circumference of a watermelon, a punishing grip when he clutched Mick's adolescent shoulder and asked him his batting stats, how much pussy he was getting from the high school girls. It was Mr. Wheeler who always seemed to be nailing some babe in the tricked-out hot tub he'd set up in his backyard, Mick taking it all in from a knothole in the wooden fence that separated their yards. Now, even from a distance and in the kindness of the late summer light, Mr. Wheeler looks ancient—flaccid flesh swinging against the armholes of his wifebeater as he raises a quavering hand to his mouth, his chest caved and his back humped, as if some god-awful beast housed in that hump is eating him alive. The only girl coming and going from his place: the health aide who stops by a few hours a week to cook casseroles and monitor his blood pressure.

It's so damn depressing, one of the worst things about checking out for a huge chunk of time—the seemingly instantaneous rot of everyone you once knew. Mick thinks he might cry, which wouldn't be such a bad thing. His mother likes it when he cries, sees it as a well-deserved penance, an admission of his abominable guilt, though he's admitted everything more times than he can count: to the lawyer; to the judge; to the prison therapist; to the Writers in the Prisons poetry instructors; to the prison chaplain; to the men in his therapy group; to the parole board, who'd rejected his parole application three times anyway; to his case manager; and, in a stupefying post-sex mind haze, to his almost-kind-of girlfriend he'd met at the strip joint Teasers the week after his release, who'd said, *Man, that's really fucked up*, right before she'd told him she didn't think it was a good idea to see him again.

"I'm sorry, Mama," he says again. And he is. He is sorry, and he is sorrowful, and some nights he lies in his twin bed, staring at the same water-stained ceiling he stared at as a boy, and he wonders what he's done with his life and what will he do with his life, and he is terrified that the answer to each question will inevitably be the same.

His mother likes this, the contrite tone, the submission. She studies him for a minute, then nods, satisfied. She cuts a piece of pie so slight it's translucent, eases it onto his plate. "Just a taste," she says. Somehow, this sounds like a warning.

It all started with a girl. Doesn't it always start with a girl? Bianca Jones and her gravity-defying ass in those stone-washed cutoffs. The summer before Mick's junior year in high school. He was young and stupid—stupider than most at that age— but he knew better than to lose himself over a girl, even then. That didn't stop him from sneaking out of the house every chance he got to monkey around on the boat landing, sipping corn whiskey from a milk jug and acting like a fool trying to get the attention of Bianca, who posed car-calendar style on the hood of her mother's beat-up Camry, chain smoking menthols with a sluggish grace so gobsmacking it was all Mick could do not to launch himself on top of her.

"Looking good, Bianca," he'd say.

"Fuck you, dickweed," she'd volley back, but she'd grin when she said it, and Mick's heart would summersault at the possibility.

Bianca never happened—not for Mick anyway. She hooked up with some surgeon's son from Montgomery, one of the rich kids partying on the lake who cruised the local hangouts for girls like Bianca, and lost her cherry, from what Mick's buddies had told him, in a porta-potty set up for construction workers building a new fellowship hall at Lakeview Baptist. Ego-bruised, the next time he saw Bianca out at the boat landing, her back pressed against the hood of a shiny BMW, the surgeon's son's hands tucked between her thighs as if he were about to take a little dive into that tan, taut flesh, Mick impulsively accepted a joy ride with a couple of older guys, aimless dropouts who'd made a career of getting wasted at the boat landing or the party cabins dotting the lake that twined its skinny fingers around their town, mean-spirited men who thought nothing could be funnier than getting a goofy, wet-behind-the-ears kid whacked out of his mind on crack.

And man, talk about immediate, body-throbbing, can't-think-of-anything-but. For Mick, it was like a switch had been flipped. After that night, Mick became so heartsick for those tiny, magical rocks he bought with his Piggly Wiggly bagboy money from some Little League-looking dad in Dockers chinos in the Kentucky Fried Chicken parking lot, he hadn't cared about Bianca, about his mother, about school, about getting canned from his bagboy gig for pinching cartons of smokes, about the baseball recruiter from Alabama Southern who'd been talking up Coach about a possible scholarship, about the kid whose go-cart he stole to get to the 7-Eleven after his mother took away his car privileges for getting fired, or about that old lady clerk reading a romance novel behind the 7-Eleven counter, her white cap of hair so sparse he'd actually seen her scalp halve like the tender skin of overripe fruit when the tire iron connected with her skull.

After submitting his guilty plea, Mick had heard through the grapevine—achingly sober and blame-gaming while waiting on sentencing in the county jail—that the surgeon's son had wrapped his fancy BMW around a tree on a country road and died, that the lovely Bianca survived but had been tossed into the branches of that tree, a human streamer. She'd hung for hours until the ambulance arrived, waiting, waiting, a tortured waiting Mick was about to learn intimately, though he couldn't know it then, the awful, interminable wait that lay ahead of him. When he heard about Bianca, he thought: *Fair enough.* He thought: *They got theirs, too.* That was before he was transferred to maximum security at Donaldson. After a week in that hell, there was no doubt Bianca and her boy had been dealt a much better hand.

This time: Tilly Daigle. Oh, Tilly. Titillating Tilly. Tender Tilly. The alliterative possibilities are endless, and Mick should know; he finds himself chanting her name to himself each time they work the same shift. If ever there was a manner in which the universe could compensate Mick for nearly two lost decades, placing Tilly at the register in the Piggly Wiggly might be it. Without a doubt, eighteen-year-old Tilly is a knockout— tall and curvy, sun-streaked blonde hair tucked behind small, elegant ears, breasts so full they graze the register keys as she rings up groceries. Her line snakes around the magazine racks during rush time, the men in their dusty work jeans waiting obediently to place their tallboys on the conveyor belt like humble offerings.

Mick went in at the same age Tilly is now, and though he'd never passed on an opportunity to watch Mr. Wheeler woo his parade of women in his hot tub, his actual interactions with women had been limited by the brief amount of time he had post-pubescence in their presence. It seems unfair that he missed not only the entirety of his youth but also the youth of his contemporaries, all of whom are middle-aged now, saggy where they used to be firm, hard where they used to be soft, a reality so distressing he avoids the few friends from high school who've attempted to see him since his release. So kill him—he can't help but notice. But Tilly's looks are not what he likes most about her. No, what he likes most about Tilly is her seriousness, her focus, her idealism, her foolish belief she can right the world, an earnestness that inspires him to be a little foolish with hope, too.

"Change must happen now," Tilly likes to say. "And I"— here she generally points a finger at Mick—"and you are agents of change." *All that youthful passion!* he thinks sometimes as she talks. *How do we ever survive it?*

Tilly's homeschooled by her mother, a retired lawyer and activist who spent her career in D.C. They were called to move here, Tilly explains, because the need is so great. Also, the property prices and tax burdens are incredibly low.

Whose need? Mick sometimes wants to ask, but he's not entirely sure exactly what he would be asking.

Tilly works at The Pig for what she calls "life experience," which apparently kids like Tilly think they have to curate, a bizarre concept to Mick, who, even after years of being told otherwise by therapists and chaplains, can't quite shake the idea that life more or less happens to you. Tilly is also saving money for UCLA, which is where she hopes to go next fall. She's aware of her immense privilege, she says. It's only ethical that she contributes toward her own education given all her advantages, she says. Her family has means, but she understands the urgent need to provide infrastructure and support to the under-resourced and underserved, she says. We must do better, she says.

She is as enthusiastic about Mick's post-incarceration opportunities, never once flinching when he explained why he was sent to prison (*you were a baby, Mick*), or how he has to live with his mom (*we all need help now and then*), or how no one in town would hire him but the owner of the Piggly Wiggly, which was generous of the old man considering Mick had stolen from him years ago (*everyone deserves a second chance, Mick*).

Tilly has made a running things-to-do-now-that-you're-out list for Mick. The highlights: mastering the art of Twitter, which Tilly says has the capacity to spark revolutions; reading the *Twilight* series, which she insists is a subversive critique of the fascist capitalist establishment; and most importantly, voting. She stayed an extra hour after work to help him fill out the petition to the Alabama Board of Pardons and Paroles to reinstate his voting rights, the criteria of which permitted only certain degrees of moral turpitude. Luckily, Mick's crime, while violent, did not involve sodomy or treason or murder— the cashier at the 7-Eleven had, amazingly, lived—and when he'd arrived at work with the thin envelope from the pardon board that contained his voter right restoration certificate, Tilly hooted and howled. It was all very embarrassing and thrilling. "What are you going to do now?" Tilly asked, as if he'd won the lottery.

What to do? What to do? That's the question. When you're on the inside and one day you know you'll be on the outside, the main occupation of the day, other than autopsying over and over again how you got there in the first place, is planning what you'll do with your New Life once Donaldson Correctional Center launches you out of its concrete womb into the bald, bright light of the free world. When it finally happened, Mick had felt as lost as a child let loose in a foreign land.

He'd tried to prepare as best as he could for a life on the outside. After wasting a few years sulking in his cell and being pissed off at the world, Mick finally got tired enough and bored enough to get his shit together. He began reading every book he could get his hands on. He earned his GED. Took vo-tech classes on carpentry and automotive mechanics. He enrolled in some poetry workshops with wide-eyed grad students from Tuscaloosa, who talked of the importance of finding his voice, the necessity of documenting his experience. His sixteen-year sentence afforded him the luxury of a few non-pragmatic curricular choices. What else did he have but time? He got baptized in an old GE fridge-turned-baptismal-tank by a preacher with an accent so thick Mick could only make out the last thing the old man had said before he'd plunged his head beneath the tepid water: *You best walk with Jesus from now on, son.* He signed up for a ten-day Vipassana retreat and meditated on a yoga mat from sunup to sundown in a fart-filled prison gym until his mind went blank as a screen, blank as his mother's eyes when they rolled back in her head those nights she got zombified drunk, blank as his father's face when eight-year-old Mick found him, one work boot still on, dead of a heart attack on the couch, blank as Mick imagined Bianca's mind when the surgeon's son rammed himself into her in that porta-potty, blank as the surface of the lake the morning Mick got arrested while he sat and smoked the last of his stash on the boat landing, the old lady's blood tattooing his palms.

"I guess I'll vote come November," Mick said. That's when Tilly invited him to the volunteer recruitment meeting for Samuel Able, candidate for Alabama's third congressional district.

Mick doesn't have a car, and his mother will rarely allow him to use hers for fear he will get himself in trouble, so Tilly gives him a lift from The Pig to the meeting in her perky VW bug. She tells him that Samuel Able won't be at the meeting—he has a fundraising dinner with some fat cats at Kowaliga Restaurant—but that Mick should be able to get a sense of where he might fit in the campaign if he's interested.

The volunteer headquarters are housed in Tilly's mother's art studio behind the Daigles' gargantuan lake house. Watercolors of the lake shingle one wall. Posters of Samuel Able and his campaign slogans paper the others: THE FUTURE

IS OURS! YOU ARE THE CHANGE YOU ARE WAITING FOR. The candidate is a handsome Black man, young and fit, his politician's smile spanning the width of the posters. The tone of the campaign is pugilistic with positivity.

Unfortunately, Ida Daigle explains, there is not quite enough interest in Samuel Able's candidacy in this corner of Tallapoosa County to secure funding for commercial office space yet. "So we're making do for now in my studio," she says. "And we can't tell you how happy we are you've decided to join us," she adds. "Now come." She grabs his hand with forced familiarity and pulls him across the room to introduce him to Tilly's father, a sixtyish man sporting a philosopher's beard and flip-flops, who is sprawled in a leather recliner in the corner, looking three bourbons past conversation and bored out of his gourd, then ushers him toward the refreshments. A pair of silver-haired ladies in sherbet pedal-pushers pick through platters of cheese and fruit. A young man in a Tupac T-shirt and blond locs sips his wine and scrolls through his phone. Including Mick and the Daigles, there are no more than a dozen people in attendance.

"In some ways this space is better," Tilly says, bouncing up to stand beside him. "We don't have to clean up the shit bombs off the doorstep like we did for Obama's reelection campaign at the Broadnax office." She has a clipboard pressed against her magnificent breasts. She hands it to Mick with the implication that he needs to fill out the questionnaire attached to it. She has changed into a white blouse and a slim black pencil skirt and is wearing red-rimmed eyeglasses. The effect is very professional. Mick is impressed. He has never seen her out of her Piggly Wiggly uniform.

"God, yes," Ida says. She is a woman of flowing linen sleeves and rippling skirts, and when she speaks, she thrums her fingers against her chin thoughtfully. She also touches Mick at the end of each sentence, like a fleshy period.

"So this guy Able is a progressive?" Mick asks. "More liberal than the other Democratic candidates? Universal income, universal healthcare, and all the other goodies?"

"That's right," Ida says, clearly impressed. "You're familiar with Able's platform?"

"I picked up the habit of reading a few papers a day over the years, ma'am," Mick says modestly, carefully avoiding explicitly referencing his time in Donaldson. It didn't take long to learn that doing so makes people uncomfortable. "From what I recall, there's a pretty popular Republican incumbent running for reelection."

"Unfortunately," Tilly says.

"Then your man's got about a snowball's chance in hell of being elected," Mick says. "You know that, right?"

"Winning's not the point," Ida says, like only a person who's pretty much already won everything worth winning can say.

"What's important is getting Able's ideas out into the world and building momentum," Tilly adds. "This district consistently votes against its own interests. Apathy and disillusionment are powerful stuff. People lose hope when hope has been systemically oppressed."

"That's for sure," Mick chimes in. Both of the women look so instantaneously mortified, as if they just realized that they are explaining faith to the Pope, that he feels bad about saying anything at all, and so he keeps his mouth shut through the informational session, in which Ida explains how to approach potential voters' homes cautiously, always standing a few steps from the front door, never entering a screened-in porch, and never invasively peering into a window to check for occupants.

Then they role-play a conversation between a volunteer and a potential voter, Tilly performing the part of the campaign volunteer, Ida the suspicious and reluctant undecided voter. Ida scowls when Tilly lists highlights of Able's campaign platform. "I'm not so sure," Ida says. "This sounds an awful lot like socialism. Hardworking folks ought to keep what they earn. I'm tired of my tax dollars paying for folks too lazy to work." Then Tilly explains how the average monthly food stamp benefit per participant in Alabama is $135.18, so no one is making lobster night a habit with that kind of money. After Tilly finishes the canvassing script, she offers Ida a flier and informs her that if she doesn't have transportation to her place of voting, transportation can be arranged.

The sanctimonious tone of the whole exchange is similar to the spiel the church ladies spout when they descend upon Mick's mother's house, every week it seems, to proselytize and inquire if Jesus has taken up residence in his heart. Even so, Mick can't fathom how anyone could possibly deny Tilly anything she asked. Hell, he'd vote for Mussolini if Tilly showed up on his doorstep with a campaign pin and a smile.

Mick claps when they finish, because it seems like the polite thing to do. Ida and Tilly offer girlish bows.

"Is Able planning on getting rid of that doughnut hole?" one of the old women says.

Tilly jumps right in, says, "He supports Medicare reform and expansion, absolutely."

The woman *harrumphs*, as if she's heard that one before. "I'm not so sure. It sounds dangerous, knocking on strangers' doors. People get riled up over this stuff. Is this kind of thing safe?"

"All real change is dangerous, right?" Tilly says brightly.

Tilly picks him up at his house for their first day of canvassing in an old Nissan minivan the Daigles use to drive voters to the polls. Mick's mother peeks through the blinds and watches Tilly pull in the driveway as Mick laces his boots.

"Since when do you care about politics? And who is this Able fellow?" his mother asks. It's approaching noon, but she's still in her nightgown and robe, the thin fabric catching the light, her body—lumpy and swollen—outlined like a monstrous shadow puppet.

"I don't know." Mick shrugs. "It's nice, I guess, to be a part of something, something positive. What else am I going to do?"

"Are you sure this is safe?"

"I'm not breaking into their homes or robbing them, Mom," Mick says. "I'm handing out fliers for Christ's sake. No one's going to shoot me or anything." But it is true that he looks menacing, no matter that he allowed his buzz cut to grow out or that he hides his tattoos under long-sleeved button-downs, even in the heat of September. Fifteen years of lifting weights have bulked his neck and chest disproportionately. His shirt buttons bulge, the fabric at his arms as tight as spandex. He resembles, his mother once said, a snake who has swallowed prey too large to digest.

"I don't mean the campaigning." His mother presses her index finger against the glass of the window. "I mean her."

"She's a kid."

"You were a kid."

"Well, she's a sweet kid."

She allows the blinds to flap closed. "That's what worries me. Don't you hurt that girl."

"Jesus, Mom. I'm not some kind of sex offender."

His mother looks him up and down. "I don't know what you are," she says.

Tilly, sweet Tilly. Who would ever hurt Tilly? The thought of it—a boy pushing a kissing session a little too far, some pervert attacking her in a dark alley—makes Mick clench his hands on the steering wheel as he drives down his street, Tilly happily organizing fliers and voter registration materials in the passenger seat.

When he'd walked out of the house, Tilly had been standing beside the minivan, dangling the keys, her face beaming. "Mom says you should drive," she said, making a show of pressing the keys in his palm. Mick knew this had been a thoughtful discussion between Tilly and her parents, whether or not they should trust him with the keys to the old Nissan, whether or not they should trust him to be alone with Tilly, and after much hand wringing and talk of the societal value of forgiveness and rehabilitation they decided they should, that doing so would demonstrate their faith in him and humanity in general, and this decision had made them feel virtuous. Mick had met volunteers like this on the inside, people who made a point of treating the prisoners as if they were men capable of goodness, as if they saw the men as something other than animals in jumpsuits, and though Mick was smart enough to know their acts of generosity were often less about the inmates and more about themselves, he was fine with it then, and he is fine with it now. He'll take his kindness where he can get it.

They drive north of the town center, toward an area primarily populated with lower-income Black families with historically low voter turnout—their target demographic, Tilly explains. Every few minutes, Tilly's phone buzzes in her lap, her mother checking in, and Tilly answers with a few punches of her thumbs, which, in a way, comforts Mick. Ida should have the good sense to be worried about the girl.

"My mom says you should be proud of yourself," Tilly says in that frank way she talks. "You're doing something with your life now. You're living proof rehabilitation is possible even after surviving the trauma of the prison industrial complex. She says you're a walking miracle."

"I'm a bagboy at The Pig."

"I work at The Pig, too."

"You're eighteen. You'll be gone in a few months."

"Well, a man's not his job," Tilly persists, parroting her mother, Mick presumes. "Look at Jesus. He was 'just' a carpenter."

"Are you comparing me to Jesus?" Mick teases, and Tilly blushes. Blushes! A glorious red glazing her cheeks. Mick had forgotten such a shade on a girl's cheeks was even physiologically possible.

"If you don't want to work at The Pig, you should go to college," Tilly says, suddenly all business, the way she gets when she identifies a problem she thinks needs solving. "You have your GED, right? Seriously, you should do it. You're one of the smartest people I know."

"Maybe," Mick says. But then what? Would he become an accountant? A salesman? It seems unfathomable, the simplicity and domesticity of such a life, days defined by work and errands and maybe, when Mick allows himself to consider it, a family's demands. But when Tilly suggests it, he thinks, why not?

They pass a defunct gas station, the pumps hooded, a small boy, his rusted bike leaning against the cement blocks of the station, beating at the stained asphalt with an old shoe he must have found somewhere. They aren't far from Highway 280, which leads to I-85, which leads to anywhere Mick might want to go.

"Let's start here," Tilly says, her excitement building in her thighs, which pump the cracked leather seat. She points to a row of modest houses, the lawns littered with tricycles and toys, the doors and windows barred.

They decide to take a methodical approach, down one side of the street, and then up the other until they reach the van again.

"I'll go first, show you the ropes," Tilly says. She's wearing a blue T-shirt with a drawing of a woman's reproductive organs across the midsection, which embarrasses Mick every time he notices it. Beneath the uterus: MINE VOTES.

They approach a little cottage the color of a worn seashell. Tilly raps on the door, then takes a respectful step back. Mick stands a few feet behind her, the clipboard they intend to use to collect email addresses clutched in one moist palm. The cement beneath his feet exhales heat.

He's relieved when no one opens the door, but ten houses later, they've still had no luck. The houses are either achingly silent after Tilly knocks, or she and Mick never even make it to the door; folks sitting on the porch to escape the un-air-conditioned heat of their homes wave them away with a flick of a wrist the minute they step into the yard. Mick's heart breaks a little for the girl, whose enthusiasm is wilting. Her shiny ponytail, usually perched on the crown of her head, droops with sweat. After nearly two hours at it, only one old man let them inside, and he had no interest in talking about Samuel Able. He put Mick to work fixing his water spigot in the backyard so he could water his heirlooms while he gave Tilly a blow by blow of his years-long quest to get the city to fill the pond-sized pothole in front of his house.

"Persistence," she says now as they walk down the sidewalk, more weed and root than concrete, Mick cradling a paper bag of the old man's tomatoes, whose delicate skin he worries he might bruise unintentionally. "We can't expect Samuel Able to work for us if we won't work for him."

"But we don't expect Samuel Able to work for us," Mick says. "You said yourself you know he won't get elected."

Tilly presses her palm against his forearm and leaves it there until she realizes they are touching. She snatches it back, fumbles with the fliers. "It's a process. Samuel's not what is important. His ideas are what's important. It's not the man that matters, Mick."

Of course, she's wrong—more often than not, it all comes down to the man—but what use is it to explain such a thing to one so young? So they try the last home on the street, a little blue house with rotting fascia boards and a porch crowded with plastic chairs.

To Tilly's obvious delight, the door opens before she can knock, a young woman in a halter top and pajama bottoms with a toddler on her hip standing behind the torn screen door, her mouth a guarded knot. She does not move to open the screen door and invite them inside.

"You tell Mr. Jones I got to the tenth on rent," she says as soon as Tilly starts to speak.

"Oh, no," Tilly says, "that's not why we're here. We're volunteers—"

"Well I ain't buying nothing."

"We're not selling anything." Tilly smiles and points at the clipboard.

The woman snorts. "Somebody's always selling something."

"Just hope," Tilly says.

"Jesus, girl. You for real?" She peers around Tilly to scowl at Mick, who stands still as a gargoyle on her porch. "Who's that fool? He your muscle? You think you need protection coming here?"

"This is a really nice neighborhood," Tilly says, and Mick knows that Tilly means it. "I'm Tilly, and this is Mick. We're here to talk to you a bit about voting in November and Samuel Able, candidate for congressman in the third congressional district." Then she launches into the rest of the pitch. When she finishes, she motions to Mick to hand over a campaign flier and the clipboard to collect her contact information.

"Where you in?" the woman asks when she spots the handless clock tattoo on Mick's wrist as he slides the clipboard through the crack in the screen door. The woman takes the flier and clipboard but doesn't bother looking at them.

"Donaldson."

The woman nods sympathetically, says, "That place ain't joking. Nobody comes out right in the head."

"Some might say I wasn't right in the head when I went in," Mick says, and the woman laughs. The toddler, who has fallen asleep, twitches his fat cheek against her breast. His eyes flicker open, shimmering with dream, as boundless as new worlds. Then they shut again.

"A major pillar of Samuel Able's platform is prison reform," Tilly interjects. "The incarceration rate for Black people is 3.3 times higher in Alabama than for white people. It's an injustice."

"No shit," the woman says.

"We're just asking you to consider voting for Samuel Able come November," Tilly continues, sticking doggedly to the script.

"So you provide transportation if I need it?"

"That's right," Tilly brightens. "We will transport you to your place of voting."

"What I need is for somebody to transport me to the store for some milk and diapers."

Tilly falters for a moment, her sunny expression wavering. "I think there's been some miscommunication," she says. "That's not what we do."

The woman hitches the corner of her lip, shifts the baby higher, presses a soft kiss on his brow, says, "I know exactly what y'all doing." She doesn't bother shutting the door; she turns and drifts back into her living room crowded with baby swings and playpens and stacks of laundry.

"I think she kept our clipboard," Mick says.

They walk down the porch steps and pause by the woman's mailbox, take sips of the bottled water Tilly brought along, Tilly fanning a stack of fliers a few inches from her forehead, barely stirring the air. Wisps of her hair, which is normally straight, curl in wet ringlets against her cheekbones. Mick thinks a girl Tilly's age should be getting ready for a date, not standing on strangers' porches, peddling a politician's promises.

Tilly drains her water, shoves the empty into her backpack, then squares her shoulders. "People are angry," she says, rallying. "Who can blame them?" She's smiling again now, the we'll-get-'em-next-time smile of a cheerleader, and all at once, Mick feels very, very tired, like he could lay down right there on this sidewalk and sleep harder and sounder than he has in years. So he's grateful that, with no clipboard, Tilly decides they should head to the van. It's getting late, anyway, the sun barreling toward the horizon. The cicadas keen their crazed melodies.

The van's air conditioner doesn't work for shit, and they roll down the windows halfway, the hot air wheezing through their sticky hair. She pokes her hand out the window, rides the breeze with her palm. They could be anybody going anywhere, Mick thinks.

"I thought helping people would feel different," Tilly says softly after a few minutes.

"Sometimes good work doesn't feel very good," Mick says.

"Maybe," Tilly says. "I just don't want to do any harm."

Mick wants to tell her what it's like to make your way in a world you've harmed irreparably, to wrestle daily with the guilt and the anger and the regret until it is impossible to distinguish one emotion from the other. But she's so young, barely more than a girl, her whole brutal, beautiful life ahead of her, and so instead he says, "You'll figure it out, Tilly. That's part of growing up."

"Do you ever think you might do it again?" Tilly says, a little shyly, in a way so he knows she's talking about what he'd done to land in prison. She watches her hand instead of him.

"Harm somebody?"

"No," Tilly says. "You know, use." She says "use" like she picked up the term watching hammy crime shows.

"I don't think so."

"That's good." Then, a minute later, "Have you seen that old woman since you got out, the one from the 7-Eleven?"

"No. But I heard she healed up more or less. Tough old bird." He laughs a little, nervous, and then feels shamed by it. "You hungry?" he says quickly. "I could use a milkshake. I can't remember the last time I had a milkshake."

This revelation energizes Tilly. She turns toward him, says, "Well you have to have one," like she's his tour guide in this strange land, obligated to reveal to him all its forgotten pleasures.

They find the Hardee's drive-thru in town and get two large chocolate shakes, sucking on them contentedly as they drive toward Mick's house. The coming night brings a touch of coolness, and it feels good on Mick's face. He forgot how much he likes this, driving with the window cracked just so, the hum of the tires under his feet. When they get to the turnoff for his road, he drives past it, not really thinking about what he's doing until he's done it.

"Weren't we supposed to turn back there?" Tilly asks.

"It's OK," Mick says. "You're always showing me things. I want to show you something."

"I don't know if that's a good idea." Tilly sits straight as an exclamation point in her seat. "I told my mom I'd be back by dark." She tugs the neck of her T-shirt up as if she's suddenly become conscious of the fact that Mick might be aware she has breasts.

"Go on, text her," Mick says. "Tell her you'll be home safe and sound before she knows it."

Tilly looks like she's going to protest, probably not wanting to offend him. But she does it anyway, thumbing the screen of her phone in rapid strokes.

He drives toward the lake. It's only a few miles out, where they're headed, but he can sense Tilly's nervousness. She fists her phone, the fliers she'd organized so meticulously earlier that day forgotten on the floorboard, the old man's bag of tomatoes rustling next to her restless feet. Finally, he turns off on a well-worn red dirt road. He would have thought it would be paved by now—people had been asking the county to do so long before he went in—but instead they've scattered it with a thin layer of gravel. Each turn of the road is as familiar to him, even after all these years, as the back of his own hand.

Mick hasn't been to the boat landing since he was arrested, and he doesn't know what he was expecting, but he feels silly as they pull into the parking lot. It's a slab of concrete littered with beer cans and fishing line and a few busted Styrofoam coolers. A blue pickup with a trailer hitched to the back idles on a slender ramp threading into the water, where a fisherman sits in his johnboat, waiting for his buddy to get the trailer angle right. The smells of decomposing fish and gasoline seep inside the minivan, smells Mick associates with his youth.

"This is where we used to hang out when I was your age," Mick says. "In a few hours, I bet this place will be packed with kids. Probably not the kind of kids you hang with, but they ain't all bad. Kids being kids. Things don't change much." He points to the left of the ramp at a patch of sandy beach. "Right there's where I got arrested. I was watching the sunrise."

"Oh," Tilly sighs. "That must have been scary."

"I was sky high. That helped. I did bad things, Tilly."

"I know."

"Not only the drugs and the 7-Eleven lady." He thinks of Donaldson, the awful hunger and rage that lurked like a boogeyman in every corner. Men became something other than men in a place like that, and Mick was not as different as he'd thought, which was, in the end, one of the hardest things to face.

"You can't do anything about the past," Tilly says. "You can only move forward."

"I guess," Mick says. "I mean, I hope so. But I do worry, you know? What if I'm not a good guy? What if I'm a bad guy who did what bad guys do?"

"I don't believe that," Tilly says, shaking her head emphatically, her ponytail whipping the seat. "What you need now is a plan, Mick. Everyone needs a plan."

"A plan?"

"Sure. Like a ten-year plan. I have one. Graduate from college in four years, maybe three if I take summer classes. Then law school. Then I want to work as a defense attorney. It's not that complicated. You need to set goals."

"I don't know, Tilly."

"Stop doubting yourself," Tilly says forcefully. She leans toward him. "I want you to ask, right now: *What do I want? Who do I want to be?*"

Mick takes a long pull on his milkshake, closes his eyes, lets the icy sludge slip down his throat without swallowing. And there is Bianca Jones, stretched across the top of her mother's Camry, her long legs golden with moonlight and summer, and Mick, a young Mick, his smooth arms lean and sinewy from hours of batting practice, dancing like a goon to Zeppelin spilling from somewhere, his face lit with longing. In that moment, it's as real and possible to Mick as anything else.

He opens his eyes. The johnboat is situated on the trailer now, both fishermen standing beside it, icing their catch in a red cooler. Tilly's studying him, waiting for his answer with that intense, contemplative expression she gets.

He just happens to see it—he easily could have missed it—a mosquito perched right there, in the lovely little dip at the base of her neck. The suprasternal notch, it's called, a term he remembers from an anatomy book he'd studied after he'd read pretty much everything else in the prison library, the name wholly inadequate in reflecting its delicate beauty. He only means to brush the mosquito away—something anyone would do—his hand moving fast, his palm barely grazing Tilly's windpipe. He can feel the scream before it's fully formed, and by the time she releases it, it's nothing more than a bleat, his hand clamped over her mouth. Her skin is unimaginably soft.

"Motherfucker, Tilly," he says. "I was swatting a mosquito. I would never hurt you. You know that, right?"

She nods, but her eyes are wide with fear, her pulse a hammer against his palm.

"You see those men over there? They don't know that. They don't know I wouldn't hurt you. You scream and they hear it and start something or call the cops, I'll be in all sorts of trouble. Do you want me to get in trouble?"

Tilly shakes her head no. Her pupils expand to overtake her irises, her eyes bottomless, a tiny reflection of Mick pinpointed in the center.

"I'm going to move my hand, and you're not going to make a sound. Everything's fine. You understand?"

Tilly nods yes, her breath warm and fast under his hand.

Mick inches his palm back, making sure she's not going to scream until he removes it entirely. They sit there for a moment, not looking at each other, both breathing heavily as if they've narrowly escaped some awful calamity.

"A mosquito," he says. "That's all."

He puts the van in gear and backs out of the parking spot. The two men wave, their faces relaxed, flushed with beer. The setting sun behind them explodes on the water, and it is every bit as stunning as Mick remembers.

No one talks. Tilly slides as far away from Mick as possible, pressing herself against the passenger-side door. She looks as if she wants to cry but will not now allow herself to do it. He's ruined everything, he thinks. He'll probably have to get a new job, or at the very least work his shifts around Tilly's until she leaves for school. The idea of Tilly fearing him is agonizing. Mick cannot think of what to say to make it right. That's all he wants: to make things right.

"Her name is Mabel Green," Mick says when they're close to his mother's house. "The cashier from the 7-Eleven. My mom had her address, visited her once or twice after she was released from the hospital. I walked to her house once right after I got out. It took half the day, but it felt like something I needed to do, apologize to her. She's nearly eighty now. A shriveled thing in her wheelchair. I found her sitting alone on her porch, staring off at nothing. She could have been on Mars for all she knew. Maybe I should have stopped and told her I was sorry for what I'd done to her back then, but I spooked, kept on walking. What would it have changed, me talking to her? I don't know if it's my fault, her being like that. Or maybe it's just old age. And sometimes I wonder, does it matter one way or the other?"

Tilly looks away from him, out the window at the gathering night. "It matters," she says.

a mother knows

Helen is driving again. It is Friday night, a tying-one-on night, something Helen has done more than she probably should well into her thirties, mistakenly thinking, until recently—until Iris—she had all the time in the world to get to the business of being a grown-up.

Aside from Teasers, a redneck joint with dimpled-kneed strippers trudging along the top of the bar with all the gusto of dog-tired moms navigating a grocery store aisle, there are only two bars in the area. Charlie's and the Rodeo Club face each other on a winding road near the lake that sits outside town, a 700-mile shoreline gem that seems, to Helen, out of place in their landscape of poverty, a miscalculation of nature, though she guesses it's not technically natural. It was formed by the hydroelectric plant nearly a century ago. Helen cannot recall even dipping a toe into its tepid water since high school, when she and her girlfriends would skip class in the late spring and find a willing boy at the marina with a boat and waste the day at Chimney Rock tanning and drinking soured beer Helen hid from her mother in the trunk of her car. She's spent plenty of time in those bars, more than her fair share these past weeks, and she's promised herself tonight she will not stop for a drink at either.

Yet here she finds herself, sitting at the stop sign; a turn to the left leads to the Rodeo Club, a turn to the right to

Charlie's. And Helen is willing herself to drive straight on. She can see the parking lot of Charlie's in the distance, the glow of the fluorescent lights, the steam of summer hazing the night. A knot of youngish men in ball caps lean against a sedan, their hands kneading the air to shape their banter. Helen is certain if she'd walked by these men two or three years ago, she would have paused their conversation, earned a few appreciative nods. She's grateful for her invisibility now, the one gift of middle age. She's never wanted to be like her mother, who, well over fifty, still dyes her hair the shade of merlot, and sports skirts short enough to reveal spongy thighs that ripple toward her knees in the same pattern a skipped rock makes on the surface of the lake. Helen cranks the radio, shrill eighties metal she once ridiculed as a teenager pinging from speaker to speaker. What she likes about the music now: its rage.

A flash of light ricochets off the rear window. When her eyes refocus, Helen sees a pickup truck behind her, its muddied cab mounted with KC floodlights. The man in the driver's seat has jutted his arm out the open window to better execute a series of obscene hand gestures. Without thinking, Helen turns right, then takes a soft left into the Charlie's parking lot, easing past the group of men and into the murky shadows on the grassy edge of the lot, where she parks and cuts the engine. Just because she is in the parking lot doesn't mean she has to go in, she tells herself. She unlatches her seat belt, grabs a crushed pack of Camels from the glove compartment. She lights one, cracking her window to release the smoke. The night is so unbearably hot and muggy, it is as if some giant beast from a child's nightmare has exhaled a fetid breath inside the car. The sudden throb of the cicadas reverberates in Helen's pulse.

Helen has a good view of the entrance to Charlie's. She watches couples trickle out, pairing off for the night. A giggling twenty-something blonde in a stamp-sized skirt and knee-high boots careens outside, her arm linked around the waist of a tall man in a denim shirt, who is laughing good-naturedly at the girl's messiness in the indulgent way of men aiming to get laid. The woman pauses a few steps outside the bar, pushing her cleavage into a crevasse with her biceps so she can snap a selfie of the two of them on her phone. Helen could put her fist between the woman's lean thighs and never touch flesh.

"She'll feel like ass tomorrow," Helen says to the empty infant seat in the back.

The blonde is doing a shimmy for denim boy now, a slow slither of hips so mesmerizing, Helen barely notices another girl—a kid, really—balancing her pink rhinestoned boots on the railroad tie a foot or so in front of Helen's bumper, her arms stretched out for balance. She has no memory of seeing this girl leave the bar or approach her car; it is as if she materialized from the night. Helen is considering whether to pump the horn or flash the lights to encourage her to move on when the girl loses her footing. Her stringy limbs scissor cartoon-style and then collapse out of sight.

Helen waits for the girl to rise, to reappear. When this does not happen, she reluctantly calls out, "You OK?" The girl's grinning face pops up in Helen's passenger-side window, as if she has been waiting for an invitation. She yanks open the car door and slides into the front seat.

Helen freezes, cigarette mid-hike to her mouth, the ash tumbling into her lap. "I don't have any money," Helen blurts out, which is true. She spent her last ten dollars buying the cigarettes that morning, the taxes more than the actual smokes. Yet another way, Helen thinks, the world manages to fuck her.

The girl looks at Helen for a moment, her eyes squinted in confusion, and then she laughs. "Oh, God, no," the girl says, "I need a ride, not money. I'm sorry if I scared you. My friend hooked up with some loser and ditched me, and the few guys who've offered me rides were all wasted. I'd call my mom, but she'd go nuts if she knew I snuck out again. She's so overprotective. My place is close, just a few miles up the road." She waves her hand against the cigarette smoke. "That shit'll kill you, you know."

The girl's wearing tight skinny jeans, a faded black T-shirt with a band's name scrawled over a ghoulish skull, her dark hair wound loosely in two braids. Her only girlish whimsy: the sparkly boots and too-bright lipstick. It is hard to tell in the dim light, but she looks young, maybe fourteen or fifteen, and Helen thinks of her own circle of friends in high school, how they snuck into this very bar, drawing on each other's wrists crude imitations of the stamp-of-the-day the doorman used to indicate an ID had been checked, though they weren't fooling anyone. What kind of teenage girl wears a T-shirt on a night out? Helen recalls elaborate rituals of reverent preparation.

The girl's underwhelming effort chafes for reasons Helen can't quite pin down. Perhaps it's because everything seems easier for kids now, all the rules loosened. Adolescence for Helen had been merciless. She'd been tall and tomboyish, completely dismayed by her friends' obsessions with boys and clothes. Each day had required of her a soul-sucking performance, and no matter how intently she studied her friends, their mannerisms, their expressions, their favored topics of conversation, she never could quite get it right.

"I don't know if that's a good idea," Helen says. Instinctively, she eyes the infant seat in the rearview mirror, and the girl's gaze follows.

"Is there a kid back there?" She pivots toward the darkness behind them, her braids thrashing the headrest. "You really shouldn't smoke around a baby."

"No," Helen snaps. "It's just me taking a drive. Couldn't sleep."

"But you're parked in front of a bar." Helen can smell booze now, something overly sweet, a young girl's drink.

"I took a detour," Helen says, irritated. "Your house is only a few miles away?"

The girl sighs in relief, her body melting into the seat. "Five or six, tops. I swear. My mom is going to go bonkers if she wakes up and I'm not there."

Helen fastens her seatbelt and turns the key in the ignition, her old Ford Focus twitching to life. "I'll take you home, but you need to be more careful. You shouldn't be out here by yourself. And you shouldn't hitch rides with strangers."

"I know, I know," the girl says, but from the look of her, Helen is certain the girl knows nothing.

If Iris were still hers, Helen thinks, she would not grow up to be the kind of girl who deceived her mother, who drank in bars, who wore garish lipstick and ratty T-shirts, who got into cars with people she didn't know. She wouldn't be like this girl. She wouldn't be like Helen. If given the chance, Helen would have raised Iris right.

They pull out of the parking lot, the group of talking men and the couple snapping photos long gone. They take a right onto the main road.

"You should put on your seat belt," Helen suggests. "Seems like someone wrecks on this road every other night."

"I'm Keshet," the girl says, ignoring Helen. She sticks out her palm by way of introduction, then, perhaps thinking better of asking someone driving to shake hands, pats Helen's forearm stiffly, as if stroking a stranger's dog. Her hand is a child's, delicate and velvety, the fingernails pulpy where the girl has chewed them.

Helen cannot remember the last time she has been touched deliberately by another person. She feels the promise of tears, always there now, searing the back of her throat. "Helen," she says. "My name's Helen. An old lady's name."

"Change it," Keshet says enthusiastically. "I changed mine. My parents named me Lola. Sounds like a porn star's name. Lola Knight. So I picked my own name. Renaming yourself is a kind of liberation. Keshet means 'rainbow' in Hebrew. It totally pissed off my mother. She named me after her grandmother. But, you know, it's my choice. That's the whole point."

When Helen tries to conjure the names she might choose, she cannot think of a single one. She wonders what this says about her.

They pass a snowball shack, the volunteer fire station, and then Mountainview Baptist, a country church housed in a double-wide trailer with a crooked cross strapped to the roof. There are no mountains anywhere. Just towering kudzu, an impenetrable wall of green.

"Keep going straight for a couple of miles," Keshet says. "I'll tell you when to turn. How old is it? The baby?"

"Six months this week." Helen's mother had removed the infant seat and stored it in the garage the day the caseworker from the foster agency picked up Iris. The next morning, Helen reinstalled it. That was four months ago.

"They're cute at that age," the girl says. "My mom says that's when a baby shows its personality. She's a stay-at-home mom. She worked before she had us, but she gave it up so she could be with us. I guess me and my sister are lucky to have so much time with her, but she drives me nuts sometimes. It would be nice if she'd get outside of the house. Find a hobby or something. What's your baby's name?"

"Iris. She was a foster kid, and she came with the name, but it seemed to fit. I manage a flower shop, so really, it's the perfect name. She's perfect." Helen's immediately embarrassed she has shared so much, but it has been so long since she's talked with someone. She quit returning her friends' calls and texts months ago.

"Iris is a pretty name," Keshet says. She directs a vent at her face, pushes her neck toward the weak stream of cool air. "She at home with your husband?"

"No husband," Helen says before she can stop herself. "Just me. Never really thought about getting married. I was having too much fun." She'd never really considered having children, either. Helen's want for a baby had come upon her like a sudden and fierce hunger absent one day and present the next. She filled out the paperwork and did the home checks without telling a soul other than her references, all people from work. She blew through her savings setting up a nursery. One day she got a phone call. That evening a lady with a grocery bag of sample formula and diapers showed up on her doorstep and placed Iris, barely two days old, into Helen's arms.

"Will she always be so dark?" her mother had said the first time she'd met Iris. "Could she lighten up as she gets older?" That was when Helen realized how terrible the world could be and how vulnerable Iris was in it.

Keshet snorts, nodding knowingly. "You'd probably end up doing all the labor anyway. Least, that's what my mom says."

"Iris doesn't feel like work at all," Helen says. "The hard part is the worry. That's what they don't tell you. All the ways a child can be harmed. Things you'd never think of."

Helen had not been prepared for the intensity of the anxiety, the fierceness of her need to protect Iris. In the middle of the night, Iris finally asleep in her Moses basket at the foot of the couch, Helen would find herself scouring news stories on the internet: a baby killed in her mother's arms by a falling tree limb in the park, a toddler's brain liquefied by an amoeba inhaled through her nose in a swimming pond, a father accidently drowning his newborn while falling asleep bathing him. She could not wrap her mind around it, the innumerable ways she might fail Iris.

In the end, it had all been needless worry. After four months of indecision, Iris was returned to the birth mother, a troubled girl not much older than the one sitting next to Helen now. "It's probably for the best," Helen's mother had said. "She belongs with her own people." And maybe, Helen considered, her mother was right. But where, Helen wanted to ask, were her people?

"You really shouldn't climb into strangers' cars," Helen repeats.

"I don't usually hitch, but you looked nice, like somebody's mom, and you are." The girl smiles sweetly at Helen.

Helen wonders what requisite traits a woman must possess to look like a mom to a girl this age: a butt crease between her brows, doughy upper arms, hair shoved in a scrunchie? She supposes that Keshet, who is quite pretty in spite of the lack of effort, finds Helen's fate an impossibility for herself. Helen thinks, with little pleasure, *You'll find out soon enough.*

"Ted Bundy," Helen announces suddenly. "As handsome as can be. Looked like the boy next door. And he butchered all those women."

"The boy who lives next door to me looks like a perv, and he is one," the girl says, giggling. "You should see the nasty old porn mags he keeps in a tackle box behind the dog pen in his yard." Keshet shudders her slight shoulders, an exaggerated gesture so adolescent Helen cannot help but laugh. "Besides, my mom says I'm such a piece of work that if anyone ever took me they'd bring back right quick. Who's Ted Bundy?"

Helen tries to think of a more contemporary example of an all-American poster-boy-turned-serial-killer, but as usual, her repertoire of cultural references is dated. "The point is, you need to be more careful. That's all I'm saying. You can't tell by looking at someone."

"Sure," Keshet says. "I hear you." But the girl's already distracted, arching in the seat to fish her phone out of her front pocket. It illuminates and beats rhythmically every few seconds like an eerie mechanical heart. "Ah, crap," she mutters. "My mom's awake." She blows into her cupped palms, inhales. "You got a stick of gum or something?"

Helen grabs a half-melted piece of gum from the coin dish and passes it to Keshet. "So, do you like school? Do you have a boyfriend?" Helen asks. It seems like a benign thing a mother might ask the babysitter when dropping her off after a date night, the exact kinds of questions she dreaded when she was Keshet's age. And as soon as she says it, she realizes its possible inappropriateness, how this girl—alone with a stranger late at night—might interpret this question and Helen's warning against sexual predators as some kind of creepy come-on.

She needn't have worried; Keshet, who doesn't seem to be alarmed by much, shakes her head. "Nah," she says. "The boys around here are so immature." Without asking, she reaches for the volume dial on the radio and flips it, some lurid ballad Helen associates with blue eyeliner and winged hair filling the car. Helen turns the radio off. The sudden quiet is loud around them.

"That's some depressing stuff," Keshet says of the song. If she wasn't smiling when she said it, Helen would have thought the girl meant to be mean. "My road's right up here on the left. Piney Lane."

Helen turns off onto the narrow red dirt road. It's uneven, like most of the dirt roads around here, which shapeshift with each new rain. Helen slows, hoping the Focus won't bottom out. They slip past a few small cabins, thin-walled, prefabricated boxes, the yards littered with trucks on cinder blocks, bowed swing sets, leaf-covered trampolines. These kinds of houses often line the access roads to the lake. The nice houses, mainly vacation homes, are always waterfront. The kudzu on this section of the road is so dense it is impossible to see an oncoming vehicle's lights around each bend, and when a truck explodes around a sharp curve, half in their lane, its high beams blinding Helen, she barely maneuvers the Focus onto the right shoulder in time.

"What a dick," Keshet mutters, not bothering to look up from her phone, which is blooming alive again.

"You should really put on your seat belt," Helen repeats. Her tone is harsher than she'd intended. She softens it, adds, "I have seen horrible wrecks on these backroads. A friend of mine nearly died in high school not far from here on a road like this. Her boyfriend didn't make it."

"If my first kid is a girl," Keshet says, ignoring Helen, the near-miss with the truck already forgotten, "I might name her Anaya. In Sanskrit it means 'completely free.' And if it's a boy, Agni, after the Hindu god of fire. He's the spark of all life, part of every living thing. Plus, I like 'A' names. Then again, I might not have kids at all. It's not really responsible. The planet's overpopulated. We're totally screwed as a species."

Later, when Helen thinks of this moment—the moment her foot punches the brake and holds it there—she will tell herself she never intended to hurt the girl, only to scare her, to remind her the world could be cruel and indifferent, the smallest carelessness bringing immeasurable heartbreak. But she knows this is not entirely true. Just as she knows that what she experiences while watching Keshet's face propel toward the windshield, her dark braids slashing her cheeks, her nose slamming the dashboard with a dull thunk, is something akin to satisfaction.

"Holy shit," Keshet says, pushing herself off the dashboard. She cups her face with her hands. "My nose—I think it's broken. Why'd you stop like that?"

Helen flips on the overhead light. Blood seeps through Keshet's fingers. One braid has come undone. She looks a mess.

"I'm sorry," Helen offers calmly, "but I told you to put on your seat belt. And see—I was right."

"What is wrong with you, lady?" Keshet yells. She searches for her phone on the floorboard with one hand, never taking her eyes off Helen. "You could have really hurt me."

"Exactly," Helen says. "You seem like a nice kid, but you need to be more cautious. People are fucked up." She gestures to the absolute quiet around them. "I could do anything to you out here. Anything at all."

Keshet throws open the door, tumbling into the high summer weeds with a yelp. She scrambles to her feet, then takes off running down the dirt road toward her house, where Helen imagines the girl's mother worries and waits—is always waiting—for her child to return home safely. The girl never once looks back.

those less fortunate

Sarah wakes to her father perched on the edge of her bed. The music she plays to put herself to sleep each night—garage punk lamentations she finds particularly comforting—is spilling from her earbuds onto her breasts. The bass burrows there, deep in her chest cavity, her heart leaping to catch the chorus's beat. Outside her bedroom window, the sun has yet to color the horizon; the moon droops in the sky, a doleful, half-shut eye.

"I didn't want to wake you," her father says.

"Then why are you sitting there?" Sarah rolls over onto her stomach, her face pressed into her pillow. The smell of her breath—peach wine coolers and weed—is enough inspiration to flip back over. "Fuck me," Sarah says. She can feel her father flinch, the quiver of the mattress.

"Because we need to get going."

"Then you did want to wake me up. So say that."

"I didn't want to wake you, but we need to go."

Before she can stop him, he tugs her ear twice, a nearly forgotten ritual of affection. He seems at a loss after this gesture. "I guess we could pray together," he suggests. "Everybody's always saying it helps." Outside of funerals and Christmas dinner, Sarah has never known her father to pray.

Sarah can hear the TV playing from the living room, the distorted roar of a crowd. She's seen all the videos often enough to know which of her brother's old game tapes is playing, that a grainy Sean is bursting across the screen right now, his right hand pumping the air with the football as he peers downfield for an open receiver.

"I saw the face of Jesus in my hamburger bun last night," Sarah says. "I'm all good for now."

"I'm trying here, Sarah." Her father sits quietly for a moment, his breathing labored, as if he's run a very long distance. Then he rallies. "Come on, this will make you feel better. It's important to remember folks less fortunate than us."

"There are people less fortunate than us?" Sarah says. "Now that's depressing."

He presses a quick kiss to her forehead and stands and leaves, turning on the light as he disappears into the hallway, past the bedroom of her younger twin brothers, who've been staying with her grandmother for weeks now; past her older brother's door, which is kept open, the dresser covered in an army of sports trophies, seamed little men clutching misshapen footballs mid-throw; past her parents' closed door, where her mother is sleeping, has been sleeping for several months now, and will be sleeping no matter when Sarah returns home today.

Sarah's father manages grounds maintenance at the Living Waters golf course on the lake, the reservoir the saving grace in their town, though only the locals who inherited property or bought lakefront lots decades ago can afford to enjoy it. Mostly, it belongs to outsiders. Everybody else lives on rural tracts outside the town limits, like Sarah's family, or in the town center, which, after her father punches an address into the GPS from a list on a half slip of notebook paper, is where they head first.

The narrow streets are empty, a ridge of red just cleaving the bruise of clouds in the east. They pass the gas-station-turned-video-store-turned-laundromat-turned-Chinese-buffet. Her dad points it out, says, "We should try that new restaurant one of these days. You like Chinese?" Sarah thinks that being with her father is like being on an awkward date with a nice boy she's really not that into.

Seven half-frozen Thanksgiving turkeys are secured carefully under a tarp in the bed of her father's truck. The plan—as her father explained it to her yesterday in a serious tone that let her know there was no escape from this day of daughter-father togetherness—is to drop off the turkeys at the homes of the guys on his crew at the golf course, then drive out to a buddy's land near Opelika to introduce Sarah to the pleasures of deer hunting.

When not working, her father usually looks like an older, heavier version of the country boys at her school: a snug Henley with low-hitched jeans and a cap with a well-bent bill shading a hank of thick bangs. Today he's decked out in full camouflage, a fluorescent orange cap tugged low over his baggy eyes. The few days' growth of hair on his cheeks, mostly white, is brilliant against his tanned skin.

"These are good men," he is telling her now.

"OK," Sarah says.

"They made some bad choices, some missteps along the way. Most places won't hire them—hell, most places ain't hiring anybody around here—but I give a man a chance to show himself."

"Like what?" Sarah asks. "What kind of bad choices?"

"Take your pick. There's a whole world of trouble out there."

Acid froths and burns in Sarah's throat. She grabs a bottle of Gatorade from the lunch cooler her father prepared and chugs the entire thing. Her swallows pound against the wall of her skull, and she thinks of Sean, what it must have sounded like when the doctor drilled a hole into her brother's head to release the pooling blood. A "cranial burr hole," they'd called it, which Sarah thinks would make a sweet name for a band.

Her father casts a sidelong glance her way from under his cap. "You're being responsible with those friends of yours, right? You're not doing anything too stupid?"

Sarah's friends are new friends, a group of perennially stoned teens who move with a sleepy languidness, as if their bodies battle some unseen resistance. Sarah, who'd always been a do-gooder, the kind of girl who ran the Toys for Tots campaign each Christmas, barely noticed these kids skulking in the hallways of the school before this year, a black-clad tribe who took her in with as much warmth and enthusiasm as they show for anything or anyone.

In part because it's a legitimate point and in part because he's annoying her, Sarah asks, "Don't you think it's too early to show up at somebody's house?"

Her father grins, his front teeth stained from the cigarettes he sneaks when she and her mother are not around. "Who wouldn't wake up early for a free turkey?" Somehow, he looks sadder when he smiles.

They turn onto a street that borders the main town cemetery. The tiny wooden cottages are the sun-bleached gray of driftwood. They park in front a house clutched in a fist of kudzu, its porch buckled. A dead fern sits on the front step, its fronds ossified into the shape of human vertebrae.

"Let me drop this one off for Mick," he says. "You stay in the truck."

Sarah's father leaps from the truck and roots around under the blue tarp, resurfacing with a gigantic turkey he hugs to his chest like a baby. Sarah watches as he navigates the decayed porch while balancing the turkey. Eventually, the front door opens, and a ripped, tatted man in his boxers emerges, his hand visored over his eyes against the new sun. His shoulders snap together when he recognizes his boss. The man seems to know the sweet spot on the porch; he moves across one board toward her father with an elegant grace. There's a lot of awkward smiling and nodding as her father rolls the turkey into the guy's cupped arms and pats his naked bicep. And then her father is back in the truck, keying the next address into the GPS.

They hit several more houses in town, most of them in a similar state of disrepair. Her father took her phone for the day, so Sarah fiddles with the radio as she waits in the truck, making it a point not to watch the gifting of the turkeys. Then they head out toward Highway 280, past the high school and the Family Dollar and the local psychic's house with the man-sized sign of a poorly painted palm print stuck to the front, which, if Sarah squints her eyes, looks as if something like God is reaching through the brick to offer her an enthusiastic high five.

They pass the Hardee's, where a bent old man with an industrial-sized broom sweeps the parking lot, a futile endeavor if ever there was one. With the students out for Thanksgiving break, the parking lot—the jock and cheerleader hangout—will fill by dusk with kids escaping their families, the boys sitting on their tailgates, talking shit about each other's trucks, the girls chain smoking and thumbing the screens of their phones while they wait for the boys to notice them, their lazy exhalations edged with a palpable anger.

Sometimes Sean allowed Sarah to tag along with him on Friday nights after his games. They would eat mountains of french fries and watch the spectacle of high school play out before them. Sean, just starting his junior year, had a drawer full of letters from smaller colleges around the Southeast, and, still juiced from the game, he'd talk excitedly about how things were going to be different for him, how no fucking way would he end up like the few other local boys who'd played college ball, coming home after graduating or flunking out and cruising the town in their tricked-out trucks hunting high school pussy.

Eventually, whichever remarkably uncheerful cheerleader Sean was hooking up with at the time would knock on Sean's window, pissed at being ignored, and Sarah would find herself displaced by the girl, waiting in the fluorescent-lit restaurant alone, watching through the window while Sean and the girl argued inside the truck, then, Sean's bulk pressed against the girl, made out, which looked to Sarah like another kind of fighting.

"Only a few more," Sarah's father says. His thighs flex against the seats with the beat of a tune about a girl digging a man for his tractor, which is about the stupidest thing Sarah has ever heard. Sarah hasn't seen him this energized in months, not since Sean's last game, when he'd paced in front of the bleachers with a rowdy posse of other dads, all of them drinking booze-spiked sodas and yelling obscenities at the other team, the coaches, the ref, and sometimes each other. This was before a 250-pound linebacker from LaFayette planted his boulder-sized head into her brother's helmet on a quarterback sneak.

They drive out of town, a few miles up Highway 280 toward Camp Hill, and turn off on a dirt road Sarah would have never noticed. It takes a good ten minutes, long enough Sarah wonders if they might be lost, but eventually a neat, yellow cottage with a bright white porch appears in the middle of a pecan grove. A little girl sits in a dented wading pool in the front yard, a throng of older boys tossing a ball over her head. A few trucks and cars are parked in front of a shed, and her father pulls up beside them and cuts the engine.

"I need to go to the bathroom," Sarah says, the two Gatorades and a can of Beanee Weenees not sitting well on her soured stomach. She doesn't really want to go inside a stranger's house, but she doesn't have much of a choice. She gets out and waits on her dad to dig out a turkey from the back. The boys, middle school age, keep tossing the football as if Sarah is not there. The little girl in the wading pool studies Sarah warily, calls out, "I'm Iris. Who are y'all?"

Sarah walks over and peers into the pool. It's filled with several inches of red dirt. The girl, who seems to be about four or so, has a naked Barbie in each hand. She drags their matted hair across the dirt, etching an alphabet.

"We brought you a turkey," Sarah says.

"We don't need a turkey," the girl says suspiciously. "We already got us one. A big one."

Sarah hears her father's name called, and she looks toward the house and sees a tall, bald, Black man leaning into the porch railing, waving. "Good morning, Mr. Trey," the man yells. "Come grab yourself some coffee."

Sarah follows her father up a well-kept stone path to the porch. He stomps the dirt from his boots at the base of the porch steps, then stands there with the turkey, staring up at the man, who towers over them.

"This is Big Charley," her father says jovially. "He's my right-hand man at work these days."

"Yes, sir," Big Charley says.

"I'd be up a creek without Big Charley."

"I sure appreciate you saying that, Mr. Trey." Big Charley grins, the gap between his front teeth large enough to show the red of his tongue. "I'm grateful for the work. Nobody else would give me a chance. All I wanted was an honest day's work."

"That's all a man deserves."

Both of the men nod their heads solemnly.

"How's Miss Bianca?" Big Charley says. "We praying for her. Holidays are hard."

"She's hanging in there," Sarah's father says. He jerks his chin her way. "This is Sarah, my daughter. I'm taking her on her first hunt today."

"Oh, I don't believe that, not at all. I bet you done killed all kinds of young bucks already." Big Charley winks at Sarah, and she feels her cheeks burn.

Her father hefts the turkey a few inches. "We brought you a little something for tomorrow. A small thank-you for all your work."

"You're a good man, Mr. Trey," Big Charley says. "A good man."

"It's the least I could do."

"You done plenty already, Mr. Trey," Big Charley says. "Let me get y'all that coffee."

Big Charley leads them through the tidy living room to the kitchen, which smells of bacon and pie crust. A young man, a kid, really, as tall and wide as Big Charley, sits at the kitchen table, drinking a glass of orange juice and reading a book. Sarah doesn't recognize the boy from school, but there is no reason she would aside from the sheer size of him. The students mostly self-segregate at assembly and lunch, the Black kids on one side of the auditorium or cafeteria, the white kids on the other, and those deemed skanks and weirdos of all races in the no-man's land in the middle. Sarah and her friends sit on the white side, precariously close to the middle.

"Will, this is Mr. Trey Grayson," Big Charley says to the young man. He hands them each a cup of coffee from the French press on the stove, and Sarah takes a sip, the taste so bitter she almost vomits on Big Charley's floor.

Will glances up from under his glasses, eyes her father, then the turkey, then Sarah. He wears a shirt with "Mississippi State" printed across the front in maroon, block letters.

"Mr. Grayson manages us men at work," Big Charley says.

"So you're my uncle's boss man?" Will says.

"I don't sign the checks," her father says, laughing. "But I hand them out."

Will doesn't laugh back.

"Will's my sister's boy," Big Charley says quickly. "He's a sophomore up in Starkville."

"What do you study?" Sarah's father asks.

"Philosophy and political science," Will answers.

"He got himself a full ride," Big Charley says.

"I'm going to set this down here," Sarah's father says of the turkey, and he rolls it onto the kitchen table in front of Will. It wobbles like a top.

Will glares at it for a long, awkward moment. "You passing out the holiday rations?" he asks.

Her father's face slackens. He stares at the boy as if he's missed something. "It's a turkey," he says. "A gift."

"It's never just a turkey," Will says.

Big Charley laughs too loudly. "You know these kids," he says. "They go off to school and come home full of piss and vinegar. Get all kinds of ideas."

"You play ball?" her father asks Will, trying, Sarah can tell, to make nice.

Will closes his book. There's a picture of a Black man riding a horse painted like an American flag on the cover. "No," he says, enunciating slowly, "I don't play ball."

"My son played quarterback," Sarah's father says, looking like he might cry at any moment.

Sarah's stomach careens against her ribs. "You got a bathroom I can use?" she asks.

The bathroom is papered in pink and gold flowers. It smells of bleach and potpourri. Sarah sits on the toilet long enough she's embarrassed to leave. Stalling, she goes through the medicine cabinet, half hoping to score, but finds only baby aspirin and laxatives.

Sarah catches her reflection in the mirror and is startled, for a moment, by what she sees there. Sarah's History teacher is always telling some horrific story—students slaughtered in China, civil rights activists murdered in Mississippi—then asking the class dramatically, *Who will you choose to be in this world?* Sarah examines herself, the dyed-black hair, the nose ring, the thick eyeliner arched up toward her brows. She knows she is staring at her own image, but it is as if she has borrowed some other girl's face. If she sticks her tongue out, there's a distinct possibility that the girl in the mirror will not do the same.

Her bottom lip is slightly bruised, a small cut puckering the fragile skin, and she thinks of her friend Andy, what he'd said last night. "All evidence of the truth, sweet Sarah Grayson, comes only from the senses," he said as he fingered her against the door of his mom's ancient Volvo wagon.

Sarah'd hooked up with Andy a few times at the cabin, a fish camp owned by somebody's grandfather who was too old or sick to use it anymore. Her friends have a communal attitude toward coupling; usually, proximity is the deciding factor. Sarah ends up with whomever is slouched next to her when she's finally too stoned to have much of a preference. Even so, Andy, with his pretentious quotes, his pocked skin and gauged, udderlike earlobes, mildly repulses her, though it takes more effort to tell him no than it does to wait out the manhandling.

"You mean my vag is the key to the great truths of the universe?" Sarah had said, laughing, and she was mainly joking, but part of her wanted him to tell her that yes, something extraordinary and unknown lay dormant inside of her, a wondrous mystery waiting to reveal itself.

Instead he'd yanked his hand from under her skirt and slapped her across the mouth. "You feel that?" he asked before walking casually up the steps back to the cabin, where she could see shadows on the porch writhing to a nasally emo song that scudded across the lake like a thousand skipped rocks.

She presses her tongue to the cut now. The sting is not unpleasant.

When Sarah finally emerges from the bathroom, she makes her way to the kitchen, but no one is there. She finds Iris in the living room, watching cartoons on the couch. Will is sitting beside her, his book opened in his lap, an index finger tracing a line on a page. He does not bother to look up when Sarah clears her throat to signal her presence in the doorway. "Your daddy's waiting in his truck," the girl says, not taking her eyes off the cartoon. A long-lashed mouse is beating a cat over the head with a toaster.

Her father doesn't say anything when she gets into the cab. They are a few miles outside Opelika when he pulls off at a gas station and stuffs the last two turkeys in the trash can by the pumps. He buys a pint of bourbon from the attached liquor store and takes a draw as soon as he slides back into the driver's seat. The jeep at the pump in front of them has a buck tied to the roof. Its bright eyes fix on Sarah. It looks as if it might reanimate at any moment, leap off the jeep, and return to whatever it is that deer do.

"Maybe your mother's got the right idea." Her father takes another sip of bourbon, turns the radio on, then thinks better of it and turns it off. "Why bother?"

"What bad choice did he make?" Sarah asks. "Why wouldn't anybody hire Big Charley?"

"Nothing worse than anybody else," her father says.

When they get to his friend's land, the access gate has not been unlocked as promised. Her father tries calling his friend, and when no one answers, he decides to scale the fence to see if it's doable for Sarah. He makes it halfway up before his boot gets caught in the wire and he falls hard, jamming his right hand. Within minutes, it swells to twice its size.

"It's OK," Sarah says. "I didn't really want to kill anything anyway. Hunting was your and Sean's thing."

"We're starting too late anyhow," he says. He stares at her for a moment, then asks, "Why did you do that to your hair, Sarah? It looks like shit." There's something mean and sad in his voice, and Sarah understands that those two things can sometimes be one and the same.

"It's hair," Sarah says. "I can change it back anytime." But her father shakes his head slowly from side to side, as if such a thing is an impossibility.

It's a nice day, the air crisp, the sky a ribbon of flawless blue, so they decide to eat their lunch on the tailgate before returning home. Her father made tuna fish sandwiches, a favorite of Sarah's, and she chokes down half of one. He eats some potato chips, but mainly he drinks the bourbon with his left hand, his right plunged into the cooler.

The cars rush by in a lulling cadence. Sarah lies back on the bed of the truck, the piney woods swaying in the breeze. Sarah's mother once told her of a woman, a mother of a classmate, who'd gone missing years ago when Sarah's mother was in high school, how she and her friends had searched with half of the town for the body in woods not unlike these, how they never located her, never knew if the woman had been killed or taken or if maybe she'd just left. Sarah and her friends would sometimes play hunt-the-body in the woods behind Sarah's house, taking turns as the dead woman, lying stone-still under some brush or in a natural depression in the earth, waiting to be found. Sarah's mother had shared the story, Sarah knew even then, as a subtle threat not to take her for granted, a warning that a mother could be gone in one way or another in a blink of an eye.

"You think Nana will bring the twins home for Thanksgiving? Maybe Mom will even cook something?" Sarah asks. She sits up, the world spinning before it steadies itself.

"No," her father says. "I don't." He shoves the bag of potato chips into the cooler. "We best be going."

Sarah packs up what's left of the lunch and slides the cooler into the cab. When she moves to climb into the passenger seat, he tosses her his keys. "You drive," he says. "It'll be good practice."

Sarah's a few months shy of sixteen, but Sean let her drive his truck sometimes, and for weeks she's been taking her mom's car on short joy rides when her dad's at work. She settles behind the steering wheel, arranging the seat and mirrors like she was taught in driver's ed.

Her father, impatient, shifts the gear in drive. "The best way to learn to drive," he says, "is to drive."

Sarah buckles up and inches into the road, taking it slow for the first mile or two, but the truck, an automatic, doesn't drive all that differently than her mom's Camry, and once she gets used to its mass, she begins to enjoy sitting so high up on the road, the powerful surge of the larger engine when she pumps the gas.

"Now we're cooking," her father says, resting his head against the passenger-side window. "Sorry today was a bust. I was trying to think about something else, somebody else, anything else," he says.

A minivan roars up on their tail, then passes on a solid line. Sarah can see child car seats in back. "Idiots," she says, feeling very grown-up.

"Why'd that kid have to be such an asshole? Take the damn turkey for Christ's sake."

The deer slams the front of the truck out of nowhere, its face pressing into the windshield with the suddenness of a ghoul in a horror film. Its lips twist against the glass. Blood bubbles from its mouth like someone is blowing in it with a straw. Sarah loosens her grip on the steering wheel, and they veer into the oncoming lane before her father grabs the wheel and yanks them back.

Sarah is shaking, her entire body spasming. Her knees bang the underside of the steering column. She manages to ease onto the shoulder, the deer still riding the hood. They sit for a moment, looking at the deer looking at them. Its breath webs the windshield with condensation. It makes an awful squealing sound.

"You got to be fucking kidding me," her father says. He opens his door and stumbles out, unsteady on his feet. "C'mon, Sarah, with this lame hand I'm going to need some help."

Mercifully, the deer, a small four-point buck, is dead by the time they try to remove it from the hood. Her father grabs one hind leg and Sarah grabs the other, and on his count, they tug. It thunks to the ground, fur and flesh still stuck in the windshield wipers and grill. Big chunks of hide are missing from one side, but he doesn't look that bad, considering.

"What are we going to do with him now?" Sarah says.

♦♦♦

At her father's instruction, Sarah parks in the same spot from earlier that day. The young boys are still throwing the football. Iris digs in the wading pool with a plastic sword now, a cloud of red dirt rising around her. Sarah can see Big Charley and Will standing on the front porch. A few women sit near them in rocking chairs, large bowls wedged between their feet, ears of corn in their laps.

Her father hops out of the truck and Sarah follows, uncertain as to what is happening. Blood and fur pepper her shirt and jeans. It took them the better part of a half hour to maneuver the dead buck into the bed of the truck, her father cussing a streak through most of it, but he seems jubilant now. He pops the tailgate, then waves wildly at the porch with his good hand.

"Mr. Trey," Big Charley calls. "Everything all right?"

"We're good," her father hollers back. "Just thought you and your nephew might could help me out here."

There's some rumbling on the porch, and it looks like Big Charley is saying something to Will that Will does not want to hear. The rhythm of the women's rocking chairs slows, their hands stilling on the corn. Eventually, Big Charley steps off the porch and walks toward their truck, Will following at a reluctant pace behind him.

"Oh," Big Charley says when he sees the deer. "You got yourself a good eater."

"We came by it the hard way," her father says. He points to the front of his truck. The grill is bent in half. Then he lifts his hurt hand, which doesn't look much like a hand anymore.

"Ouch," Big Charley says, releasing a low whistle. "You need some ice for that?"

Sarah's father taps the pint of bourbon in the breast pocket of his shirt, says, "I took my medicine."

Will stops a few feet away, kicks at the ground with his sneakers. His eyes are swollen and red, the way Sarah's mother's eyes always look now.

Her father's eyes flicker from Will's face to Big Charley's, where he meets and holds Big Charley's unblinking gaze.

"Looks like you could use a drink, too," her father says, extending the bourbon toward Will.

"No thank you," Will says faintly.

"With my hand busted, I ain't worth much." Her father gestures toward the deer. "I thought y'all might be willing to help me dress out this bad boy."

"I've never dressed a deer," Will says. His eyes widen with alarm. "I don't even know what that means."

Big Charley stands next to Sarah's father. He's a least a foot taller, his biceps the same diameter as her father's neck. His fists tighten, and then he smiles widely. "We'd be happy to, Mr. Trey."

"Excellent!" her father says. "Where's your skinning hoist?"

Big Charley points to an oak at the right of the shed; what looks like a hanger with hooks on the bottom corners dangles from a rope strung over a branch. Her father jumps into the truck and backs it up to the oak's trunk, then Big Charley and her father, who isn't much help, work the buck toward the tailgate. When the deer's sprawled half out of the bed, Big Charley pulls a fold-out knife from his jeans' pocket and gouges a hole in the big joint of each hind leg. He finally gets the buck's legs, slippery with blood, lodged on the hooks. The younger boys have crowded around the carcass, and they poke it with sticks, giggling and shoving each other.

Big Charley strains as he winches the deer off the bed of the truck, but eventually the deer rises, its head and front hooves hanging limply toward the ground, and Sarah doesn't want to, but she can't help but think of her brother after the accident, of the long days he spent lying, unmoving, in the hospital bed, half his head shaved where they'd drilled the hole into his skull. Before they took him off life support, the doctors explained everything to her family, how Sean was no longer Sean, his brain a jumbled network of highways to nowhere, a miscarriage of neurons. But there was still something inside her brother—that miraculous and unnamable thing. Sarah sensed it when she held his hand before they turned off the machines, and then later, when she kissed his cheek before they took his body, it was gone.

"I think he's up there good," Big Charley says, stepping back to admire his handiwork. "Let me get my skinning knife from the shed."

"I got mine," Sarah's father says. He fishes in his toolbox and finds a long, leather-handled knife. Big Charley reaches for it, and her father says, "I thought I'd let Will here give it a try."

Will looks petrified. He stares at the knife as if he's never seen one. "I told you," he says, "I don't know anything about cutting up a deer."

"This'll be your first lesson, then," her father says. There's a firm resolve in his voice. His expression beneath the bill of his hat is almost reverent. "Every man should know how to dress a deer."

"Sure enough," Big Charley says. He tugs the boy toward the buck, then points at the pelvis, tells him to start below there and move toward the ribs, using only the tip of the blade so as not to rupture the gut sack and spoil the meat.

The deer—its legs spread wide, its genitals a tender swelling—looks indecent to Sarah, a heinous violation.

Will takes the knife and places its point hesitantly against the lower abdomen. His shoulders shake, but it is hard to tell if he is crying. He jabs the blade in too far, then yanks his hand away. The knife stays put, like a dart stuck in a board.

"You can't hurt it," Big Charley says. "It's already dead. Gut the damn thing."

Will takes a deep breath and grips the knife handle with both hands. He braces himself, turning his head away from the deer's belly, as if he can't bear to release what's inside.

"Go on, son," Sarah's father says, not unkindly. "We all had to learn somehow."

the lives of diamonds

Why Lola is at the Lakeview courthouse: she has a hand-ful of parking tickets, her grandfather's, shoved in the belly of her crocheted purse, and her purpose, as dictated by her grandfather, is to see if something can be done about them other than payment. It would do you good, he'd told her earlier, to learn the art of negotiation now, while you are young enough it is a luxury rather than a necessity.

This statement sounded, to Lola, fair enough. And it is June, summer break. And her grandfather did take away her phone and iPad after he found her sneaking out again. And she has watched 10,000 *Jerry Springer* reruns on her grandfather's ancient TV, learned about babysitters who shake babies, sisters who sleep with sisters. And she is bored. A trip *anywhere*, especially a place with the potential for exciting, unexpected encounters, seems promising.

When Lola arrives, the female officer behind the desk in the lobby doesn't look up from her computer screen and waits a full minute before speaking, not bothering to hide the fact she is shopping for shoes online. "You here for the Law Enforcement Explorers meeting?" she says finally.

"Sure." Lola shrugs. "I'm here for the meeting."

"It's next door at the station. In the conference room. You can't miss it."

The conference room in the police station is like every conference room in all small-town police stations: cement blocks, cheap plaques, graying tile floor, an old pine table with mismatched chairs. In these chairs hunch two plain, teenage girls and an attractive, youngish officer. The Alabama heat saturates the room; the drowsy swirl of the fan above them does nothing more than blend the soupy air and the smell of the girls' too-sweet perfume.

The two girls, whom Lola does not know—and she knows every teenager in this town—ignore her. But the man smiles broadly, says, "Take a seat. This here is Savannah and Madison. They're sisters visiting their grandparents for the summer. I'm Lieutenant J. B. Loomis." Lieutenant Loomis nods in greeting, hands Lola a brochure, the coarse hairs on his forearm brushing Lola's wrist.

Lieutenant Loomis explains that the Law Enforcement Explorer program is meant to bridge the gap between youth and police by educating and involving them in police operations. He reads off the brochure: *Members can volunteer at community events doing security work, directing traffic, fingerprinting small children, and helping with Crime Prevention Programs. Members can also learn firsthand how police officers do their jobs. Officers and Detectives with special skills are invited to meetings to explain how the police department investigates major crimes such as homicides, narcotics violations, and gang activity. Explorers also make in-person visits to such units as K-9.*

"We don't have our own K-9 unit," he says. "It's run by an independent nonprofit, and I haven't had a chance to arrange a visit, so I guess we won't be doing that for a while. And we don't have the budget for a child fingerprinting program, so we won't be helping out at schools, either."

"They have a K-9 unit at home," the girl named Savannah says. "German Shepherds. Big ones."

"I like Willy best," Madison adds. "He has gray eyes."

"Blue," Savannah says.

"Light gray," Madison says. Lola can tell they've had this argument before.

Lieutenant Loomis chuckles uncomfortably, points at the bright green folder with *Law Enforcement Explorer Instructor Guide* printed in gold letters on the top. Beneath the words there's a picture of a balding, jovial cop with his arms wrapped around two scrawny teen boys with high-top fades. "It says here that the first get-together is a meet-and-greet and an introduction to the process of taking fingerprints during bookings." He tugs at his bottom lip with his front teeth, a nervous, boyish tic. Lola decides he is entirely cute.

He whips out an inkpad and several white cards, tells Madison to give it a try. While Madison inks her fingers, he confesses, "This really wasn't supposed to be my thing. Captain Benny went to a conference about building relationships with the local youth and came back really inspired and committed. But then he had a heart attack." Lieutenant Loomis smiles at Madison's smeared fingerprint on her card, motions for her to try again. "Not that I'm not excited," he says. "I'm just not quite as on top of things as I'd like to be."

"But we're not from here," Madison says in a tone that makes it clear she does not want to be considered a local.

"Well, you're here now," Lieutenant Loomis says with a weary politeness.

"Are we going to have a background check?" Lola asks. "This brochure says all Explorers will have their backgrounds checked." Lola loves this, the idea of someone hunting for her dark secrets. She hates the fact that she doesn't have any.

Lieutenant Loomis takes a brochure from the stack of extras he'd placed in the center of the table and skims the paragraph about background checks for members, then slips the brochure under the instructor manual he clearly has yet to read. "No," he says. "You girls look like good girls. No need for that."

"But that's not procedure," Savannah says, and Madison scowls, her top lip catching on her braces. The sisters are all business. "That's not how our group does it at home."

"Your turn," he says to Savannah, handing her a fingerprint card and the pad of ink. "Now press your thumb steady and slow. Kind of rolling it, like." Savannah fills all the blocks on her card intently, then passes the ink pad to Lola without looking at her.

"How old are you?" Lola asks as she writes her name on her card, Lola Knight. She dots the "i" in her last name with a heart, then decides this is corny. She fills in the heart until it transforms into a giant blob that eats half the stem of the "i."

"We're both thirteen," Madison says. "Fraternal twins." Madison, who has a mouth full of braces, is blonde and squat, with a wide nose and a gap between her teeth. Savannah is dark and tall and skinny but shares the gap and braces. "Fraternal means we each had our own egg."

"No," Lola says, rolling her index finger in the ink. "I mean you." She lifts her eyes, brown and lucent, her best feature, she knows, and smiles at Lieutenant Loomis, whose tanned skin looks jaundiced under the fluorescent lights.

He smiles at her uncertainly. "Ancient to you, I'm sure. Half in the grave."

"You don't look ancient to me," Lola says.

"What now?" Savannah interrupts. "We've got a whole hour left."

"Like forty?" Lola says. "My parrot is about forty, and if I take good care of him, he can live for anther ten years."

"Like thirty-five," he says. "And hopefully, I'll last longer than your parrot."

"Are we going to dust the room for fingerprints now?" Madison asks. "Find match points with the ones on our cards?"

"I hadn't thought of that," Lieutenant Loomis says, slapping his hands together. "But it sounds like a plan to me."

In the span of five minutes, the girls cover the small room in grainy, graphite shavings.

"See," Lieutenant Loomis says, pointing at the table, "that's what we call a latent print. It's an impression of the friction ridges on your fingers."

Savannah leans over the fingerprint, examines it closely, says, "That one must be yours, Madison. Look how fat it is! That's a fat finger."

"Well, now," Lieutenant Loomis says, "we really can't be sure until—"

"My fingers aren't fat," Madison says. She waves her stubby fingers in the air. "Mom says I have piano player hands."

"What about pictures?" Lola asks quietly, feathering a fingerprinting brush over the bridge of her nose. The two girls, their gawkiness and uncontrolled blabbering, are annoying her. She worries Lieutenant Loomis won't be able to separate her from them, will lump them all together as silly, immature teenagers. "Maybe you can show us some pictures of crime scenes. I'm finding this all really fascinating. I mean, this program has got me thinking I might want a career in law enforcement. You must help all sorts of people."

"Jesus," Savannah snorts. "You've got stuff on your nose." Lola shoots the girl a nasty look. She doesn't wipe the graphite off.

"I don't know," Lieutenant Loomis says. "Those files are kind of confidential."

"Even the solved cases?" Madison asks, the possibility of seeing actual crime photos too tempting to pass up. "Or maybe something simple like a good old car wreck. Something where there's really no crime."

Lieutenant Loomis looks at his watch, then opens the instructor manual, flipping through a few pages before closing it again. There are at least thirty minutes left in the meeting, and Lola can tell he doesn't have anything else planned for the night, has seen the same look of confusion and desperation on her teachers' faces when a lesson plan has gone awry and they are facing a possible classroom mutiny.

"Just a little peek?" Lola says.

"Well, I guess it wouldn't hurt." Lieutenant Loomis rises from his seat. He is tall and muscular, his forearms tanned, a tattoo of a dolphin on the underside of his left arm. Lola thinks this shows sensitivity, the dolphin, and she imagines him at home with his wife, perhaps with the small children she assumes he has, frolicking in one of those cheap aboveground pools, the little ones in floaties, slapping at the water, screaming at him to put his arm in the water again, to make that dolphin swim.

While he's gone, Savannah slips the ink pad and a fingerprinting brush into her purse. Madison walks to the wall, plucks off a dusty plaque, and drops it into her bookbag.

"Working from the inside, I see," Lola says.

"What?" Savannah says.

"You really shouldn't do that," Lola says in an exaggerated voice she associates with mothers on sitcoms. "J.B. has been nothing but nice to us, and you could get him in trouble."

"J.B.," Madison mimics.

The sisters scramble for their seats when they hear a door down the hall close. Lieutenant Loomis returns, a file folder beneath his arm. "Now we can only look at the pictures of the wrecked vehicles," he says, "not of the actual victims." But when he moves to sit down, the contents of the folder spill onto the table, and all three girls dive at once, searching for the shiny, slick photos.

"Oh my God," Madison squeals. "Look at this boys' legs! They're, like, not even attached."

"Drunk driving accident," Lieutenant Loomis says. "I chose this particular case because it had a great impact on me. This happened before I even joined the force, when I wasn't much older than you are now. A girl from my class was a passenger. She lived, but her boyfriend died at the scene. She was lucky. Remember that photo the next time you get in a car with someone who has been drinking behind the wheel. You might not be so lucky. Now, please, you really need to give those back."

But Lola is looking at an image of a shoe, a single sneaker, its laces dangling from the mulberry bush that cradles it. There's not a smudge on it. Not a drop of blood. Not a streak of dirt. It is inexplicably unscathed.

J.B. gently takes the photo from Lola. "There's no rhyme or reason to it," he says. "What survives and what doesn't."

Madison giggles. "Like, that's so tragic," she says.

"Everything. Now." Lieutenant Loomis holds out his hands, and the sisters reluctantly hand over their contraband. "Next week," he says, "we'll take the patrol car out and I'll show you how to run the radar gun."

"We've already done that," Savannah says. She crosses her arms across her flat chest.

"Yeah," Madison adds. "We've already done all of this before."

When J.B. arrives home, his wife, Dana, is sitting on the floor in the den, sucking on a Popsicle, the local newspaper spread in front of her. She's dyed her naturally dark hair light blonde and cut it short. She looks faded, like she's been left out in the sun too long.

"You like it?" she asks, one hand propped behind her head. "I paid too much for it, for sure. And none of the stylists here know their heads from their asses. But what the hell. I thought it was time for a change."

"Sure," he says. "You look very Marilyn Monroe-ish."

Dana frowns. "Marilyn Monroe was pudgy. They say she wasn't, but I've seen the pictures, and pudgy is pudgy, no matter how famous you are." She puts a protective hand over her own tiny pooch.

"Well, Meg Ryan-ish then. Pixie-like. No one can call her fat."

Dana considers this for a moment. "But she's cute. Cute is the curse of death. No one wants to be over thirty and cute.

And she's got that weird, squishy face thing." Dana draws up her nose, pinches her brows together to illustrate.

"Please," he says, unbuttoning his uniform. "What do you want me to say? I love it. I mean I really, really love it." It doesn't really matter what he says. The banter is merely a formality. They've been married for twelve years, and aside from the first few tenuous months, J.B. cannot remember one time when he felt like he possessed the ability to honestly hurt Dana's feelings, though he sometimes tries to see if he can get a rise out of her. When they first moved to J.B.'s hometown, when things were still new enough change seemed possible, they sometimes talked about Dana's remoteness. Now it just is.

Dana bites off the end of her Popsicle, points a finger at the paper. "Lilly Smith spent the night with Mia Krink last Friday. They made snickerdoodles and watched *The Notebook*. Can you believe this crap is news? Are these people serious?"

"No news is good news for me," J.B. says. Dana is from Mountain Brook, one of the wealthiest zip codes in the state. She considers herself somewhat worldly and cultured. They met at Samford when J.B. went back to school in his mid-twenties to get a degree in criminal justice. Dana studied interior design. Now she helps wealthy ladies decorate their vacation homes on the lake that borders their town. J.B. wants children, but Dana is ambivalent—about having kids and, increasingly, about J.B. Years ago, after they'd eloped impulsively on a graduation trip to Vegas, his mother had cautioned him about the perils of a wife with lofty ambitions. He suspects she was right.

"How'd the meeting go?" Dana asks. "I still can't believe Benny stuck you with that assignment. If the fat fuck would have laid off the fried chicken like his doctor said, he could do his job."

"He had a heart attack, Dana. Give the man a break. Besides, the meeting was kind of fun. We dusted for fingerprints. The girls seem really enthusiastic."

"Girls?" Dana arches an eyebrow, winks lasciviously. She sets her Popsicle stick on the newspaper, crawls between his open knees. "Girls, is it?" She presses her mouth against J.B.'s belly, and J.B. reaches for her. This they do well. Dana assures him marriages have been built on far less.

"So tell me about them, *the girls*," Dana says later. Her new hair is spiked with sweat, and in the anemic light of the lamp, she looks like a young punk J.B. might shoo away from the boat landing on any given night.

"I think Benny's intention was to connect with some of the more disenfranchised kids in town, but I ended up with a set of spoiled twins parked with their grandparents at their vacation house for the summer," J.B. says. "Barely teens. Mouths full of metal, although that doesn't keep them from running them as frequently as possible. God knows why they're interested in law enforcement, though I wouldn't be completely surprised if we found their grandparents tied up and tortured in their basement by the end of the summer. Something is off with those girls."

Dana laughs, and J.B. loves to make Dana laugh.

"There's one other girl. A little older. Seems like a loner. Thinks she's prettier than she is, although she is pretty. But she'd be prettier if she didn't try so hard. I found out after the meeting that she was over at the courthouse asking about parking tickets, so she might have wandered in." J.B. thinks of Lola, her dark brown eyes, her garish lipstick. "She seems lost."

"Who wouldn't be, in this town?" Dana says. She slips from the couch, pads naked across the room, opens the freezer and pokes her face into the cool swirling air. Her shorts, which lay pooled on the floor where she'd peeled them off, still retain the shape of her rear end.

What J.B. wants to say is that he's not your run-of-the mill, small-town, redneck cop. Sure, he's from here, but he's always been different, dreamy and curious in a way that worried his poor mother, who would have been satisfied with him graduating high school, the first in his family to do so. Before Dana, he'd gone to art school at Carnegie Melon on a full ride, worked a summer as a bike courier in New York, spent a semester in France at an art colony. He smoked opium in street alleys in Paris with a blade-thin French girl who didn't shave her armpits, for God's sake. But he's already said this to Dana before, shown her pictures of him standing first in front of the Louvre, then a bohemian gallery in Soho, hoping she'd recognize something in him in those images she refused to see in their everyday life.

In truth, he couldn't stand art school or New York or Paris, all the noise and chaos, all the snotty, opaque people, every act and utterance studied and analyzed until J.B. could never be certain what was real and what was performed or if there was even a difference between the two. What he'd loved was comic books, their beauty, their directness, their boldness, the worlds of escape they'd offered him as a boy in this very town. But in the end, as much as he'd hated himself for it, all he'd wanted was to come home. He'd flunked out his junior year, moved back in with his mother and worked at the mill long enough he would have given pretty much anything to leave again. He was sitting on a bar stool at the Living Waters clubhouse, shooting the shit with the old golfers, settling in for another long shift of day drinking, when he saw the towers coming down on the bar's big screen, the garish plumes of smoke cartoonishly grotesque, and like so many others, he found himself consumed with a need to *do something*. He enrolled for the spring semester at Samford the next day, declaring Criminal Justice as his major, a pragmatic path that also allowed him to feel as if he were useful during a time when so many people felt helpless.

Dana turns to face him, the freezer door still open, her cheeks pink with cold. Her eyes are solemn. "I want us to be happy," she says, "and I don't see how that can happen here." She plucks a bag of frozen peas from the freezer and presses it against the soft nape of her neck. In this exact moment, J.B. is crippled with love.

He is struck all over again with the same desire to win her he'd felt the first time he saw her reading on the steps of the student union the fall of his last semester, the knuckle of her thumb sucked into her mouth, the left strap of her tank top slipping slightly down her shoulder. He'd thought to walk over to her and push the strap up with one finger, say something witty, offer her a smoke.

Instead, he'd sat a few feet away from her, opened up a book, pretended to read, and waited for her to talk to him, which he assumes she did out of boredom or amusement. They made love that evening in a cloud of incense in Dana's bedroom, her roommates ranting about Nietzsche and the virtues of hydroponic weed in the living room, Dana, even then, looking slightly blasé while they'd shared a smoke afterward, her mouth lifted at the corners, a half-smirk she wore often, moving through the world as if she were in on some fantastic joke he couldn't quite understand but hoped she might explain to him.

Now, when he thinks about it, none of it feels like winning.

"It took you long enough. How did it go?" Lola's grandfather asks. His parking tickets are shoved deep in a trash can outside the police station, and he is sitting at the kitchen table, a model car spread in parts before him. "1932 Ford Roadster," he says. "Now that's the real thing." The TV blares from the next room, a music video. Vintage Duran, Duran: "Hungry Like the Wolf."

"It was cool," Lola says. She opens the fridge door, looks to see if there are any beers she can steal later after her grandfather has gone to sleep. "The receptionist lady said she'd get back to you about the ticket thing. She has to talk to her supervisor." She takes three cans of Budweiser and shoves them into the crisper, behind the lettuce, so her grandfather, who occasionally has a beer before bed, won't drink them. Later, she'll steal them, sit on the back lawn and get slightly buzzed, a ritual she's developed over the last year.

"See," her grandfather says brightly, a tube of glue in one hand, a fender in the other, "that's better than nothing. You never know until you try." He seems so pleased with her that Lola almost feels as if she's honestly accomplished something. She smiles back at him, kisses him on the cheek.

"I joined this club while I was there. Law Enforcement Explorers. We learn police stuff. Next week Lieutenant Loomis is taking us in his patrol car up on Highway 280 to show us how to run the radar gun."

"Excellent!" her grandfather says. "You're moving and shaking and making connections. That's what I like to see. Can you hand me that towel over there? I'm leaking glue on the hood."

"Shut up," her sister Mary yells from the living room, where she's sprawled out on the couch, her huge belly towering over her like a fleshy volcano. "I can't hear anything." Her boyfriend, The Father, as Lola calls him, sits at the end of the couch, Mary's bloated feet in his lap. He is oafish and dimwitted but was the captain of the football team a few years back, and in this town, that means her sister hasn't done all bad. Since he inserted his DNA in their gene pool, he spends most of his time catatonic on their couch.

Things were rough for Lola at school before her sister—the head cheerleader—got pregnant her senior year. Now they're even worse. But she's acquired a kind of bad-girl rep from association, and in Lola's opinion, there is something to be said for having a bad reputation rather than none at all. Technically, she is a virgin. But she's never placed much value in chastity, which seems to her a stupid thing to praise, the encouraging of inaction.

"Leave Lola alone," her grandfather calls to Mary. "She's done something productive today. Have you?"

"I'm building a human being, Pop-Pop," Mary says, wobbling into the kitchen. She kisses him on his fuzzy crown, and his expression softens. "I'm always doing something productive." She opens the pantry, grabs a sack of Doritos, shoves a handful in her mouth. "I'm eating for two," she says to Lola, who watches her sister with open disgust. "What's your excuse?"

"Girls," Lola's grandfather says absentmindedly. *He is a broken man,* Lola often writes in her diary. She likes the sound of it—*broken*—as if people were simply ill-made machines that could be taken apart and put back together like one of her grandfather's model cars. But really, her grandfather's general happiness is, by all appearances, indestructible; he greets each disappointment with a Bible verse and unwavering optimism. Lately, she hates this about him.

As usual, Lola escapes to her room. The sign on Lola's door reads WELCOME TO THE JUNGLE, a birthday gift from her mother, who lives, the last Lola heard, somewhere in California. Lola hasn't seen her father since he took off when Mary was six and she was four. A few months later, Lola's mother went to L.A. for a long weekend to visit a man she'd met online and called to say that she wouldn't be coming home yet, that she thought she'd try her hand at acting. So far, the closest she's come to stardom is playing a corpse pulled out of a cooler on *NCIS: Los Angeles*, an episode Lola has watched no fewer than a hundred times, marveling at how her mother, a heroin addict for close to a decade now, could still be so beautiful, even with a bullet hole in her temple and her mouth painted blue. When the NCIS agent, the one played by the actor with baggy eyes and a square chin and a dozen kids in real life, slides her mother from the cooler and peels the sheet from her face, he shakes his head soberly, says, "Life's a bitch sometimes."

When Lola was small, she used to cry a lot for her mother, but now she finds solace in her menagerie of pets, all rescues abandoned at the local vet's office. The family pet rejects. She has a blind guinea pig; a painted water turtle missing a foot, who paddles in awkward little circles; a cancer-ridden ferret; an iguana with severe socialization problems; and her favorite, a one-legged parrot named Uno, who suffers from separation anxiety and greatly resents Lola offering affection to any of his sibling pets. According to the vet who gave Uno to Lola, some middle school kid razored off Uno's leg when his father told him he couldn't afford a PlayStation. That was three years ago, and Lola has loved the lopsided bird ever since.

"UNO," he squawks when she enters the room. "U-NO."

She immediately walks to his cage, opens the door. He throws himself at her hand, rubbing his velvety head on her fingers.

"That's a good boy," she coos. "Uno mad at Lola?"

He promptly jumps from his cage and on top of the iguana's tank, hopping on one foot across the wire mesh cover. "Uno mad," he says. He shits into the tank, the iguana staring placidly in the distance, suffering the humiliation with admirable fortitude. He knows the drill.

"Uno mad," the bird repeats. It took Lola three months to teach him this particular phrase.

"Bad Uno," Lola says soothingly. "No shitting on George. No, no, no." She plucks Uno from the tank, nestles him against her breasts. "No, no, no," Uno says.

Lola laughs. She can never really get mad at him. She admires him. She thinks there is something to be said for such devotion to one's rage.

This time, J.B. is prepared. When all the girls are gathered around the police car, he passes out a printout he made explaining how radar guns function. He added a visual aid at the bottom, a sketch of the inner workings of the radar gun. He is pleased with how it turned out.

Madison glances at the handout, then stuffs it into her purse.

"We've already done radar guns," Savannah says. She has something green, a piece of salad maybe, stuck in her braces, which makes J.B. inordinately happy.

"Look—" J.B. begins, but Lola interrupts.

"I haven't done radar guns," she says. "I think it sounds interesting." She claps her slender hands together. "Let's get us some bad guys."

"Oh, we won't actually be able to pull anyone over," J.B. says. "Too dangerous. But I'll show you how it works."

"You're kidding me!" Madison balks. She's sprayed her blonde bangs into massive wings, the style the girls used to wear in the 80s, which J.B. surmises is back in fashion from the flouncy, too-bright outfits of the twins. "Why the hell would we go out in the patrol car if we can't stop anyone?"

"Watch the mouth," J.B. says. It sounds like something he should say.

"Well, if we can't stop anyone, who's out policing the streets?" Madison says. "What if something really bad happens? Like a murder?" She seems optimistic.

"Nothing will happen," J.B. says. "And if it does, I can call backup."

Dispiritedly, the girls slide into the patrol car, the sulking sisters in the back, Lola in the front. When J.B. pulls out of the station's parking lot, Lola rolls down the window, pushes her head slightly outside to catch the nonexistent breeze.

J.B. drives toward Highway 280, passing a boarded-up grocery, an abandoned gas station, a video store with a going-out-of-business banner draped across its front.

When they pass the red brick high school, in such a sad state it looks like it should be condemned, Savannah turns to Madison, says, "Can you *imagine*," a comment J.B. knows is for Lola's benefit. He's visited enough high schools over the years to never underestimate the savage cruelty of teenage girls.

"It's worse than anything you can imagine," Lola says quietly, her face still shoved outside the window. "We moved here to live with my grandparents after my mother died last year. But I swear, going to that school is about as bad as losing my mom."

Madison, who J.B. has decided possesses an impressive mean streak, is suddenly all butter with Lola. "I'm so sorry," she says, placing one consolatory hand on Lola's shoulder. "How did it happen? How did she die?"

"Orangutans," Lola says. At first, J.B. thinks Lola is kidding, and he laughs nervously.

"No, really," Lola says. "She was a primatologist. She studied orangutans in Africa. One day, she got too close, and the Alpha Male, Moby—she named him Moby because he was big as a whale—he jumped her. Shredded her to pieces."

The twins are stunned into silence.

Not knowing what to say, J.B. pats Lola on her knee, then yanks his hand away, unsure if such an intimate gesture is appropriate.

"Orangutans are surprisingly humanlike in their grieving behavior," Lola continues. "They mourn like us. When a loved one dies, sometimes they climb up in the trees, make a nest, lay down, and just die."

"That's so unbelievably cool," Savannah sighs. "I mean—not about your mother. But the orangutans and trees and stuff."

For the first time that evening, Lola pulls herself from the window and twists toward the back seat, fixing her eyes on the twins. "Yeah, well, when my mother got mauled, not a one of them climbed up a tree."

"Well, now," J.B. says, sensing danger. "We're about there."

When they reach 280, J.B. turns east toward Auburn and drives for a mile or two before he pulls off on the side of the road, aiming the car at oncoming traffic. He flips on the radar gun. They all stare eagerly down the road, waiting for a car to come into range.

Five minutes later, a handful of cars have passed, all moseying along at granny speeds.

"What's the most bizarre pull-some-idiot-over story you can think of?" Madison says, leaning forward into the front seat. Now that she wants something from him, a dark tale of police heroism and human misery, she's all smiles. "I mean the *absolute* strangest one," she adds, in case he thinks he's going to skimp on the gory details.

J.B. mentally flips through his work anecdotes, tries to decide which ones are teenager friendly and instructive. "Well, there was this one lady, a young woman, mid-twenties. I pulled her over late one night clocking 105 in a Honda Civic. When I asked for her registration, she started crying. I mean, really crying. Said she was speeding because she had to go to the bathroom."

"Oh, please." Madison rolls her eyes.

"Well, I learned not to be so quick to judge, not to assume everyone doing something idiotic is just an idiot. Compassion is a major part of wearing the badge. It turns out, she wasn't lying. In fact, she urinated all over herself. I felt so bad for her, I let her go."

"No one should be humiliated like that," Lola says, as if she's old enough to have endured similar moments of abasement. Even so, J.B. is impressed with her generosity.

"That's it?" Savannah pipes up from the backseat. "That's gross."

What J.B. doesn't tell them is that he led the woman to the closest open gas station so she could clean up, and after she'd wiped herself down in the bathroom as best as she could, she'd sat in his cruiser for a good half hour, the scent of urine overwhelming, and divulged her life story, which included all manner of woes for someone so young, including a diagnosis of terminal kidney cancer. This was early in J.B.'s career, before he fully understood that half of his job consisted of listening to stories of suffering that people seemed compelled to share when in trouble, perhaps out of the need to sort how they got there.

"What's up with everyone? Where are all the cars?" Lola asks. "Hel-lo," she whispers out the window. "Anyone out there?" The forlorn way she speaks lends the last question a melancholy subtext, and her tone moves J.B., who's been told more than once by Dana that his tender heart is nigh near worthless. But what really touches J.B. is the vulnerability of Lola's soft, dusty feet, which she's slipped out of her flip-flops and perched on the dashboard, her toes painted a sparkly pink.

"This is so dull," Madison says.

"Nobody's doing anything bad," Savannah says disappointedly.

J.B. doesn't panic. Not yet. This time, he's come prepared. He turns toward the twins, narrows his eyes in what he hopes is an ominous expression. "Want to see something really disturbing?"

The twins nod yes.

He opens his car door, instructs the girls to slide out of the cruiser on the side farthest from the road. Once they are all standing outside the car, he leads them off the road to where someone has erected a white, wooden cross. It's his intent to explain how three drunk sorority girls from Auburn rolled their SUV in this exact spot two summers before, how the parents identified the girls by their class rings—the implications obviously horrific—which, unfortunately, turned out be a tragic mistake. Two of the girls had switched rings. This very story has brought more than one teenager to tears when he's shared it at various high schools around the county, but before he can begin, Madison screams, "Motherfucker!"

"There's no need to be disrespectful—" J.B. begins.

Savannah cuts him off. "It's her foot. She's totally mutilated her foot."

And true enough, when J.B. pushes Lola and Savannah out of the way to examine Madison's foot, he blanches at the sight of blood pulsing from Madison's wound, the cut nasty and deep. He fights hard not to gag; this has been a constant embarrassment in his law enforcement career, his wooziness around blood.

"That's going to need stitches," Lola says. She picks up the broken beer bottle that caused this fiasco, examines it intently.

A Mustang whizzes by them fast enough to ruffle Madison's plastered bangs. Madison cries violently in Savannah's arms. There is so much blood—a pool of it on the ground, Madison's foot and ankle swimming in it—that J.B. has to remind himself to stay calm. But as fucked as J.B. feels right now—his teenage charge bleeding to death on the side of 280—he's comforted to see that, beneath all their rancorous disdain, the twins are ultimately just scared girls who are savvy enough to associate their own blood with mortality.

Savannah glares at him, says, "We could sue you for this, you know. This is your fault."

"We can worry with that later," J.B. says. "Let's get the cut taken care of now."

J.B. thinks that, if the twins' grandparents are anything like their grandchildren, litigation is entirely probable. But when the twins' grandparents, tanned and in matching teal Izods, arrive at the community hospital, neither of them appears too upset by the whole affair.

"These things happen," the grandfather says jovially. He seems invigorated by all the commotion, has already flirted his way into the hearts of two loitering nurses.

"Might as well get used to it," the grandmother says to Madison, who is turning her foot to and fro, admiring her new stitches as if she's gotten a snazzy tattoo or piercing. The grandmother yanks up the front of her Izod, revealing a shoelaced scar running across her doughy abdomen. "When you get older, they keep cutting things out of you."

◆◆◆

Later, when J.B. is driving Lola back to the station to get her car, she turns down the radio, which he had turned up to avoid conversation. "Do you think we could drive for a little bit?" she asks. "Madison's accident kind of freaked me out, and nobody's home at my place. I don't think I want to be alone right now." She rolls down her window, assumes the same position from earlier that evening.

"Just for a minute," J.B. says. He watches her long dark hair whip against her face in the breeze, how it catches in her mouth, how she leaves it there, chewing on the silky ends. He thinks he might be slightly scared of this morose, somber girl.

It's past nine, and the night has mercifully cooled. J.B. lowers his own window, lets the breeze and the strains of the cicadas wash over him. The communities along 280 are sleepy and shadowed. The darkness blurs the harshness of the abandoned buildings, evoking a romantic, ghostly feel.

"Pull off here," Lola says, pointing to a narrow dirt road. "I want to show you something."

Without thinking, J.B. does exactly what she asks, and he decides that Lola will grow into the kind of woman men want to take care of, to please, that perhaps she already is.

They drive slowly, the patrol car's undercarriage scraping the deep dips and hollows formed by hard rains. It takes him a minute to recognize where they are, an access road to a landfill no longer in use. He's been here once before, many years ago, when he was a senior in high school. A classmate's mother had gone missing, the scarf she'd been wearing when she disappeared found on this very road. J.B. had joined the search party along with half his high school. J.B. had always been a quiet, uncertain kid, given to hiding in his drawings and comic books. But searching for that woman, something righteous and fierce lit inside him. When Dana asked him why he wanted to be on the job in a town like theirs with its good-ol'-boy bureaucracy and shit pay, which she did with some frequency, he often thought of that day, of that first time he felt as if something he did might make his world, however small, a bit better.

"Stop here," Lola says, pointing to a little clearing.

J.B. parks the car on the side of the road and peers into the darkness. He can see nothing, not even with the aid of the headlights. He takes his flashlight out of the glove compartment, shines it out of Lola's window. There is a bent, rust-eaten, wrought iron fence surrounding a few markers, most of which are covered in weeds. If you didn't know it was there you would miss it.

"It's a pet cemetery," Lola says. "I have a guinea pig named Checkers and a rat named Sammy buried here." Her voice quivers.

"I'm sorry," he says, although he can't imagine what kind of home life this girl must have to feel so intensely for rodents.

"I have a parrot named Uno," she says. "When he dies, I'm going to cremate him and turn him into a diamond so he can be with me always. There's this company that does it. You send them the ashes, and they compress them down to a diamond." She twists toward J.B. He can make out the delicate curve of her chin. "All living things are carbon based, just like diamonds."

"That sounds nice," he says.

"When I called the company to ask about the process, the guy said that most of the inquiries they get are about pets, not people. At first I thought it was strange. If you really love someone, wouldn't you want to keep them with you forever? And then I meet people like the twins, and I wonder how anybody loves anybody, really. I mean, what's the purpose of those girls existing?"

J.B. starts to laugh, but Lola seems serious, and he doesn't want to insult her. "They're young," he says. "Give them a chance. We won't always be what we are now."

"Really? You really believe that?"

"Maybe," he says. He thinks of Dana, her constant disappointment in him, her restlessness filling their house like an unwanted guest.

"My sister's pregnant," Lola offers out of the blue. It takes a moment for J.B. to register what the girl has said or to question why she's said it.

"Well, congratulations," J.B. says. "I have two nephews myself."

"No," Lola says. "You don't understand. She was raped. In a Walmart parking lot in Birmingham. She was buying beer after a Radiohead concert. Some dude jumped her. Anyway, that's why I joined Explorers. Maybe I'll learn how to help people like my sister one day." Lola shudders, wraps her arms around her chest. "Life's a bitch sometimes."

"That's pretty hard stuff," J.B. says, and this is all he means to say or do, but he reaches for Lola's soft shoulder, to cup it for a moment in comfort. She surprises him by covering his hand with hers, holding it there.

"I'm really sorry," he whispers. "Sincerely," he adds, as if such a qualification is needed, which leads J.B. to suspect there is very little sincerity left in the world.

He thinks of his job, of his small, tidy house, of Dana sitting on the back porch he built. And then he thinks of nothing.

When J.B. gets home, Dana is sprawled on the floor in her underwear, the newspaper spread before her. She has a portable fan placed so close to the side of her face she can barely hold on to the fluttering pages of the paper.

"The Eagle Creek Fire Department had a cake sale," she says as he takes off his hat. "Mrs. Mulcan's layered coconut cake brought in twenty dollars." She whistles under her breath. "That's news, alright."

"Why do you read that thing if it pisses you off so much?" he says. "Why torture yourself?"

She looks up, a frown forming. "I don't know. Maybe I like getting pissed off. Maybe it reminds me I'm still alive."

J.B. sighs, collapses onto the couch. "Not tonight, please. I'm worn out." He'd driven around for an hour after he'd dropped Lola off at her car at the station, trying to stop shaking, trying to wrap his head around the night's events.

"If not tonight, then when?" Dana says. "Are we going to die in this town? Because if we are, let's be honest about it. I'm tired of pretending anything is going to change."

"One of the girls got hurt tonight." He thinks of Lola, of how she turned her head away from him on the ride home.

"How?" Dana says. She seems genuinely alarmed.

"She cut her foot on a bottle on the side of the road. I had to take her in for stitches."

"Do you think you'll get in trouble?" Dana scoots over to him, rests her chin on his knees.

"I doubt it," he says. He can tell by the slight wilt of her face she is disappointed. If he got in trouble, they would have an excuse to move. He suddenly has the urge to tell her about Lola, to see if it hurts or shocks her. He wants her to know she doesn't have him all figured out, that he still has some surprises left.

"Well that's good, I guess," she says.

"I'll think about it," he says. "Put some feelers out there."

"Think about what?"

"Transferring to another department. Although with Benny maybe out for good, I might be giving up a promotion."

"Really?" Dana says. "You'll really look into it?"

"Sure," he says.

She pulls up to her knees and presses her cheek against his chest, gives him a hard, rare hug. Perhaps, he thinks, this is a kind of living, too. As much as most of us can endure.

Lola's grandfather is hunched over the kitchen table when she gets home, the parts of a new model car spread in front of him, his bushy gray brows drawn in concentration. "This one's going to be a challenge," he says, not looking up.

He seems so pleased with his task. Lola tries not to resent him for not being angry at what little life has offered him. "How did the meeting go?"

"It was lame," Lola says. "I don't think I'll go to another one."

"I didn't raise you to be a quitter," her grandfather says.

"No?" Lola says, pointing to her sister, who is passed out in front of the flashing TV, The Father asleep on the floor.

Her grandfather lifts his gaze, his kind eyes the nondescript blue of old people. "Oh, honey," he says. "Don't be so hard on her. Mary's got her whole life ahead of her. Same as you. And trust me, the good Lord will surprise you more often than not. It won't always be like this. The one thing you can count on is change."

"That's more or less what Lieutenant Loomis said," Lola says.

"Well, then he's a wise man," her grandfather says, turning back to his model.

Lola walks to the fridge, opens it, takes out a beer without trying to hide it, figuring her grandfather won't notice it missing anyway, then goes to her room. She wants to see what she looks like. To see if she looks different.

Uno starts squawking the minute the light flips on. She walks to his cage, opens it, lets him hop onto her shoulder. "Uno," he says.

"Sweet Uno," she says, nuzzling him. "You get it, and you're a little bird. What's wrong with everyone else, huh?"

She stands in front of her antique mirror, her mother's mirror before she left, and studies herself, looking for a sign, anything to show she's something other than what she was hours before. But she still looks like Lola.

"Uno MAD," Uno says.

"I know, baby."

She thinks of her mother, how on her last visit, on Lola's sixteenth birthday, she'd given Lola a more elaborate version of "the talk," telling her daughter it was time she identified with her as a woman before she identified with her as mother, a declaration so absurd Lola didn't bother to object. Her mother had been high as a kite, loopy and erratic and boundary-less—that Lola was used to—but there was a new softness about her, a nostalgia, an air of regret. She'd taken Lola to the only decent restaurant in town, a steakhouse on the lake, and ordered two screwdrivers, making a big deal about buying Lola her first drink, and for some reason Lola didn't have the heart to tell her mother she'd been sneaking into bars for years. They sat on the patio all afternoon, sipping screwdrivers like two old friends, her mother telling her about the first time she'd had sex when she was fourteen, a drunken encounter with a college boy from Auburn she'd met party-boat hopping on the lake. She advised Lola to be more cautious, but not to be afraid or ashamed of sex, that the sharing of her body is a sharing of her life's path, however brief the encounter, and there is beauty in the connection.

While she talked, all Lola could think about was her mother's body being pulled from that morgue cooler, the glossy pale globes of her shoulders, how her mother dead on screen seemed more real than her mother alive in front of her.

But now, Lola understands a little of what her mother meant. And she has a story to tell her own daughter if she ever has one, the story about a small town she will barely be able to recall, and they will laugh together at the absurdity of it all.

lessons

S andy and a few of the other teachers are congregating in
Lakeview High's faculty lounge the day before Christmas
break, milking the last minutes of their planning periods. The
kids maraud the hallways, pressing each other against lockers
in tonguing sessions, stuffing their pocked faces with Christmas
cookies and holiday-themed candy the teachers purchased
with their own money, singing lewd versions of holiday music,
like "Here Cums Santa Claus," a rendition that apparently
originated in Jill Hobart's British Lit class. It's no surprise,
given her dogmatic devotion to "the creative process."

Jill, a Teach for America wunderkind with a degree from St.
Olaf's, sits in a wooden-backed chair in the corner of the room,
shaking her head ruefully, as if she is deeply disappointed, but
Sandy can tell the young woman finds pleasure in her students'
clever innovation. She is that stupid.

"At least they are *thinking*," Jill says, massaging the bell on
her elf sweater. She smiles hopefully at the room.

"Yeah. Thinking about—" Gary Biddescombe, the local-grown
Geography teacher/football coach, jams his tongue against his
cheek and drills his thumb in the air to simulate fellatio. He laughs
at his own joke, his burly shoulders quaking. He has a nean-
derthal look—heavy-browed, full-bearded, dense-boned—some
women find virile but Sandy thinks vulgar, lacking in subtlety.

Jill shoots him a betrayed, wounded glance. He shuts up. Everyone knows they're sleeping together. The rest of the faculty are of two opinions on the matter: Gary's a sleaze carrying on with a naïve first-year teacher ten years his junior, especially considering his wife and young daughters at home; Jill should close her legs to married men, and if she's foolish enough to get involved with a douche like Gary, she deserves what's coming to her. Sandy has no dog in the fight, but she enjoys the gossip.

"Any big plans for the holiday?" Tag Miller, the History/Social Studies teacher queries the room, polite and deft at diffusing tense situations. Tag is another TFA savior from some city up North—Chicago or Boston, Sandy can never remember which one. But unlike most of the TFA recruits, who, stunned by the poverty of Lakeview and the rabid apathy of the student body, often flee the school before the end of the first nine weeks, Tag has stuck around for over a decade. He is a pleasant, finely formed man, a snappy dresser who favors the kind of lightweight suits and jocund bowties one might encounter in Savannah or New Orleans. Sandy finds his debonair flair uplifting, particularly given the students' attire since the dress code was modified by the new principal: the boys in their increasingly tight T-shirts and low-slung jeans, the ravines of muscles leading to their pelvises exposed, the girls in their skirts that drift higher and higher until they can't bend over without revealing the halfmoons of their buttocks. That they live in the deep belly of Alabama doesn't help matters; winter offers no relief to the onslaught of flesh.

"A hundred essays on the nature of love and vengeance in *Wuthering Heights* and about as many beers to get through them," Jill says. Sandy interprets this as a plea for sympathy, but no one bites. In addition to resisting affairs with idiots, Sandy thinks Jill should lay off the beer. Her pink-skinned face is rounding.

"Taking the girls down to Pensacola to see Cynthia's mother. Two weeks of free babysitting. Woohoo!" Gary punches the air with a balled fist.

Immediately, Jill's face storms. She stalks to the old coffee maker, wrenches the filter holder from its slot, and bangs the coffee grinds into the plastic trash can. "Pensacola's an armpit," she says, shoving a sponge into the bowels of the coffeepot.

"I'm headed to Utah to spend some time on the slopes with my brother," Tag offers quickly. "I'll probably take out a tree with my skull." He raps his knuckles against his high forehead. "But he's been asking for years, and I thought, *Why not?* I've got the money and the time. I should live a little."

Sandy considers her winter break options: go to her mom's place and watch game shows in the morning and Dr. Phil reruns in the afternoon until dinner's served at five (throw in a little the-liberals-are-wiping-their-asses-with-the-constitution-and-stealing-Christmas-to-boot rant from her mother and a needling reminder from her grandmother about Sandy's nose-diving fertility); spend the holidays in Selma with her younger sister, a clever domestic who is pretty enough to have married a dentist from the kind of family who would never willingly engage with Sandy's kind of family if not obligated by marriage and shared grandchildren; or, most likely, sit by herself in her apartment with her dog snoring in her lap, a medical mystery show on the TV, Sandy well on her way to getting tanked on gin.

Sandy examines her hands, which are resting on a stack of her third period's half-graded Anatomy exams. She's surprised to notice the ropy knots of her veins bulging under her papering skin. She stares up at her colleagues questioningly, as if to ask, *How have I not seen this before?* But the lot of them look so haggard, so horrifyingly beaten down—a pretty accurate reflection, she realizes, of her own disheartened state—she can't speak.

"How about you, Sandy? Any big plans?" Tag asks politely. Everyone stares at Sandy expectantly.

Outside the lounge window, Sandy spots two slender forms weaving through the sea of sun-silvered vehicles in the parking lot, arms entwined. Sandy knows their tricks. She attended this very high school, was the type of girl who didn't think twice about skipping class to smoke a joint or take a few shots or mess around with a boy in the back seat of a car. And then a classmate, whacked out on drugs, landed in prison for beating an elderly cashier over the head for a few bucks, and a close friend, stupid drunk, nearly got herself killed in a car wreck that did kill her boyfriend. Sandy thought: *enough*. She cleaned up her act, extricated herself from the raucous crowd, tried to make the right choices. Look where that had gotten her. Right back here, perpetually stuck in her adolescent nightmare.

She considers raising the alarm on the AWOL students, but really, little would be accomplished today in class, and she's come to understand kids probably learn more about the delicate and indelicate negotiations of life in the back seat of their cars than she can ever teach them. Perhaps she has always known this.

"I'm beginning the treatments," she announces to the room. "The radiation."

The details Sandy offers are sparse—tumors, radiation, an uncertain prognosis. The group wants to press for more specifics, but feels it inappropriate, macabre even, to pry. Of course, they're shocked by Sandy's admission, clustering around her on the stained lounge couch. Gary, at a loss for words, thrusts a pastry in Sandy's face. Jill pushes his hand away with such force the pastry slides to the floor, hitting Sandy's low-heeled pump.

Tag engulfs Sandy in a bear hug, then sits very close to her, intently studying her pinched face. He is concerned about everyone to excess, mostly because he has come to suspect he isn't authentically concerned about anyone. Or, if he is authentically concerned for his fellow human beings, especially his students, whom he sometimes loathes, how can he know for certain if his concern is authentic and not just performed to satisfy societal norms? Does he stay in this godforsaken place because he truly believes in the kids, or does he stay because he needs people to think he truly believes in the kids? He grips Sandy's hand with his own, overcome, and he sees himself doing this as he does it, a drawn, tired, not-so-young man wearing a sappy smile and a cheap suit, and he worries he sits too close or too far away, his hand on hers too familiar or too contrived. Is he feeling empathy for Sandy, whom he likes most of the time, except when she dumps her lunchroom duty on him to nap in her car? Or is he devastated that he can't know if he's truly experiencing empathy, which means he's vacuous and self-serving (an accusation his most recent ex-girlfriend tossed at him in a parting email), a shell of a person lost in the wasteland of the human condition? Regardless, his eyes water as he gazes into Sandy's horsey face.

Jill is moved by Tag's tears, again reminded of the brevity of life, the brutality of the body, its ruthless determination to self-destruct. Although, as she strokes Sandy's back and arms, murmuring the phrases one should murmur when a relatively young woman confesses she's very, very ill, Jill notes the tautness of her own bicep, the pleasing way it pulses under her tan, smooth skin, and feels comforted by her youth, the time she has to right any wrongs she's committing against her body. But still, she's frustrated by Sandy's reticence to confide, to offer up the details, the symptoms, the warning signs, the contributing lifestyle factors, the likelihood of her own affliction in ten or so years, which she knows, from reading many memoirs, will pass with a merciless ferocity.

Gary thinks of his mother, who died from ovarian cancer the year before, how ravaged she'd been at the end, a dry, wheezing husk, unable to even sip broth, which is why he'd offered Sandy the pastry, as he's come to associate food with good health, vitality, abundance. It was a sincere, heartfelt gesture, but clumsy, and now, with Jill glaring at him for the pastry, for the off-color comments about the students, for being married to someone else, he feels like a boorish ass, which he knows he probably is. Here sits a woman, a good woman, riddled with cancer, stoically and bravely facing her uncertain future, and he can't muster up the courage to end it with Jill, or end it with his wife, or even sign up for the guitar lessons he's been talking about for years. All he can manage is the gift of a stale, grocery store apple turnover.

The bell rings, and Sandy gathers her papers to head to next period. When they offer their help, their condolences, and she says, quite cheerily, "Don't worry about me. I'll be fine. Y'all enjoy your break," everyone feels like shit. But they are also grateful and relieved Sandy has taken this bullet for them.

Driving home late that afternoon, slightly buzzed from the drinks she'd had with Tag at the Rodeo Club, where they'd talked, initially about Sandy, the tragedy of it all, and then about Gary in thinly veiled terms, and then, slightly drunk, about how much they detested pickup trucks and mayonnaise-based potato salad and slurred diphthongs, it is the recollection of that gesture, the thrusted pastry, that convinces Jill to break it off with Gary. Life's too vast, too fragile, too short to waste on a man who will never leave his wife, and really, would she want him if he weren't married and unattainable? She doubts it. He is not, as they say down here, her kind of people. It's time to take stock, to quit her navel gazing and think of a world larger than her own, to give of herself to people like Sandy, and the elderly, and the battered women at the shelter she'd read about in the local paper, and those poor orphans in the commercials on TV, who could be fed for forty cents a day, less than she spends on gum at the Texaco each morning to hide the smell of her commute cigarette.

The first weekend of break, Jill works through the Bronte essays at an impressive rate, pausing only to grab another beer from the fridge and email some of the gems to her college buddy, a high school English teacher at a better school in an adjacent state. (*This book makes the reader, me and you, see that incest in some cases is different then you might normally think and maybe we shouldn't judge different kinds of love just because most people don't crush on a brother or sister, even unreal ones.*)

She cleans her one-bedroom apartment, completes half of a yoga workout, calls her mom and explains, again, why she can't just pick up and move home, then unearths her writing journal from a mound of Signet Classics and starts brainstorming ways to help Sandy. At first, she considers hosting a fundraiser to offset Sandy's medical expenses, but although the state barely pays teachers enough to buy name-brand cereal, she has to admit it provides pretty good healthcare benefits.

Finally, after nixing a watercolor class, dance therapy, a spa day, and hippotherapy, all of which seem underwhelming gifts for such an overwhelming diagnosis, she thinks of sending Sandy on a Caribbean cruise. A cruise! Sandy could rest on the lido deck, a colorful scarf wrapped elegantly around her balding head, and no one would even notice. Everyone wears scarves on a cruise. She could drink cocktails with fanciful umbrellas, read books that had nothing to do with class prep, dance at all night discos with the young, foreign men Sandy imagines work such cruises.

Gary repeatedly warned her not to contact him during the break, but after vacillating for a few minutes on whether or not to break his rule, she decides her idea for Sandy's cancer cruise affords her legitimate license to text him at the very least.

She quickly thumbs: *DY wan2 giv $ 2wrd cruz 4 Sandy? TMB*

Her cell rings a few minutes later. "Why are you texting me here?" Gary hisses before she even says hello. She hears the squeals of kids, someone singing off key, *he's making a list, checking it twice,* the chorus punctuated by a faint *ho-ho.* "I told you not to try to reach me during break. My mother-in-law is like a dog with a bone when she's suspicious, and when it comes to me, she's always suspicious."

"Not everything is about us, Gary. I'm trying to do something nice for somebody. Don't you think it's time we do something nice?" Jill hears a sharp cry in the background, as if someone has really been hurt. "What's that sound? Where are you?"

There's a long pause. Gary breathes heavily, a raspy, greedy intake that annoys her when she allows herself to dwell on it, which she does now. She remembers the way his hands feel on her breasts, which he enjoys gripping, like a climber clutches handholds, for the duration of sex, a quirk she once found unabashedly boyish and exuberant. Now, she shudders at the thought of it. With a clarity she has not experienced in some time, she understands Gary has been placed in her life journey for a purpose, to offer her an important lesson, and now it is her duty to discover what that lesson is, and thankfully, the process of this discovery will not require her to sleep with him ever again.

"We're at the mall getting the girls' pictures taken with Santa. Some kid fell off Santa's lap," Gary says finally. "It's North Pole hell up in here. We've been waiting for two hours to get pictures with a Santa who weighs a buck twenty and looks like he glued some cotton balls from his medicine cabinet on his chin. And I can't imagine a woman who's just had her insides nuked would want to wear a bikini and bake in the sun, but fine. I'll throw in a couple hundred bucks."

Gary is having a rough go of it. The kids are jacked up on sugar his mother-in-law practically mainlines them, and his wife has spent most of the vacation holed up in her childhood bedroom, sifting through old high school yearbooks and photos, emerging only to sigh and pat the girls' heads listlessly. If he has to spend one more day attempting to claw sand out of the crack of his ass while hauling fifty pounds of beach gear, he thinks he might lose it.

Now he's promised Jill money he doesn't have and has no idea how to back out of a pledge to send a dying woman on her dream cruise or how to explain to Cynthia where the two hundred dollars went if he gives it to Jill, especially considering he already raided their savings account to take Jill on that weekend trip to Vegas when he'd told his wife he was at the coaches' prayer retreat. How could he have known Jill would be such an enthusiastic and spectacularly bad blackjack player?

He'd taken the money and the trip without much thought of how he might explain their anemic bank account other than a hazy half-hope Cynthia would discover the missing money and start asking questions, to which he would respond forthrightly. (When he imagines this scene playing out, he is always wearing a hangdog but honorable expression, and he says something like, "I know I've hurt you, but I'm here to make it right, and if making it right means I need to let you go, I'm willing to do that for you.") And then he supposes Cynthia would kick him out, and he would move into an apartment close to the kids, where they would have their own bedrooms, which he would let them decorate any way they wanted. They would spend glorious, giggle-filled weekends together, frequenting water parks and movie theaters and skating rinks in Birmingham and Montgomery. After a year or so, Cynthia's anger toward him would cool, and when it was time to drop the girls off at her place at the end their visit, he might even come in for a while, sit in the Florida room and have a cocktail with his ex-wife, and they would chat about how fast the girls were growing up, then maybe reminisce fondly about the good times—their first apartment, their honeymoon in Key West, the girls' births—carefully avoiding the not-so-good times, like Gary's affair and Cynthia's decision to move, wordlessly, all of his things into the guest room a week after they brought their younger daughter home from the hospital. On Cynthia's weekends with the kids, he would sleep, long, deep naps on the couch in front of a muted TV playing porn or baseball.

But watching the girls examine the pinto beans Cynthia left soaking in a pot on the stove for a week in her abject depression, their small fingers stroking the nascent tendrils of roots sprouting from the beans' bellies as they selected, with the focus of a fertility specialist choosing the most well-formed embryos for implantation, the sturdiest ones to plant in a soil-filled coffee can, he's struck by a feeling of love for his daughters so intense he almost vomits. The idea of being apart from them for days at a time for years on end is unbearable.

There are so many miserable fuckers in the world, he thinks, and he seems determined to join them. People like Sandy, for instance, whom he imagines sitting alone right now gestating her tumors in her child-free house, which he pictures as clean to the point of sterility, with stain-free furniture and blinding white tile that makes Gary think of hospitals and then his mother and then the way she kept shitting herself in the end and how he'd turned his head as the nurses cleaned her with a brisk, rough efficiency instead of doing it himself, even when she'd cried out to him to make them stop.

Then it occurs to him: he is sick, too. Something in his head has broken. He must be sick to think of that bachelor pad—of the soft perfection of that couch—while his daughters squeal in delight as he flicks water from the pinto bean pot into their shining faces. But still, he wants it: his wife crying in a bedroom in a house other than his, the numbing relief of a flickering TV in a dark, motionless den.

It's the day after Christmas, and Sandy's watching *Mystery Diagnosis*, a profile of a woman who keeps passing out every time she experiences a feeling of love or joy. The poor lady can barely look at her husband, who isn't much to look at, without transforming into a bleary-eyed, drooling zombie. It turns out that she has some kind of narcolepsy with cataplexy triggered by love, and she battles it by focusing on horrible things, like gutted puppies or maimed babies, whenever she feels tender toward her husband.

At first, Sandy finds the woman's mawkishness annoying. No one should like another person that much. It isn't healthy. But as the program progresses, depicting the woman's total incapacitation—she can't drive, work, attend family events, eat out—Sandy becomes enraged that this woman's husband, a hook-nosed, wobbly-chinned man, could inspire such a remarkable reaction in his wife when Sandy can't even convince the forty-year-old balding barista at the Starbucks in Auburn to have a cup a coffee with her, which really, would have been more like a break for him than a date considering he works in a coffee house, something she actually pointed out to him, much to her mortification.

She's brooding about the woman's story, wondering if she could ever inspire a narcoleptic love fit, when Principal Philips calls to suggest she take medical leave for the next nine-week cycle.

She has no idea why Principal Philips—another transplant sent to their school to save its lost kids and dispirited teachers with progressive ideas such as afternoon meditation and kinesthetic learning practices—would offer her leave. Then she remembers the cancer confession in the teacher's lounge the week before, after which she'd felt briefly wretched, placing the blame wholly on these stupid medical shows she can't stop watching.

To be fair, she has been diagnosed with a severe case of benign fibroid tumors, which will require outpatient surgery. But she can think of no reason why she lied to her colleagues, only that her fibroid tumors seem so banal, too tedious to even mention, and she decided, in the moment, she deserved a cataclysmic affliction, the kind that garnered a dazzling, rapturous sympathy. Frankly, she feels cataclysmically afflicted each time she walks into that school.

She'd intended to return to work after the break with the news of a misdiagnosis, a sound plan that would simultaneously get her out of a prickly situation and offer her colleagues a bit of much-needed affirmation that indeed sometimes things go right in the world, a win-win for all involved, really. And she hasn't thought of it again.

But apparently others have because Principal Philips's voice is filled with the kind of grave concern reserved for the dying. She's tempted to take him up on his offer. It wouldn't be difficult to get a doctor around here to sign off on the leave request. Hell, half the town has been prescribed enough opiates to down a horse. Still, it doesn't seem right. But each time she rejects his offer, he volleys it right back.

"Let me be honest with you, Sandy," he says finally. "I truly believe in atmospheric toxicity. Do you know what atmospheric toxicity is?"

"Pollution in the atmosphere?" Sandy ventures.

"Exactly. But the way I'm using the term is in relation to the kind of emotional and mental pollution that poisons the body in other ways, and that pollution can manifest in physical form, like, for instance, cancer. Do you understand what I am saying?"

"The students gave me cancer?"

"Not exactly," Philips says. "It's more like your weakened body allowed the students to give you cancer. Which is why you need this break. To cleanse yourself, to find a way to build an emotional shield, if you will, that protects you from atmospheric toxicity. Let us do this for you. You deserve it. And besides, you earned the sick leave."

Sandy deserves many things: a man who loves her with enough passion he would pass out if afflicted by narcolepsy with cataplexy; a house with a yard and a pool and a gazebo; students who know more about anatomy than what fits where; sensitive, thoughtful consideration from her colleagues without having to threaten death to get it; a soundly constructed emotional shield; and, she supposes, nine weeks off from teaching.

The ride down to Orlando passes pleasantly enough. They wait with the masses to check in and board, riding a wave of flesh and bloated carry-ons over the plank and onto the ship, Sandy beaming in her hot pink linen shift dress, her bald head wrapped festively in a sheer, peacock-colored scarf. For a sick woman, she looks better than he's ever seen her in the decade they've worked together, and for the first time since Tag obligated himself to go on this trip, he considers it might be a good time.

When Sandy called Tag and started talking about her cruise, he thought she was offering a roundabout thank-you for his contribution toward her vacation, which, if he were completely honest, he'd ponied up to please the lovely Jill. But when she kept listing the virtues of *The Adventure of the Seas*—the ice-skating rink, the golf simulator, the climbing wall—it dawned on him that she was working toward asking him to accompany her.

"Look," Sandy finally said, getting down to business, "I'm not propositioning you. I'm asking you to sleep in your own bed that happens to be in the same room as mine on a fantastic, luxury cruise. Jill raised enough money to get me an interior room the size of a closet, or half of a double occupancy with a balcony. I want a balcony. My mother is scared of water, and my sister doesn't really like me very much. I tried to come up with the person who irritates me least, and you are the winner. We can go during spring break, so it won't interfere with your work schedule."

A painful silence followed. Sandy had asked Tag out before, to brunch, to the movies, and he'd always found a way to decline politely. But that was pre-cancerous Sandy. This was cancerous Sandy, and cancerous Sandy wanted him, Tag, to be her partner on her recovery voyage, an idea Tag found very frightening, but also, if he thought about it, quite flattering. Here was a possibly dying woman, a woman who might have limited time on this earth, and she wanted, for whatever reason, to share that time with him. It was in his power to give her this, to offer himself to her, and who was he to deny her? He could—as the kids say—sac up for a sick woman.

That had to be one of his more narcissistic musings, he'd decided a few seconds later, and according to his most recent ex, he was a certifiable narcissist, evidenced by his unwillingness to engage in activities she liked, such as kickboxing and church. Besides, Sandy said she didn't want to sleep with him, and he had to take her at face value, and even if she did want to sleep with him, he'd hooked up with far less attractive women in college (although, to be fair, that had been a numbers game), perfectly healthy women with no last requests other than he not sleep over.

"I'll go," Tag had said before he realized he was going to say it.

And here they are, standing in the doorway of their shared cabin, which is, as Sandy promised, very nice, two twin beds and a balcony large enough to pull a couple of chairs out on to watch the sun set. Sandy claims the bed closest to the balcony, flopping onto the crisp, blue bedspread, kicking her heels to the floor. She closes her eyes, sighs. Then she cracks one eye open, studying him. "You going to be that uptight the whole trip?" She points at Tag's linen summer suit and pink-dotted bowtie.

Immediately, they're intercommed to the main dining room, where they suffer with the rest of the travelers— honeymooners, retirees, ass-grabbing college kids already half tanked—through the sobering how-to-get-your-useless-life-jacket-on-in-case-we-go-down-like-*Titanic* drill. Afterwards, Sandy turns toward him, still in unflappable good spirits, and says, "Let's get wasted."

It's awkward at first, sitting arm-pressed-to-arm next to Sandy, the handsome Greek bartender asking them good-natured questions about their cruising intentions—what shows they think they'll see, which adventure excursions they'll take, if Tag is going to enter the hairy-chest contest that evening. But the bartender moves on to spread his cheer to other customers, and after their third cocktail, Tag finds himself deep in conversation with Sandy about their jobs, then their families, and finally, the nature of true love, a circuitous route so effortless Tag never realized where they were heading.

"My great-grandfather met my great-grandmother when he was thirty and she was twelve," Sandy is saying. "Her parents owned a boarding house, and he stayed there sometimes when he was on the road for his work on the railroad. He loved her the minute he saw her. Waited a few years for her to come of age—this *was* the early 1900s—then married her."

Tag thinks of his own young, female students, some of whom don't look so young, which he tries not to notice.

"The thing is, you'd think she would have outlived him. But she died in her early thirties. Childbirth. And do you know what? He never married again. My Grammy said that every time they moved to a new house, he dug her up and carried her with them and reburied her on the property. Now that's devotion. That's love."

Sandy stares at him, her brown eyes wide and earnest, and Tag notices Sandy is a decent-looking woman, quite attractive, really, especially with the scarf, which makes her look a little biker babe, a little dangerous, and the lovely, tiny birthmark or freckle nestled in the dip under her nose, no larger than a grain of coarse ground pepper. Then he wonders, what kind of degenerate would think about such things when a woman, a very ill woman at that, offers her example of transcendent love? What kind of man is he? That, he decides, is the million-dollar question.

"That's your ideal love?" he says. "You want someone to exhume your corpse and replant you in the backyard?" He realizes what he's said, and who he's said it to, and is immediately remorseful, his hand on her bony shoulder in consolation or embarrassment or apology.

"Pretty much," she says. She happily drills her over-iced Sex on the Beach with a straw. He marvels at her verve, her breezy insouciance.

How could this woman be so uncomplicated by fear when Tag fears everything: what his students text about him in class,

that his students don't think of him enough to text anything
about him, that he will always feel disconnected from the world
because he can't stop himself from analyzing what is happening
while it is happening, that he will never find a woman who
"gets" him and doesn't leave after the getting, that his job
shaping the minds of the youth of America means nothing in
the big scheme of things, that there is no big scheme of things.

"Were you scared about, you know...?" he says, gesturing
toward her head. "It must have been hard. Losing the hair."
What he wants to ask her, what he needs to ask her: is she
terrified of what grows inside of her?

Sandy presses her palm to the edge of her scarf and
contemplates his question. "Yes and no," she says finally. "I
shaved it myself, before treatment for the tumors, and I kind
of decided it was an opportunity to shed the old me, to become
someone else. And really, who I was sucked." Sandy kicks off
her sandals with the glee of a girl shedding her Sunday shoes,
then smiles, brilliantly. "This has all been an unexpected gift,
really."

Tag has the urge to touch her. He places his fingertip on
the mark cradled in the groove under her nose. "What's this
called? This indentation right here."

"The philtrum," she says, her breath warm on his fingertip.
"But you know what your problem is? You need a name for
everything, a neat ordering." She lowers her voice reverently.
"What's happening to me doesn't have a name."

They settle up their tab, then tumble out of the bar into the
day, the sea dimpling in the late afternoon sun. They stand at
the railing, watching the last of Florida disappear into the rim
of the horizon. Tag's head is spinning a little, from the booze,
the movement of the ship, the intimacy of the conversation
with Sandy, and perhaps sensing his slip into introspection,
Sandy announces, "Enough of this water gazing. We're not
dead yet. We're going dancing."

"It's still daylight."

"Why not?" she says.

They end up at a disco named Jesters, which is ringed with
stained-glassed windows showcasing bare-breasted queens.
Aside from the lone bartender prepping the bar for service,
no one else is there. The place isn't really even supposed to be
open, but the bartender turns on some music for them anyway,

and they flail on the dance floor to the electronic music their students favor, blue and green lights strobing over Sandy's face. Tag isn't much of a dancer; when he moves too quickly he feels as if his limbs are a beat or two behind his brain. But Sandy's abandon on the dance floor, the rhythmic writhing of her hips and arms, her joyous smile when she opens her eyes periodically to find him swaying in front of her, inspires him to lose himself, and for a moment, the pump of the base synchronizes with the pumping of his heart, as if the workings of his body generate an external beat.

And eventually, he reaches for her, his mouth on hers, her lips moving against his without hesitation as if she'd known this inevitability. She takes his hand and leads him solemnly out of the disco. When they finally reach their cabin and Tag lays Sandy down on her bed, easing her skirt up around her thighs, he tries not to think about whether or not he's resting too heavily on her, or if she might prefer another position, or if her illness makes this painful, or if her tumors are still there, right in the vicinity of where he's probing, which almost puts an end to the whole endeavor.

Instead, he focuses on the flowered print of the pillowcase propped behind Sandy, and then at the grain of the wooden table next to them, and then at the blinding blue of the ocean outside the balcony window. Then he chastises himself for not existing in the moment, for thinking of anything other than the woman beneath him, whose closed eyelids are twitching with pleasure at this very moment, their tiny violet-colored veins tracing an intricate pattern under the translucent skin.

"Stop," Sandy says. She clutches his hips to still him.

"Am I hurting you?"

Sandy doesn't answer. She lifts her hand and tugs at her scarf, unwinding it from the globe of her head, laying bare the delicate skin encasing her skull. She watches his face the entire time, and Tag understands he is witnessing a kind of nakedness no other woman has been willing or able to offer him. Hairless and startled-eyed, she looks like a creature just born, or something ancient and rawly formed, and really, aren't those one and the same?

When their bodies quiet and Tag eases himself next to her, Sandy notices it, the brown-winged bird perched on the railing of the balcony. It studies her with red-rimmed eyes, not judging, just observing in the thoughtful, unblinking way of birds. It unhinges its long orange beak as if trying to speak.

"Look, Tag," Sandy whispers, nudging him with her shoulder.

Tag raises his head, eyelashes matted, and searches in bewilderment in the direction she pointed.

"It's a bird."

"Yes," Sandy says. "Isn't it amazing?"

It's an Oystercatcher. Sandy knows because she once took a continuing education course at the community college on the birds of the Gulf Coast to impress a man who knew the name of all living things except her. An Oystercatcher is a coastal bird, not a seabird, and they've been traveling for hours now, no land in sight; it has no business being here.

The bird stares at them with its hard eyes, then turns its head toward the water with a jerky, unnerving motion. It shuffles its feet, seeming to consider launching into flight. Sandy starts, as if to warn the bird the sea is too vast, too treacherous to navigate, that there is no possibility of reaching shore, and even to attempt it is a foolish and futile endeavor. But what, really, can be said or done? The bird stomps its feet once more, huffing its chest in anticipation or preparation, and then it lifts itself gracefully into the air, throwing its pitiful wings wide over the shadowy sea. And it flies, and it flies, and it flies.

collateral damage

We never considered she'd show up. We'd been nothing less than cruel to her all those years ago. But there Mandy is on Helen's front porch at the funeral reception, talking with the pink-scalped church ladies, a paper plate of deviled eggs and chicken salad seesawing on her knees, her blonde hair upswept into a perfect cone. Mesmerized, we watch her pop one egg after the other into her mouth. Her manicured eyebrows—winged dramatically over each eye, nearly meeting at the bridge of her nose—flutter on the plump expanse of her brow as she chats gamely: Yes, she'd been gone too long. Yes, she'd finished school. Yes, she'd gotten married, though it didn't work out, but she'd learned a lot in the process. Oh, she'd lived all over, a little while here, a little while there. Everyone waits for the church ladies to ask what we really want to know: Did she ever find out what happened to her mother?

This middle-aged Mandy is obese, her torso and limbs rung in layers of fat, her bulk contained by a horizontal-striped, silk shirtdress of primary colors. She resembles an oversized toy stacking tower. Yet she seems to retain that haughty flair of her nostrils we'd always resented in high school. We resent it even more now. We are old enough to know better than to say it in polite company, but none of us thinks a woman that size has the right to put on airs.

We retreat to Helen's bedroom to debrief and take drags off Helen's smoke, lifting our skirts and aiming our own dimpled thighs toward the oscillating floor fan, the July heat vicious. In an impromptu rebellion, we wrench off our black nylons and toss them onto Helen's comforter, then stare at them warily, as if monitoring a coil of snakes. All around us, the murmur of consolations and grief buzzes, punctuated only by an intermittent keening from Hank in the backyard, which swells and ebbs like the passing of sirens on nearby Highway 280.

None of us looks at the empty crib beside Helen's bed. It squats there in its pink-bowed bumper like an obscene ghost. No one has the heart to suggest she take it down, the baby she'd hoped to adopt from foster care back with the birth mother for almost a year now.

How will Hank ever be right again? Helen says. How could anyone be right in the head after what he saw? She chugs from the pint of Beam she'd kept clutched in her hand for the entirety of Stella and the boys' funeral. She'd napped on our shoulders for most of the preacher's eulogy. He's fucked for good, Bianca agrees, and there is really no platitude I can offer to make it less true.

And what is Mandy doing here? Helen asks. Like we don't feel shitty enough, she says. Like we need her here making us feel worse. She thunks her cigarette butt into a Coke can overflowing with ash.

Our sweet Stella, the best one among us, mowed down along with her three sons by a drunk driver while crossing the street in the middle of the day at the town Fourth of July picnic, Hank, a few steps behind his family, witnessing it all. Who knows the many kind things she'd done in that quiet way of hers? It would have been just like her to keep in touch with Mandy and never mention it to us.

You'd think at least *one* of them would have made it, Bianca repeats for the twentieth time since we first gathered at the hospital after the accident. A single truck takes out four people? And the baby—he was protected by the stroller, right? They have, like, reinforced, bionic bars now. That doesn't even make sense, she insists, and Helen rolls her eyes, says, Quit with the stroller, Bianca. It was plowed down by a fucking truck. It might as well have been made of toothpicks.

Girls, I caution, and Bianca knots her lips, the bronzing powder she's applied religiously to her cheekbones since we were preteens caulking the little Cs that cup her mouth. Bianca is still beautiful, but she looked old and tired even before Stella's accident, which makes me feel old and tired in her company. She has a husband she barely tolerates, her unhappiness made all the more complicated because he is a decent husband and father, and people feel compelled to remind her of that fact often. *Trey's so good with the kids, Trey's such a hard worker, You sure are lucky to have a man like Trey.* Like he's doing me a goddamn favor, Bianca complains. She has four kids, three of them boys, wild, magnificent creatures who roam her house and neighborhood with an electric, restless intensity that completely cows her. We recognize the extra layer to her grief: sometimes, she wishes her family away, and the accident seems like a horrific misplaced conjuring of Bianca's dark, private wants.

It's plain rude. Waltzing uninvited into someone's house after nearly two decades. What has Mandy been doing all this time? Helen says hotly, perennially irritated by Bianca's indulgent discontent and lack of gratitude for her domestic privileges. Helen has spent her twenties and half of her thirties pulling fifty-hour weeks and downing car bombs on the weekends, actively avoiding any kind of domestic entanglements. We were all shocked when she'd shown up last year with the foster baby, a beautiful newborn she'd doted on with manic tenderness.

But when Helen speaks now, she directs her anger at me, not Bianca, her soupy blue eyes narrowed accusingly. I abandoned my girlhood friends both geographically and intellectually, first on scholarship to Auburn and then graduate school out west for my master in social work, and they make no bones about holding it against me. It doesn't matter that I settled not two hours away in Atlanta, and I return home, devotedly, every holiday, passing most of those visits on the porch on which Mandy now sits, trying to maintain some semblance of camaraderie with my old friends, who are yoked to me in a shared history of childhood trauma: overworked and ill-equipped mothers, derelict or dead fathers, and a general lack of resources ranging from school shoes to housing to compassion. Classic survivor's guilt, explains my husband, the beneficiary of a solid two-parent upbringing in a nice Seattle suburb with an HOA and a community pool.

She's been eating, it appears, Bianca says meanly, and we all laugh like the girls we once were, but it doesn't feel very good.

Shouldn't we talk to her, to be polite? I say. She came all this way.

Actually, I have no idea where Mandy Miles lives now, what distance "all this way" might be, but when I thought of her over the years, of her mother, who'd disappeared the summer before our senior year in high school—mysteriously vanishing after a trip to the local Piggly Wiggly—I always imagined Mandy as tragically beautiful with protruding cheekbones and expansive, limpid eyes fixed on the horizon, as if forever in search. I also imagined her as stick thin as she'd been in high school when she'd hacked up her lunch daily in the last stall of the girl's bathroom, and her unexpected girth unsettles me. Her defiant indifference, the bold way she pops those deviled eggs in her mouth, seems outrageously extravagant. And a little dangerous.

Bianca sighs. What in the world would we have to say to her now that we didn't say years ago?

Oh, I don't know, maybe something humane, I say, watching my two happy and well-adjusted daughters cartwheel on the side lawn, the skirts of their matching navy dresses tucked into their sashes, their strawberry blonde hair alive in the landscape of scorched lawn. My husband, John, slightly puffy in the shoulders and gray at the temples but handsome in a professorial way, observes them in the studied manner he observes all things, as if the image of them in that moment—the juxtaposition of the girls' vitality against the dank sorrow of a funeral reception—might make for a compelling description in the sci-fi novel he is writing late at night after bedtime rituals.

I mean, really, I press, aren't y'all a little curious?

Mandy corners us on the porch, the picnic table beside us a graveyard of congealing casseroles. She'd lingered after our husbands left with the kids, after Hank passed out in the hammock, stone-cold drunk, and someone shepherded him home; after the church ladies made their offensive comments about the dead being in a better place and Jesus taking for himself those too good for the world and how at least Stella and the boys were together; after Stella's mother and siblings and aunts and cousins said their weary thank-yous and wandered to their cars, dazed by grief.

We were, I think, expecting some kind of confrontation, a deserved if mistimed reckoning for the years of bullying we should have regretted far more than we did. Mandy's offense: having a father who didn't desert her, a beautiful mother who threw her birthday parties with cakes shaped like Barbies, a fancy house on a hill overlooking the lake, a new car on her sixteenth, an easy path to a future somewhere other than here. Mandy thin and young and rich, or Mandy fat and middle-aged—neither version inspires in us any great empathy. Mainly, we feel a keen protectiveness for our adolescent selves, girls pushed to ruthlessness by crushing neglect.

It doesn't seem possible, Stella gone, Mandy says, poking a thick finger into what was left of a bowl of macaroni and cheese. She picks up a jug of sweet tea and drinks from its wide spout, amber liquid trickling down her chin, which she sweeps away with the tip of her pinkie. Then she pokes a noodle into her mouth and chews glumly. She seems entirely comfortable in her sorrow, as if we were old girlfriends, as if we had not gutted the tires of her apple-red Miata with hunting knives and posted drawings of her emaciated body in the boys' locker room.

You want me to wrap that up for you to go? Helen offers.

Oh no, Mandy says, clumping another bite onto her fingertip. This is fine. Let me help you clean up.

She begins collecting dishes, stacking them next to the single basin sink in the adjacent kitchen. Helen slumps onto the couch, a potholder in her lap. Bianca and I fall into an easy rhythm of washing and drying dishes while Mandy clears, her movements brisk and efficient; she maneuvers her mass magnificently, pirouetting around the scattered chairs. The spectacle of her is spellbinding.

She slips the last plate onto the counter, then stills, hovering directly behind our backs. Her breath grips my neck. OK, after all these years, I have to ask, she says. Bianca's freckled hand pauses mid-wipe on a pie dish. She is bracing herself, I know, for what we all expect: the litany of our transgressions, the details of their collateral damage, the demand for amends. Mandy says, How in the world did a girl from Alabama get the name Bianca?

Bianca shrugs. My mom had a thing for Mick Jagger, she says. I know this to be untrue. Bianca's name is Leslie. She renamed herself in third grade with supermodel aspirations.

I also know there comes a time in your life when you are so diminished you are unwilling to give any more of yourself away.

I got a burning question for you, Helen says from where she's sprawled on the couch, her eyes still closed. How did you get so fat? Did you eat a horse? One of those Quiverfull families? Her eyes spring open. Your mother, maybe? she adds, and I say, Enough, Helen, and Helen says, Mind your own fucking business, she's just here to tell us what bad people we are, and Bianca tosses the pie pan like a Frisbee onto the dish towel and says, If I wanted to listen to a bunch of fussing I'd be at home. She looks like she might start crying again.

Mandy actually smiles, her capped teeth a perfect wall of white. Mom never let me eat anything, she says. After she disappeared, I ate everything. And I kept it down. It was my own small revolution.

I thought your parents were nice, I offer, recalling a soft-spoken man with a Magnum PI mustache and pockets full of candy, and a dramatic woman with flyaway curls and plunging necklines. Mrs. Miles called us *darlings*, complimented our thrift-store clothes we ripped and studded Madonna-style. She had been the closest thing to a celebrity ever to grace us, a former weather-girl on a regional station in Georgia who'd snagged a pharmacist and moved to our tiny town in search of simple living and lakefront bliss when we were in elementary school. Her disappearance nearly a decade later, and the subsequent failed search, had been both heartbreaking and thrilling, and every now and then at a BBQ or Sunday supper, someone, in the process of inventorying our history—who died, who stopped going to church, which church splintered into two churches, who divorced, who ran off, who went batshit crazy, who stole from whom, who fucked whom, which offspring or spouses were lost causes—would ask if anyone had heard from Mrs. Miles, as if, much like Mandy, she might be inclined to show up at a party or a funeral.

Did you ever learn anything more about what happened to your mother? It comes out before I realize I am speaking, the tone horrifyingly casual.

Mandy blinks. She rests her pudgy hands on the table of her belly. She shakes her head from side to side. She opens and closes her mouth several times before actually making a sound. She's dead, Mandy finally says. My father confessed to me before he passed last year. It was sort of an accident. He buried her in the backyard under the hot tub. It tore him up, what he'd done. But honestly, she was a real bitch.

We fall silent. The running faucet roars like a waterfall. Bianca's pulse thrashes the ropy vein in her neck. I can hear the liquid slosh in Helen's bottle of Beam, her long swallow.

And then, as if on cue, a chorus of laughter, all of us, even Mandy, nervous at first, then wild with a terrible mirth.

We take Bianca's minivan on what I assume is a booze run, Mandy riding shotgun and me and Helen crammed on top of the camouflage-print booster seats in the second row. Helen leans into the front seat and fishes around in Bianca's CDs, popping in *News of the World*. In honor of Stella, she announces, a nod to our teenage years of belting out Queen at furious decibels. We take turns singing lead to "We Are the Champions," one voice fading and the next seamlessly rising until we explode into the refrain. There is a long spell of quiet when Bianca punches the pause button after the song ends. We think of Stella, of our children, of ourselves, both then and now. You sing really pretty, Bianca says to Mandy, breaking the quiet, and Mandy blushes a dreadful red. She hits the backwards track button, and we do it all over again.

When we reach town, Bianca veers into the ABC parking lot and leaves the motor running while Helen slides out of the side door and trots into the liquor store, the cheap fabric of her black skirt hiked to her knees. I tug at the hem of my own linen dress, self-conscious of its good quality.

Maybe this isn't right, I say. I evoke the serious, earnest faces of my disciplined, socially minded colleagues at the nonprofit where I work as a therapist with at-risk girls, counseling them to avoid situations just like this. I think of my husband, his polite, white-collar mannerisms, characteristics that attracted me to him in the first place. John had become for me, over the years, by no fault of his own, the omniscient eye of propriety, and like some feel the relentless gaze of a judging God, I can never seem to shake the feeling of being observed by my husband and deemed white trash unsalvageable even by a good education or a tony zip code.

We just buried our friend and her three children, I say softly. We shouldn't be carrying on like this. Bianca spins to face me, her eyes bright with pain. They're dead. You tell me how to make this right, and I'll do it. Not expecting an answer, she turns back around and hunches down in her seat. An old lady in ill-fitting Sunday attire drags a rolling suitcase through the parking lot toward the liquor store, ostensibly to fill it with alcohol, and we watch her inch along before us like a living metaphor we can't quite decipher.

Helen's head appears in the frame of the van's sliding door. She thrusts a large brown bag toward me. Get to mixing, she orders. I peer into the bag. It contains eight Gatorades of various flavors and a gallon of vodka. Like old times. Helen grins, the first time I've seen her smile in days.

Jesus, Helen, we'll be vomiting in an hour, I say, but I obediently open four Gatorades, passing two to Helen to sip down to make room for the booze, taking on the task myself for the other two. Helen clamps each Gatorade between her knees while I fill the bottle an inch from the opening with vodka, then she replaces the top and shakes them like a martini, the long-ago ritual unnervingly familiar. Helen dispenses the drinks to all of us, and we hold them aloft in a silent toast.

This actually doesn't taste half bad, Mandy says. Bianca punches the gas, and we pitch out of the parking lot.

Sort of an accident, I think for the hundredth time since climbing into the van. How did someone sort of accidently kill his wife? Surely, I reason, Mandy had been joking, though I can't wrap my mind around a daughter making light of the death of her mother.

We pass our old high school, which looks as it did when I graduated—maybe a little more worn, smaller, the way a childhood home appears to shrink with time. We pass the old Hardee's, where we used to loiter on weekend nights, flirting with the jocks. Then the town center, two square blocks anchored by the county courthouse, most of the retail space vacant. Not a soul walks the pitted sidewalks. I experience a spear of shame. Occasionally, at social gatherings in Atlanta, I speak about my hometown as if it were a prison I'd escaped, an anecdote of suffering I trot out with ironic distance, and somehow, riding through it with my old friends and Mandy, a Gatorade cocktail plugged between my knees, seems an unforgivable farce. But here's the thing about leaving the kind of place where I grew up—while it's true you can never go home, you never really go anywhere else either.

The other women barely glance at the town; Bianca cruises briskly through, taking a left on Highway 49 toward the lake. It occurs to me that everyone seems to have a shared destination in mind but has failed to share it with me. Where are we headed anyway? I yell over the stereo, and Bianca says to Mandy, Turn it up, I love that song, and Mandy obliges, singing along to every word as if she's been practicing for years.

Where we are headed is Mandy's old place on the hill over-looking the lake, a decision I guess was made while I was clearing paper cups and plates from Helen's lawn. The house is now owned by a family from Birmingham.

Trey does their landscaping for extra cash on the side. They only come once or twice a summer, Bianca assures us as we roll into the circular driveway.

I haven't seen the house since Mandy's mother disappeared. Even then, we girls had enough decorum to resist TP-ing a grieving daughter's dogwoods. But it looks pretty much the same: red bricks and a peaked roof, the shutters, flanking the floor-to-ceiling windows, painted a rich forest green. All those years ago, I had thought it a castle, something right out of a book, but it isn't that impressive, really, no more grand than the houses in my suburb in Atlanta.

We sit in the van for a minute while Mandy takes a few deep breaths, as if preparing herself, though I am uncertain for what. Then she says, Let's go.

We unfold from our captain's seats, stunned by the bright sun, weak-kneed from the vodka. We stand in the driveway, acclimating to the fierce heat and finishing our neon drinks, tossing the plastic bottles onto the van's floorboard. Then Mandy walks to the basement door, digs behind a railroad tie used as a retaining wall for the shrubbery framing the front porch, and pulls out a key. Still here, she says, dangling it victoriously.

Surely, they changed the locks, I say, but then the door swings open, and we all cheer like we've won something. What exactly are we doing? I ask, but the other women are already filing into the dark basement. Mandy bolts down the wood-paneled hallway, pointing from room to room in the narration of her youth—here's where I read Dad's porn, here's where I hid the bags of puke in high school when Mom started stalking me every time I went to the fucking bathroom, here's the closet where I sat and ate Little Debbies I stole from Dad's pharmacy—and then we are up the stairs to the main floor, Helen hitching the brown paper sack of vodka and unopened Gatorades on her hip like a toddler. Other than the furniture and new black granite countertops, the house is unchanged from what I remember of the one time we'd been inside for a birthday sleepover so awkward we were never invited back.

I hate the granite, Mandy says, running her hands along the length of the kitchen island. How can you hate granite? Bianca says. Everyone loves granite. And Helen says, For fuck's sake, Bianca, it's not about the granite. Her mother died here. She pins a challenging stare on Mandy. She did die here, right? In the house? In this very kitchen, maybe? Or downstairs? Or the master bedroom? That makes the most sense, the master bedroom. That's where all the dirty fighting happens.

Cool it, Helen, I say. She grabs my hand and squeezes until the bones of my knuckles collide, says, Shut up, and I do, as awed by her fury as I'd been as a girl. Helen has always been the unopposed leader of our motley crew. Bianca is the pretty one. Stella was our conscience, the one who talked us back from the brink as best as she could. And me, by sheer luck of random genetics, the smart one, a gift I did my best to squander for years. But there is something powerful and magnetic in Helen's unbridled rage, and being in its vortex allows a kind of delicious, forbidden liberation, the repercussions of which the rest of us never have to bear fully. If born into more favorable circumstances, she could have easily been a politician, a successful CEO, a fascist dictator. As it stands, she runs the same flower shop where we purchased boutonnieres for our dates to homecoming and prom.

I love this house, Bianca says, opening an oak cabinet. She raps on the door. Solid wood, she says. Real quality stuff. And then she is dabbing at her eyes with the sleeve of her dress. How can I be talking about cabinets on a day like this? she asks us. What's wrong with me?

Outside the wall of windows in the dining nook, the lake shimmers. The lot is precipitously sloped, the house sitting high on a ridge. A pier and boathouse, the pontoon boat lifted for storage, extends into the deep water. A little garden shed with yellow siding and lime green trim, as quaint as a playhouse, sits next to a mature elm, under which rests a cedar-planked planter, a riot of bougainvillea filling its tub, and two sea blue Adirondack chairs. Trey does a good job with the landscaping, I say appreciatively, though I know any spousal praise chafes Bianca, and Bianca says, I guess so, though it doesn't pay for shit, and Helen says, For fuck's sake, are you ever going to forgive that man for marrying you? You could have said no.

There, Mandy says, pointing in the direction of the planter. That's where the hot tub was.

We stare at it for a moment, no one knowing how to react when faced with the remains of someone's mother hidden beneath sod, and then Mandy announces, OK, I'm ready, her tone resolute. She moves toward the door that leads to the screened-in porch, and Helen and Bianca follow. What are we doing? I ask again. Bianca throws over her shoulder, Mandy needs closure, which clarifies nothing, and I say, OK, but what are we doing? When Bianca does not answer, I reluctantly follow them out the door and through the porch and down the narrow stairs that lead to the lawn and the planter and, according to Mandy, her mother's gravesite.

Helen unloads the bag of Gatorades onto the seat of an Adirondack. We arrange ourselves in a ring around the bougainvillea, as if we are readying to engage in some ancient and exotic ritual of mourning and spiritual restoration. The heels of my sandals sink into the tender grass. Sweat rivers my spine.

Apparently, whatever closure Mandy requires does not necessitate our active participation. She studies the planter, her mouth moving but no words coming out. She inhales deeply, exhaling through her flared nose. She peers out toward the lake, ski boats skimming its surface, the roar of motors thundering from all directions. You know what I hated most about living here? she asks. What I really couldn't stand? She sweeps her arm toward the water. The lake, especially during the summertime. Because summer meant warm weather and the lake meant swimming and swimming meant bathing suits, and nothing, not even what you all did to me, was more punishing than a bikini.

When Mandy begins unbuttoning her silk shirtdress, I presume she is seeking relief from the heat, a button or two undone to circulate the air, but she keeps going the length of her dress, her hands as steady as a surgeon's, until she stands proudly in front of us, a terrain of fleshy hills and valleys, wearing nothing but a very nice purple bra and panty set and a pair of lipstick-pink pumps.

I'm going for a swim, Mandy says. Anybody care to join me? She fishes around in the paper bag, retrieves a Gatorade, replaces most of the Gatorade with vodka, and then kicks off her heels and heads toward the beach area next to the pier, her back inked in Latin I can't quite read, the cheeks of her buttocks, bared by her thong, twin suns. She wades elegantly into the water, then plunges under, her cone of blonde hair unraveling into a liquid curtain. She bobs up, says, This feels amazing.

It is hot, Bianca says, her tone more question than comment. Why not? Helen says. Unlike Mandy's, our undressing is slow and hesitant. We drape our clothing neatly over the back of the chair. We line up our shoes beneath the elm tree. We avert our gazes like tentative lovers, none of us wanting to see ourselves reflected in the aged bodies of each other. We sprint toward the lake and wade gratefully into the cover of the water. It feels spectacular, like stepping into a fall breeze.

We dog paddle around for a bit, at first trying to keep our heads above water to preserve our hair and what is left of our makeup. The coolness of the water is too tempting, and eventually we are diving beneath the surface, doing flips and handstands like kids, Mandy an impressively strong swimmer. Tiring, we find ourselves gathering together, replicating the circle we'd formed on the lawn, my feet barely grazing the sandy bottom. Mandy passes around her drink, and we take turns gulping swigs, the vodka burning a hole in my gut. I feel more than a little drunk, unsure if the sway of my body is provoked by the alcohol or the sun exposure or the waves from the boats.

So you're married? Mandy says to Bianca, and Bianca nods, giving a brief summary of her life post-high school—a little community college, then Trey, then one kid, and another, and another, and another. That's about it, Bianca concludes. I do the same—a ridiculously high ACT score that surprised no one more than myself; eventually college after pissing away half a decade drinking and working at the marina; then graduate school in California, where I met John; a job in Atlanta; two sweet, healthy girls; a new house last year. I work at Pearson's Florist, Helen says curtly. Nothing else worth telling.

When it is Mandy's turn in the rotation, she dunks her head, spouts a plume of water, and gazes past us toward the big water, with the exact expression I've always pictured her wearing in whatever life she leads, as if searching for something in the distance. I regret I never appreciated how beautiful it is here, she says.

It really is a lovely view, the belly of the sun cradled by the water, the surface ablaze now with light. I guess it's nice, Bianca concedes. Her eyes dart toward the yard, the planter, the supposed grave, which I had done my best not to stare at for the duration of our swim. Doesn't it seem wrong, Bianca says, to leave your mother there all alone? Can't you tell the police now that your father's gone? It seems indecent not to give her a proper funeral.

Helen snorts. Slaps a wall of water at Bianca's pensive face. Grow up, Bianca. No one is buried in the yard, she says. You really think one man moved a hot tub by himself, stuck a body in the ground, then moved the hot tub back? And the police never thought to check the house and yard? We're here so she—she shoves a water-logged thumb toward Mandy—can shame us, make asses out of us.

Who would do such a thing on a day like this? Bianca insists, and Helen shifts her thumb toward me, says, Ask her, she's the one with the fancy degrees in human psychology.

Meanwhile, Mandy slides beneath the water, her hair fanning behind her, her body brilliantly white, its outlines blurred and shifting. She reemerges at the shore, her shoulders held back, so much water cascading from her skin it looks as if it originates from some replenishing source within her. The tattoo sprawls the small of her back: *vita non est vivere sed valere*, melancholic sparrows circling the words. Mandy walks casually to the small garden shed, pulls the door open, disappears inside, then reappears, holding an armful of yard tools. She thrusts them in front of her. I only found one shovel, she says. But the hoes might work.

That's all it takes. Helen is halfway out of the water before I can open my mouth to stop her, Bianca slinking in her wake. You coming? Helen calls to me, and it is clear from her tone that any choice I might make other than enthusiastically hacking up some stranger's lawn will be deemed an indefensible betrayal.

Which is how I find myself standing in my wet underwear in the yard of Mandy Miles's old house, dragging a planter of bougainvillea a few feet across the grass. The hot tub was right here, Mandy says, pointing to a large indentation in the earth. She shrugs her broad shoulders indifferently. I don't know how far down she is. Understandably, my father did not go into great detail.

Helen plunges the shovel into the earth before Mandy finishes speaking. She digs diligently and methodically, her wiry calves caked in black topsoil. Bianca and I are left with the less effective hoes, more or less rearranging soil Helen has already displaced. Within ten minutes, we are down to the Alabama red clay, dense and unforgiving. Mandy sits in an Adirondack chair, watching us, sipping vodka out of the bottle, smoking a cigarette she's swiped from Helen's skirt pocket. She appears serene, like a woman having a cocktail and a contemplative smoke on no particularly significant afternoon.

Stella hated the water, too, Mandy says. It scared her when she was little, its movement. She thought those puny waves would sweep her away. It's funny, the things we believe as children.

Bianca's hoe nearly hacks off my toe when she punches it into the ground so she can properly turn to confront Mandy. Stella loved the water, she insists. She and Hank got married on the lake. You made that up.

Mandy takes a lazy drag on the cigarette, says, I know what I know.

This is ridiculous, I say. What are we trying to prove?

Helen's wet head shoots up. She doesn't look angry anymore. She looks frail and small, like the scared kid we all once were. And she is crying, weeping really, her entire body shivering with sobs. Her shovel never stops moving.

Dig deeper, Helen says, and we do.

_f_rom _a great distance_

Hank Yost never intended to stay in Alabama, to marry his
high school sweetheart the summer after graduation, to
have three kids, to buy a cottage adjacent to the elementary
school he'd attended as a boy, to BBQ on Saturdays with his
old varsity football buddies and their softening wives, to work
for his father laying carpet in the beastly, Tuscan-style vacation
villas rising en masse from the iron-rich, red shores of Lake
Martin like a legion of stucco beasts. But he'd done it all the
same and had been happy enough doing it. If he'd harbored
grander ambitions, a knot of want in his gut—boyish dreams
of moving out West, of living off the land at the base of a
mountain with a peak as ragged and massive as he imagined
God's eye tooth—they had unspooled with age. His main
regret: how easy it had been to let it all go, what that said
about the measure of him.

When the black Ford Ranger ran the stop sign and plowed
through the intersection in front of Liberty Park during the
Fourth of July community picnic, pitching Stella and the
boys—little Davey napping in the stroller, his fat, toddler
cheeks spangled in red blooms of heat; Jake, the spitting image
of his mother, taking great stomping steps to ignite the bolts
of lightning on his light-up shoes; James, already growing lean

and hard at twelve, sullenly thumbing a video game on his mother's phone—ten feet into a drainage ditch, Hank had stood on the sidewalk and watched, stupidly holding a sippy cup, the item he'd paused to retrieve from the edge of the road, on the hook of his thumb. They were there, his wife and boys, and then they weren't. The truck continued on its way, a piece of Stella's new red-white-and-blue dress fluttering from its front bumper.

Their town was small enough that a witness recognized the truck, and the police confirmed the driver's identity using security camera footage from the bank across the street from the park, locating the man, just twenty-one, holed up in his mother's basement in a neighborhood where Hank had warned Stella never to venture. When the driver killed Stella and the boys, he'd been coming off an all-night bender at Teasers, a strip joint a few miles up Highway 280 that most of Hank's friends frequented before other demands were made on their money and time, a place Hank had visited once or twice himself for bachelor parties, though the women, their sadness, somehow made him feel like the one being exposed.

Everyone Hank knew and many he didn't turned out for the funeral, hundreds of people solemn and plaintive surrounding a quartet of coffins, the smallest no larger than a toy chest, a boot box, a Rubbermaid bin. Hank could not stop cataloguing the comparably sized household items throughout the duration of the ceremony. Someone read a poem about footsteps in the sand, and a few kids from a youth choir sang a song about lambs and Jesus, and a little boy in an ill-fitting suit from Jake's class released a clutch of white balloons that hovered in the sky for a long moment before fading into the distance like a wisp of smoke. When it came time for Hank to say something, he inched toward the maws of the graves, the coffins suspended within them. He stood there as stupidly and silently as he'd stood on the side of the road with the sippy cup hooked on his thumb. Then he nodded his head, as if he'd been asked to approve the placement of the coffins and found things acceptable, and folded back into the crowd of mourners. Hank had nothing left to say.

The driver of the black Ford Ranger was named William, a strong, old-fashioned name Hank and Stella had considered for their first son, and in the frenzied days that followed the accident and funerals, Hank often found himself thinking of William's mother, all she must have imagined for her son the day she'd held him, newly born, in her arms. When he thought of his own boys—their yeasty breaths against his cheek when he rocked them to sleep as babies, the supple fat over hard boy muscle when he gripped their arms to lift them above his head as toddlers, the cut of their shoulder blades as they hunched over their Legos or bike handlebars or remote control trucks—the pain was so agonizing he could do nothing but sit, as winded as if he'd been running for miles in the summer swelter. And Stella—for weeks he could not say or hear her name without sobbing, a reaction that often motivated his friends to place a glass of strong, antiseptic liquor in his shaking hands. Long after the chaos of those days dissipated—friends and their wives returning to their homes to tend to tasks long overdue, Hank and Stella's parents retreating into their own grief—the glass of liquor remained. No one had the heart to caution Hank of the danger there.

Their town was the county seat, and there'd been a trial in the old Federal-style courthouse where Hank had taken school field trips as a boy to learn the machinations of justice. Hank attended the trial daily, someone arriving at his home each morning to help him dress in one of the suits that had materialized in his closet and then drive him to the courthouse. He remembered little from the trial but the back of William's head, the tidiness of his hairline, the perfect V it etched on the meat of his nape. That and the image of the mangled stroller the prosecutor had flashed onto a screen, the navy blue canvas ripped, a wheel flapping loose like a broken wing. William got his time—twenty-five years—and though everyone said that it was not enough, could never be enough, Hank sensed the collective relief that things could more or less move on. That Hank sometimes found himself, his mind loosened by the unnatural quiet of his home, feeling a pang of sorrow for the young William, wondering what the man—who had once been a boy like all boys—suffered in prison, terrified him. How could a decent father give up on his vengeance so easily?

Aside from the drinking, for months after the accident Hank continued the routine he'd kept for years. No matter how hungover, he rose at dawn, ran for five miles on the neighborhood sidewalks, the houses lazy with sleep, the blinds pulled down like pursed lips. After he showered, Stella's jars of bath salts still rimming the tub, he poured a bowl of Cheerios from a full box that somehow replenished every week, one of his wife's friend's doings, he supposed, though he never recalled anyone coming by. He passed the day working side by side with his father, hauling rolls of carpet up the marble steps of the lakeside McMansions, his cuts, when he laid carpet, more or less sure.

Hank kept a small rubber ball in his pocket while he worked, a cheap toy from a birthday party favor bag or a grocery store coin-operated dispenser, the last toy he recalled the boys playing with, James kicking it around the kitchen while Jake scrambled at his feet and Davey clapped from his high chair. Poorly made, the molding seam's hard ridge worried his thumb as he stroked it throughout the day. He'd found it in the bowl of rotting fruit on the kitchen table the day after the funeral.

The ball was colored like Earth from a great distance, a swirl of green and blue rubber, a crude globe. When he got home from work, he would sometimes sit on his front porch, his glass sweating beside him, spinning that rubber ball in his palm for hours, and he would think of those mountains out West, the way they must gouge the swathe of endless sky, what a man must experience standing atop one, the world below him in blurred miniature. But to go now felt like a betrayal of sorts, an admission that all that had come before—Stella, the boys—had been nothing more than a detour, a turn in the path of his life that his father had begun reminding him would be very, very long, hoping, Hank assumed, to reignite a spark in his son. Somehow that reassurance, that there was more to come than grief, felt like a punishment.

The Friday afternoon Hank Yost left work and found himself driving away from his home—where the boys' clothes still hung in their closets, where ride-on toys and BMX bikes had settled into the soil like lawn art, where the washcloth Stella had last used remained draped over the tub faucet, stiff as papier-mâché—had been no different than the days that had come before it.

He'd finished a job double-padding and carpeting a workout room for a woman so fleshless her clavicles erupted from the skin of her chest like a hanger of bone. "Why do rich women have such skinny asses?" his father had asked as they rested for a moment on the tailgate of Hank's truck, the swollen sun leaking its red on the quivering water of the lake. Once, when Hank was a small boy swimming at Wind Creek State Park, a water moccasin had wrapped its sinewy body around Hank's thigh and hung there for a long moment, as if seeking a respite from the obligation of keeping its body afloat. Hank had been too scared, too mesmerized, to say a word long after the snake released its hold and transformed into a slithering shadow, a shift of light, moving toward the brush fringing the shore. The thought of it made him shiver, even all these years later, and when his father felt the trembling in him, he gave a cautionary shake of his head, said, "You need to take care of yourself, son. Lay off the hard stuff."

Hank's father had a rib cage like a truck grill and arms that grazed his knees, an anatomical oddity that earned him a few cruel nicknames as a child, including Ape, which strangely suited him; he could staple a cavernous walk-in closet from a fixed point in the center of the room. He'd become a father barely out of high school, like many in their town, where, other than work in the now shuttered textile mill, there wasn't much to do other than drink or fish or hunt—game and women. Ape hadn't allowed fatherhood to hamper his other pursuits, and Hank had few childhood memories of his father, who was gone more often than not until he was gone for good.

Ape's liver eventually fattened enough the doctors advised him to dry out or else, and for once, he listened. When Hank was fourteen his father showed up at Hank's mother's house, towing a rust-mottled 1956 Chevy 3110 pickup behind his own truck, a thermos of black coffee lodged in his coat pocket. Outside of football season, when Hank had practice and weightlifting after school, they spent every evening together for two years, rebuilding that Chevy from the tires up, an act of forgiveness, on Hank's part, his mother wildly resented. She wouldn't allow Ape in her house, not even to go to use the toilet—he pissed in the front hedges in protest—and some nights when Ape and Hank would work too late, cheek to cheek under the hood, she would lock Hank out of the house, too, forcing him to sleep in the garage or the cab of the Chevy, a price he gladly paid for a relationship with Ape. Such is the way between fathers and sons, his mother often said, her bitterness somehow more of a burden for young Hank than his father's years-long absence.

Ape was not a man of many words, but after Stella and the boys had been killed he'd been given to moments of introspection like these, sometimes laying down his top cutter or pausing in the rhythmical pounding of his knee kicker to pepper the quiet with a few cryptic insights, like the one he offered next, the lake gathering the last of the day's light before them. "You owe it to your boys and Stella to find some peace. That's the only thing you can do to honor them, the only way to make their deaths mean anything. Are you listening to me, son? You understand what I'm telling you?"

Hank had nodded that he did, but he understood nothing, and he wanted to understand more than he'd ever wanted anything, and maybe that is why, he would think, much later, with Crystal asleep next to him in her brass bed, he'd made his way to Teasers that evening after work.

At first, Hank had just thought to have a drink at the bar where William had, according to the state prosecutor, partied for hours before shredding Hank's family with his truck and driving on as if nothing had happened, as if the world as Hank knew it had not been rendered unrecognizable. If it was a ghoulish desire—the want to sit on the same bar stool William had perhaps sat on that day, to sip a bourbon from the same kind of glass, to take in the same parade of third-rate strippers—Hank did not allow himself to consider it.

Teasers was in worse shape than he'd remembered, though the few times he'd been there his mood and perception had been bolstered by booze and youth and possibility. It was a cinder block building painted a chalky, hospital-room green, the only two windows on the front strangely small in proportion to the size of the building, like a drunk's squint. A giant neon sign pulsed Girls Girls Girls, its tempo erratic, as if uncertain of its promise. When he opened the door, the few men in the bar, laborers still in their work clothes, turned their heads toward the entrance, their brows furrowed against the intrusion, then went back to the business of their drinks. The walls were covered in red velvet aged by wear and cigarette smoke to the color of dried blood. The bar itself, which stretched for about thirty feet, the entire length of the building, served as the stage for the girls. It looked like a sidewalk upturned by roots, the wood rupturing in chunks where the strippers' heels doweled its flesh.

Hank worked his way through a labyrinth of tables and mismatched chairs in the center of the room to the shadows at the end of the bar where a serrated, plastic, gold curtain hung car wash-style, the entry point for the strippers. A lone girl with a plume of red hair worked the bar now, wearing only a pair of pointed cat ears on a headband and a G-string with some kind of limp, feline-looking tail attached to the back strip. She meandered along the top of the bar, stopping every few steps to give the air a spiritless pawing. Some dance song Hank had never heard before directed the sway of the girl's hips. Occasionally, she would pause in front of one of the men, lock her knees, bend at the waist, and press her breasts close to the customer's face. The bartender, a young woman with broad cheekbones and a wholesome blonde bob, nodded her head to the beat of the music and flipped through channels on the TV hung over the top-shelf liquor. She brought Hank a sweating can of Budweiser and set it in front of him without bothering to take his order, said, "That'll be $10.50." Hank paid without protest, and the beer, to his surprise, was ice cold, hitting the back of his throat with a pleasing punch.

"This place is fucking depressing," a female voice said from beside him. "Makes you want to go home and blow your brains out and be done with it."

Hank hadn't noticed anyone sitting next to him, and it took him a moment to locate the source of the voice, a small woman, her hair tied in a haphazard bun towering atop her head sumo wrestler-style. A layer of cigarette smoke as thick as seeded clouds clotted at eye level, but even so, Hank caught the woman's scent; she smelled overwhelmingly of flowers, like a funeral home.

"Helen?" He recognized his old high school classmate, a member of the group of girls Stella had run with for years. Hank vaguely recalled that Stella and the boys' funeral reception had been held at Helen's place, though that was the extent of what he could remember of the day. A lot of people were wary of Helen, a brusque woman who rarely smiled, who never married or had kids and kept living hard past the point of what most considered decent. But Stella always had a soft spot for Helen, swore there was a depth to her, a heart so big she didn't quite know how to wrangle it. It was a mystery to him, what bound women together in friendship. "What are you doing here?"

"I got kicked out of Charlie's and the Rodeo Club. This was my last option." She stabbed a finger into the opening of her beer can. "I lost my job at the flower shop today. It's a long story, Hank." She did not seem inclined to elaborate, and thankfully, she did not ask him the same question or show surprise at his presence. "I'm sorry I said that to you, the thing about blowing your brains out," she added. "You're the last person I should have said that to. We're all heartbroken about Stella and the boys. I'm too far gone today to say the right things, so you'll have to cut me some slack."

"Sure," Hank said, relieved Helen was not handling him with the polite stiffness of condolence.

The stripper sashayed her way toward them, pausing in front of Hank. Her tremendous breasts levitated at her neck. It looked as if she could lay her head down and take a rest there if needed. She slumped over and rotated her head in staccato circles to the beat of the music, her red hair a roiling flame. Hank could make out the telltale stretch marks of childbearing beneath the slit of her bellybutton, and the pang of tenderness they elicited took his breath away. Hank's heart blistered in his chest.

"Mosey along," Helen said, shoving a five-dollar bill toward the stripper, who seemed to instinctively know it was being offered, even though her view must have been blocked by the mass of her hair. She jerked up straight, her thin face expressionless, then grabbed the money, folding it expertly in half with one hand and slipping it into the satin patch of her panties before trudging down the bar.

"That's Crystal. Her real name, not her stripper name. Convenient, huh? She was always around the boat landing senior year, stealing everyone's beer. She couldn't have been more than twelve," Helen said. "She was a skank then, too."

Hank didn't recognize Crystal, but he grunted as if he did.

"I heard she's got a kid. A little girl." Helen picked up her Bud and drained it, then leaned toward Hank, her face so close he could see the twin grooves that trenched her forehead. Her aged face surprised Hank. He didn't remember

Stella having wrinkles like this. He'd known Stella his entire life, had begun dating her in eighth grade, and the idea struck him that perhaps when a person knows another person like that, they lose the capacity to see each other as they are. The thought—that his Stella might not have been his Stella at all, merely a projection of what he wanted to see or was capable of seeing—was unbearable.

"Does that piss you off?" Helen asked. "That she gets a kid? Because it pisses me off. Why does she get a kid? I don't get a kid. Your boys are gone. But her—" Helen jabbed her thumb in the general direction of the stripper. "She gets a kid."

Hank understood the anger, felt it at unexpected times, like when he stopped at the gas station that morning for a Powerade after his run and saw a harried mother impatiently wrestling a gas nozzle into her sedan, two kids strapped in car seats in the back, the domes of their heads barely clearing the back seat. And the mother, blank-faced with boredom, as if this day and its sweet labors were guaranteed, and the next, and the next. Hank had hated the woman as much as he hated himself in that moment, the fury rising inside him, volcanic. But he could say none of this to Helen, could say only, "I didn't even know what it all meant until after."

Helen nodded, as if she understood. "I had a baby, a foster baby," Helen said, and when she said it, her eyes went soft. "Maybe Stella told you about it. I was supposed to adopt her, but her birth mother took her back." She lifted her hands close to Hank's face and opened them palm up to show him they were empty. "Poof. Just like that."

"I'm so sorry, Helen," Hank offered, and Helen slid back onto her stool, spent.

"It's OK," Helen said. "I would have been a shit mother." She fisted her hands into her eye sockets like his boys used to do in the aftermath of a long tantrum. "I took a kid, Hank. A while back. That boy on the news, missing from the duck pond in Living Waters." She spoke so quietly Hank could barely make out her words over the dull thump of the music, and he thought, at first, he'd misheard what she said. "I was driving around. I drive a lot these days to get my head straight. And I pulled up next to that pond to watch the kids and ducks and smoke a cigarette, and this little boy, no more than two or three, was strolling through the parking lot, no parent in sight.

I couldn't believe it. What parent doesn't pay attention to a toddler near water? I guess I thought a parent like that shouldn't get to be a parent, so I opened my car door and scooped him up and drove off, as easy as you'd pick up a stray dog. He didn't cry or anything. I took him home. Fed him a boatload of hotdogs. He fell asleep on the couch. He didn't seem scared or unhappy. But then his face was all over the news. So I drove him back to Living Waters and dropped him off by the side of the road. I told him I was a fairy or some bullshit. I guess he wandered into the woods. That's where they found him. Who does that? Drop a baby off on the side of the road?"

"I don't know," Hank said. And there, unbidden, was his last image of James, stepping into the crosswalk, punching the screen on his mother's phone, not paying attention, and Hank hadn't said a word, had stood there and watched it all.

"I'm not a bad person, am I? I mean, I did the right thing, didn't I, Hank? Taking the boy back. Everything turned out OK in the end, right?"

"Of course," Hank said, "you did the right thing." But he couldn't be sure of anything.

II

How Hank ended up in Crystal's bed was somewhat of a mystery to him. Helen left Teasers an hour or so after he'd arrived, and then another girl, this one blonde and anemic-looking, replaced Crystal in the bar, and then Crystal was sitting beside him, quietly sipping a bottle of water, and then he was asking her if she knew a William, and she said she knew many Williams, and they were all, for the most part, asshats. Her voice possessed an unusual, rich texture, the kind that promised a good choir alto, and Hank recalled being surprised by this, though he wasn't quite sure why. He bought a few rounds of shots, and things got spotty after that. He remembered vomiting in the shit-smeared bathroom; Crystal shoving him onto a floorboard of a vehicle and then onto a bed; his chest sliding across her breasts, which, sweaty from tussling on the sheets, were as hard to navigate as wet pool floats; and then him mumbling a string of apologies when things didn't work like they were supposed to. The only clear memory: weeping for a long time afterward, Crystal stroking his back and singing a lullaby, her voice as beautiful as he'd imagined.

Hank woke once, in the middle of the night, and watched Crystal sleep in the moonlight. He thought he should be ashamed of himself, though he wasn't, and wondered what Stella would say, seeing him here now, drunk, a stripper in bed beside him. But Stella wouldn't and couldn't say anything because Stella was dead. And when he fell asleep again, he did not dream of Stella and the boys as he had all the nights that had come before; he dreamt of standing at the base of a mountain, of a path of blinding white snow that unfurled before him as far as he could see.

When the sun split the room open Hank found himself lying in a soured bed, a freckled girl looming over him, her angular face unnervingly serious. Hank grabbed the sheets to cover himself, almost hitting the girl with his clenched hands.

He managed a smile for the girl. She did not make eye contact. She did not smile back.

"I'm Hank," he said. "What's your name?"

The girl studied the wall behind him. She gave her left ear three quick jerks.

"That's Lucy," Crystal yelled from another room. "She doesn't have many words."

Hank's first thought: *Who took the girl's words? Who would do such a thing?*

He could hear Crystal jangling pots and pans, and his stomach flip-flopped at the idea of food. Outside the bedroom window the sun had reached mid-sky. He knew he was late for work. His father would be worried, might be sitting on Hank's front steps right now, wondering where his son was, if he'd find Hank's body behind the locked door. That option, ending his own life, had been a comfort to Hank, though he'd thought better than to admit it to anyone, including the grief counselor he'd seen once, a terribly young woman who, in spite of her training and the string of initials behind her name on her door, had seemed so shaken by the horrors that had been visited upon Hank he'd had to pause from time to time in answering her questions while she masked her tears with fits of coughing.

Hank's clothes had been washed and folded and placed on the end of the bed. Lucy, who'd bored of him after a few minutes, finally wandered out of the room, dragging her fingers along the wall, teasing the dips in the old plaster as if reading a secret message with her fingertips. He dressed quickly, stripped the bed of the fouled sheets and put them as neatly as he could on an old cane-backed chair in the corner of the room because it seemed like the polite thing to do, then sat on the end of the bed, unsure of what to do next. It made no sense to him, why Crystal would take him home over all the other drunks, why she would permit his awkward fumbling, why she would allow him to spend the night. He wondered if she expected to be paid, or if she'd already helped herself to what cash was left in his wallet, but when he located his wallet in his boot, the hundred-dollar bill he kept behind his driver's license for emergencies was still there.

Crystal appeared in the doorway in faded jeans and a man's white undershirt, her face scrubbed clean, her bright hair pulled back into a low ponytail. Her nose and chest were splattered in dark freckles as if someone had flung a handful of mud there. She looked distinctly un-stripper-like. "It's OK," she said, as if coaxing a child. "Come on and eat. You'll feel better."

And so he did, sitting at the small wooden table in Crystal's eat-in kitchen, which was tidy and cheery, the windows dressed in homemade yellow curtains, overlooking the garden. He found himself suddenly starving, eating three of the canned biscuits and most of the eggs. Crystal sipped coffee and watched him eat. Lucy, a stone-faced little girl of about three or four with huge green eyes widened as if she were perpetually alarmed, hummed to herself, methodically lining up five saltine crackers on her plate. When she had them just so, she would mix them up like a deck of cards and do it again.

Crystal watched Hank watch her daughter; he kept his face neutral, but he did not look away like he guessed most would when caught staring at Lucy, and this seemed to please Crystal. "That's her way," Crystal said, dumping a package of generic Sweet'N Low into her coffee. "She eats other things, too. Pop-Tarts. Popcorn. Dried spaghetti. Raw vegetables, even. But crackers are her favorite." Crystal did not appear overly concerned by this. She unfolded the *Montgomery Advertiser* on the table in front of her and read it in order, not skipping a single section. Every now and then she would snort in disgust or look up at Hank and shake her head in disbelief, and say "Damn politicians" or "What the fuck is wrong with everybody?" But for the most part, she read and he ate in silence, watching the girl arrange and rearrange her saltines while humming, all of it, the girl, the mother, the kitchen, strangely natural to Hank, as if he'd sat there many times before.

When the food was gone, Hank figured it was time to go, and Crystal, who he was beginning to recognize as extremely perceptive, perhaps a necessity in her line of work, said, "I drove us home in your truck. It's out back in the shed. I thought you'd prefer not to park it out front. Don't worry about getting me back to Teasers. I can catch a ride with one of the other girls for work tonight."

"Thank you," Hank said. He didn't know what else to say.

He put his hand out and cupped Lucy's head, the heat of her rising into his palm. "It was nice meeting you." She responded only by not pulling away.

"She likes you." Crystal smiled fully for the first time since they'd met, at least that he could recall, her front teeth slightly crooked and crossed at the bottom inner edges, reminding Hank of pigeon toes. "Lucy doesn't like anybody."

Crystal walked Hank through the tiny living room, just big enough for the faded floral loveseat and an ancient TV set the size of a small stove, and then out the back door to the carport, a sheet of corrugated aluminum on four metal poles.

"I didn't do that to Lucy, in case you were wondering," Crystal said when they reached his Chevy. "I stayed clean when I was pregnant with her." She smoothed her bright bangs from her forehead nervously. He could tell it was important to her that he believe her.

"She seems like a good girl," Hank said. "You're lucky to have her."

Crystal cocked her chin, studied him for an uncomfortably long spell, then said, "I don't work tomorrow if you want to come over for dinner. We usually eat around six. Keeping a schedule is good for Lucy. You don't need to decide now. Come if you want."

Hank nodded, then opened the door and slid into the truck, uncertain of how a man says goodbye to a woman he doesn't really know after spending the night in her bed; there'd never been anyone but Stella, and their love had been fueled by the flame of adolescence. Not seeing one another again after the first time they'd made love in the cab of this very truck had seemed an impossibility.

"Thank you for breakfast and the ride and everything," he said, hearing the blush in his voice. He leaned over and pecked Crystal on the cheek and then shut the door quickly. Crystal stood there, her arms crossed, watching him try to steady his hand enough to insert the key into the ignition. She rapped her knuckles on the driver's side window. Reluctantly, he rolled it down.

"Give them to me," she said. She held out her hand. He passed her the keys, shamed for the first time that morning. She twisted into the truck surprisingly easily, plugged the key into the ignition, and spun it. For once, the truck's old engine started on the first try.

Crystal's mouth was close to his now, her breath a mixture of coffee and toothpaste. "I know who you are, Hank," she whispered. "What happened to your family. I hope it's OK that I know." Then she spun and sprinted toward her little house, her soles of her bare feet as red from the Alabama dirt as her hair. She was, he thought as he watched her disappear into the house, terrifyingly lovely.

It wasn't until Hank pulled out of the alley that he recognized he was in the part of town where the police had found the boy, William, hiding, where Hank had warned Stella never to venture.

III

Hank showed up for dinner at Crystal's house the next evening and the evening after that and most of the evenings that followed for days, then weeks, then months. He was always careful to sleep over no more than an occasional night, not leaving so much as a toothbrush at Crystal's place, his way of stating the boundaries of their relationship without stating them at all.

He'd asked, only once, why she'd brought him home from Teasers and lain with him as drunk and pitiful as he was. Hank did not know much about women, but he could gather it was not Crystal's habit to bring home men from work.

"You were so alone, Hank," she'd said. They were in her big brass bed, Crystal half reclined against the wall, Hank stretched between the V of her thighs, his head cradled in her lap. When she looked down at him to speak, her hair curtained his face as if they were children creating a secret, private space.

"I'm betting there are plenty of lonely men at Teasers." He'd wanted to sound jealous, because he suspected she needed to feel as if she were a rare and precious creature in danger of being poached. But Hank didn't feel this way about Crystal, couldn't conjure up those proprietary jealousies, and though this made things easier and kinder on him, the same could not be said for Crystal.

"I didn't say 'lonely.' Everyone's lonely." Crystal lifted her head, her hair uncloaking his face. "I said 'alone.'"

Together, they were still lonely, perhaps, but not so alone, and they'd both lost enough to value the mercy of another's abiding presence.

On afternoons when the Alabama heat hung heavy and moving felt like wading through tar, Lucy would nap in the hammock in the backyard, its gentle sway supplied by Hank's big toe, and he and Crystal would light a joint and sip its smoke greedily until the roach burned the tips of their fingers and the sun bled out. Hank would tell Crystal about his solitary childhood, his fantasies of heading out West, how the first time he read Maclean's book, he read and reread the descriptive passages of the brothers fly fishing in the wilds of Montana, their lines threading the implausibly vast skies, like some teenage boys savored porn, resting the open book on his chest to close his eyes so he could daydream himself there, thigh-deep in mountain waters, the pulse of the river the pulse of life.

And then Crystal, unusually talkative when stoned, would tell the stories of her childhood, which were more or less the same as his, all of them ending with Crystal heartsick and alone in her bedroom, wishing for something else. She told Hank how she hitchhiked to Montana at nineteen with a trucker who could have asked her to compensate him for his trouble in a variety of degrading ways—a price Crystal was more than willing to pay to escape their town—but only requested that she comb his thinning hair each night and sing to him the way she sang to Hank the first time they'd met. The old trucker had wept at the beauty of her songs, too. She told of roasting a rattlesnake she killed herself with nothing more than the heel of her boot and eating its sweet meat in the monstrous shadows of the Rockies. She told of spending the night in a sweat lodge with a shaman and a wealthy divorcee from Arizona who, high on peyote, tried to gouge out her own eyes with one of the steam rocks, her hands burning so badly her palms fell off in charred chunks. She told of cleaning condos at ski resorts in the winter and selling beaded bracelets on the boardwalk at Flathead Lake during the warm months, of the ambitious and talented actors who came through each summer to work at the famed local Shakespeare Theater, of the handsome actor who'd tied her off with a scarf from his Othello costume and pumped her vein full of Dilaudid the first time. That time and every time after, she talked with God and the universe and all that had come before and all that would come, including Lucy, who, in her vision, was a beautiful young woman of about sixteen, given to speaking in verses of poetry so divine her tongue illuminated with each articulation. She told of how that summer waned and the actor went back to being a student at some university, and Crystal, Lucy planted in her belly, came home as a passenger in a string of other semi trucks, several of whose drivers had no problem asking her for what they considered just payment for her fare.

Crystal had been brave enough to do what Hank had not been able to accomplish after years of planning and wishing and daydreaming, and this said enough about her that Hank allowed himself to overlook the troubling facts of her life. On the rare occasions he doubted the wisdom of getting involved with a woman like Crystal or considered what his choice said, if anything, about how much he valued his marriage and family, he would find himself retreating to his own house, reaching for one of the bottles he kept stashed in strange places—in the laundry room closet, Davey's diaper pail, the curio cabinet that held Stella's doll collection from childhood—not knowing why he bothered to hide a transgression no one was there to witness. So he chose not to think, taking pleasure instead in the movement of his body, the pull in the muscles of his shoulders as he cut and fitted a roll of carpet, the vibrating firmness of the gear shift in his palm as he drove his old truck, the pressure of the pavement rolling against the length of each foot on his morning run, the feel of the sun tightening the skin of his forehead as he sat with his father in the late afternoon after work, and yes, the give of Crystal's flesh as he slid inside her atop her big brass bed.

A neighbor usually watched Lucy while Crystal worked, but now and then Hank filled in, stepping into the role of caregiver with ease. Lucy was a mystery to Hank, so different from his chattering, rambunctious boys. She rarely spoke, though she made certain sounds Hank learned to decipher—two grunts for juice, a short, clipped howl for a stack of saltines. Lucy was unlike any child Hank had ever known, and she intrigued him with her ability to exist in her own world, content, for the most part, unless something—a neighbor's vacuum, a police siren—intruded. Then she could be inconsolable, banging her head against her bedroom door with frightening intensity, Hank unable to soothe her no matter what he tried. And so he quit trying, allowing the girl to wrestle her emotions on her own, barely noticing the thuds, regular as a metronome, as he flipped through the channels on the TV.

On her good days, he would read to Lucy the one book she tolerated, a story about a little mouse that woke up from a nap and could not find his mother, who had stepped outside the log in which they lived to fetch some water from the nearby stream.

Lucy always cackled in delight for the duration of it, her stubby fingers working her left ear as if trying to dislodge something there. She would sometimes sit in his lap while he read, and if he was tired enough or drunk enough, he would close his eyes and recite the story from memory. The pressure of her little limbs against his thighs, her bones digging into his worn muscles, allowed him to remember the exact weight and feel of his own boys when he'd held them and read to them in this way. There was always the price to pay, a piercing hurt when he opened his eyes to Lucy, but for a moment, the topography of his eyelids a silky blankness, Hank felt at peace, as if he recognized the life he was living.

When Crystal saw Hank like this with Lucy, her face would soften with gratitude, and she would say, "You're a good man, a good father, Hank Yost," and Hank would thank her, but he believed none of it.

Crystal didn't ask to be introduced to Hank's family, who knew nothing of their relationship, and Hank never offered. Crystal's father had managed to drown himself in the bathtub on a binge when Crystal wasn't much older than Lucy, and her baby sister was strung out somewhere in Florida, but her mother still lived in town, and when Crystal took Lucy to visit her, she didn't invite Hank along, and he didn't request to join them. Lucy's father was not in the picture, and Crystal never explained why beyond her stories of Flathead Lake, and Hank never asked her to elaborate. Hank didn't criticize Crystal's choice of work or her occasional absences—days-long gaps in their surprisingly domestic life when she never came home, until she did, the neighbor taking in Lucy as if intermittent abandonment were rote—and if Hank's drinking was a problem for Crystal, who'd been in and out of treatment for opiate addiction for over a decade, she chose to get past it. They never spoke of Stella or the boys. But there was a kind of love between them, and from it Hank learned there were many ways to endure a day and then another, and he was both grateful and bitter for the lesson.

As it turned out, Crystal was no great talent as a stripper. Hank had watched enough movies to assume strippers made cash hand over fist, but Crystal was either blasé or almost confrontational with customers, wielding her breasts threateningly on stage, like a man sometimes raises his fists to show the power there. Her boss, a kind, elderly man with a slew of children and grandchildren, including a grandson not unlike Lucy, kept her on out of compassion, knowing her work schedule allowed her to be home during the days when Lucy was not at Head Start or was sent home from school for being disruptive, which was often. But the money stunk, and there was never enough, certainly not enough to send Lucy to the private preschool in Auburn for kids like her, a magical place from the way Crystal spoke of it, where the instructors would teach Lucy how to free the girl imprisoned inside her, a desire that unsettled Hank because what if there was no girl trapped within the girl? What if Lucy was just Lucy, and it was everyone else who was in need of liberation? Besides, Hank sometimes wondered if finding the girl lost in the girl would end in disappointment, but he never said as much to Crystal, who, at night, after lovemaking, draped herself across his middle, her fingers twining his chest hair, and spoke in wistful tones of the golden-tongued daughter of her vision she hoped to meet again one day.

Crystal's love for her daughter was a raw, festering thing. The house fevered with it. There was no perceivable logic to how Lucy processed her world, no map to her particular neurological wiring. A frustrated slap on the butt from Crystal might launch the girl into a fit of uncontrollable giggling; the inability to find the yellow socks with the giraffe on the heels could trigger a tantrum so violent Crystal was forced to lock Lucy in her room for her own safety. Simply put: Lucy as Lucy broke her mother's heart.

And if Crystal sometimes spanked Lucy a little too hard and bruised the skin of her daughter's buttocks, or left the girl in her room, wailing and thrashing, for an entire day, who was Hank to say he knew better? As far as Hank was concerned, a father who'd stood on a street corner with a sippy cup in his hand and watched, unmoving, as his entire family was slaughtered didn't have the right to say much about anything.

Hank had money, and a good bit of it, from an insurance policy his father had provided for Stella and the kids through his flooring business, but Hank saw no reasonable way to spend it. He couldn't bring himself to buy a new television or a pair of running shoes with money earned in such a way. He'd used the funds only to pay for the funeral and the grave lots and the tombstones, nice ones with ceramic, oval-shaped photos of the boys and Stella, though he'd only visited the cemetery once since they were erected, and that one visit, he had decided, would be enough to last a lifetime.

His mother, he knew, disapproved. She tended the plots weekly, leaving flowers on holidays and birthdays, a practice that mystified Hank. Each time he saw her she whipped out her phone and scrolled through the photos she took of the gravesites and the flower arrangements she left there—shaped like footballs or teddy bears—with a chatty eagerness, not unlike a grandmother showing off the latest school pictures and snapshots of grandbabies. Hank did not know where his family was now, if there was some other layer to the universe, a life on the other side, a heavenly shepherd who'd guided his family to His everlasting kingdom, but of one thing he was certain: no part of his wife and boys was in that cemetery.

He never told Crystal about the money, for obvious reasons at first. He'd been unsure of the kind of woman she was, if she'd feign interest in him in hope of a payday, a notion so depressing and awful he could barely entertain it. But the fact of the money also shamed him, that he'd not made it through ingenuity or hard work or exceptionalism, unless one considered the spectacular demise of his entire family in an instant exceptional.

So when he dropped by one morning for breakfast and handed Crystal a check as she read the paper, Lucy stacking her saltines on the table across from him, Crystal stared at it suspiciously for a long time, the pink, jeweled nail of her index finger tracing the looping zeroes.

"Is this a joke?" she finally asked. Her eyes narrowed in Hank's direction, the skin beneath them the muddied brown of stagnant water. The night before had been long—an altercation with a handsy customer at work, then Lucy waking from a police siren in the middle of the night, her wails and head-banging lasting until morning light. She'd emerged from her room on her hands and knees, covered from head to toe in her own shit. They had to dig it out from under her fingernails with toothpicks.

"I thought it would help Lucy," Hank said. "She can go to that school you've been talking about."

Crystal exhaled and placed the check on the kitchen table in front of her, as if she were scared to touch it now she knew it was real. "That's a lot of money," she said. "A person could do almost anything in the world with that much money." Then, "Thank you, Hank." But she did not sound thankful at all.

He returned to his own house after work that day, emptying the stack of mail from the Noah's Ark-shaped mailbox Stella had made at a ladies' spiritual retreat, tossing the mountain of papers on the front step into the trash bin. A few children in after-school care were playing on the elementary school's playground, their laughter cascading over the fence. It used to drive him nuts, all the noise. He stood there and watched them for a spell, finding himself searching for boys the ages his sons would be now if alive.

He took some time to wander through the sunny rooms of his home, which were growing increasingly unfamiliar, as if he were a guest in someone else's house. He went to each boy's closet and fingered the clothes that still hung there, burying his face in the soft fabrics. Then he took a bath in the master tub, carefully unscrewing the lid to one of Stella's salt scrubs, rubbing the gritty mixture over his calves, sore from the day's labor. The water smelled of Stella: honeysuckle and jasmine. He wept in the tub until the water cooled.

After putting on a clean change of clothes, he made himself a drink, then sat on the back porch and sipped it, watching the branches of the shade trees swirl lazy shadows on the overgrown grass. He could hear the neighbor on the other side of the privacy fence, working in his garden, but the man didn't call a greeting like he once would have done; people had a tendency to avoid Hank now, as if his sorrow were contagious. Even his high school buddies, men he'd known his entire life, had eventually drifted away, barely calling every month or two, a dutiful checking-in. Hank couldn't blame them. They all had their own families, and who needed a reminder of the worst that could happen?

An hour before Crystal's shift at Teasers, he drove over to her place, his mood improving the closer he got. He turned the radio up, belting out a country song about chew and solo cups, feeling self-conscious while doing it but needing to experience a moment of buoyancy, the pure grace of levity. He parked in the carport, pulled the trash can to the alley for pickup the next morning, then entered through the back door. Lucy sat on the area rug in the living room, spinning the wheels on her battered Tonka truck. The neighbor who sometimes watched her, a young woman named Octavia, bounced her own dimple-cheeked toddler, Iris, on her lap. The girl's plaits were clipped at the end with tiny plastic barrettes shaped like hearts.

"Crystal said she needed to run a quick errand," Octavia said, visibly distressed. "That was four hours ago." Iris grabbed at her breast, her hair. Octavia swatted the girl's hands away gently. "I got my sister visiting this week. I can't take Lucy right now."

"Vroom, vroom, goes the truck," Hank said to Lucy in way of greeting. She didn't look up.

"It's not a good time for me," Octavia said, already rising from the couch and gathering her phone and Iris's blanket. "I got work and Iris to mind."

"Of course," Hank said. "I can handle Lucy for a while. I'm sure Crystal will be here any minute."

Octavia shook her a head a little, but she smiled kindly, patted Lucy on the head as she passed her on her way to the door. She paused in the doorway, turned to face Hank as if she were considering whether or not to say something. Finally, she said, "Crystal takes off sometimes, sure. But this feels different. She sounded different." She shrugged. "Maybe it's a feeling I got. I don't know. But think twice before you call CPS. They took Iris from me, and it was months before I got her back. People like me, people like Crystal, we don't always fare well with the folks supposedly helping us." She kissed Iris on her crown, tugged the girl's body a bit closer to her own.

"You're a good mother," Hank said.

"I know," Octavia said. "And you probably mean well, but I don't need anybody telling me that to make it true." Then she slipped out into the warm afternoon light, the screen door slapping behind her.

Crystal didn't come back that night or the next. She didn't call. She didn't answer her phone. She didn't show up for work. Hank stayed with Lucy, getting her ready for school in the morning, cutting his day short to be home in the afternoon. He slept on the couch. It seemed too strange, too intimate to sleep in Crystal's big brass bed without her in it. Some mornings, he'd find Lucy curled like a cat in the center of the rug on the living room floor. Other mornings she'd be in some stage of undress in her bedroom, the sheets ripped from the bed, the mattress askew, all her clothes dumped from her drawers.

It would have been simpler to take Lucy to his place. But he didn't want her there in his house—his boys' house, Stella's house—and he didn't know if this said something about how he felt about his family or how he felt about Lucy.

After three weeks he went down to the county courthouse where they'd held the trial for the boy William, and he filed a missing person's report at the police station, the concern of the officer taking Crystal's information visibly dissipating when Hank mentioned where Crystal worked, a slight so inhumane Hank considered jumping the counter and pummeling the man. Hank didn't tell him about the money. He didn't tell him the check had cleared.

"Hank," the officer said, touching Hank on the hand, "it's not what you think." When the officer used his name, Hank recognized the man as J.B. Loomis, a fatter, softer version of an old classmate. In a town as small as theirs, he must have been aware J.B. had joined the force, but as with most things lately, he had no recollection. He remembered J.B. as an artistic, intelligent boy who spent most of his time sketching in his notebooks, the kind of kid who should end up in a city somewhere selling his artwork in some pretentious gallery, sipping coffee at cafés with brooding, complicated women. He felt disappointed, seeing J.B. here in uniform, the feeling similar to hearing an old acquaintance had passed without your knowledge, the tiny shock that lives and dreams and love affairs begin and end with little fanfare.

"You're a police officer," Hank said. "I guess I knew that."

J.B. fiddled with his badge. "Captain now. Just promoted." He smiled gently. "Listen," he said, "it's not uncommon for someone in Crystal's line of work to take off for a while. Those girls sometimes live pretty hard. It's a high-risk lifestyle. Does the minor have a father?"

"Somewhere."

J.B. shifted his jaw, the indentation at its base the width of his thumb. "Well, can you get in touch with him?"

"No. But I can call her grandmother."

J.B.'s face relaxed. "It's just a lot of paperwork, and once the wheel gets turning, it's hard to stop. If you can't get in touch with her grandmother, you come back and ask for me. We'll get children's services involved."

J.B. shoved a business card in Hank's palm, closed his notepad, plunged it into his breast pocket. "I'm sorry about your family, Hank. Stella was a fine woman." He looked past Hank when he said it, as if the whole situation—a missing stripper, a dead wife and kids—embarrassed him. It dawned on Hank that J.B. was probably there at Liberty Park, had seen his wife and boys in the drainage ditch. It was too much, knowing what J.B. knew.

If allowed his preference, Hank would have gone straight to the liquor store, bought a pint, then sat in his backyard and drained the entire thing. But there was Lucy to consider, and so he drove to the house he and his father were working that day, laid a football field's worth of top-of-the-line Berber in some pediatrician's weekend retreat. He cut the day short, heading, anxiously sober, to Crystal's place, where he searched her papers and mail for her mother's contact information, finally finding it on a copy of Lucy's Head Start registration materials. He waited in the front yard for the bus to drop Lucy off, yanking some dandelions out of Crystal's flower beds, running the push mower over the few scabs of grass.

When Lucy got off the bus, she didn't acknowledge her mother's absence or Hank's presence. She trudged inside without a word, dragging her miniature backpack behind her. Hank found her in the kitchen, her head shoved in the cracker drawer.

He dialed Crystal's mother's number, and a voice, rich and deep like Crystal's, answered.

"Gone?" Dawn said after he explained, with as little detail as possible, what had transpired. "Stupid, stupid girl."

"Can you come get Lucy?" Hank asked.

There was a silence, a shaky inhale. "Caring for a little kid, especially one like Lucy, ain't cheap. Money don't grow on trees."

"I can help out here and there," Hank said. "The main thing is Lucy needs family. She needs a familiar routine."

"She don't know me from Adam," Dawn said. "Not that I can tell, anyways. Stares through me like I ain't there. What can I do for her?"

"Lucy is a smart kid. She knows more than you think." Hank eyed the girl, who was still fumbling in the drawer where Crystal kept the supply of saltines.

"I'll be there," Dawn said, "but no good'll come of it."

Hank packed a few of Lucy's things—several changes of clothing, pajamas, a toothbrush, the Tonka truck, a sleeve of saltines, the book about the lost little mouse, a snapshot of her mother—into one of Crystal's gigantic, bedazzled handbags. They sat on the front stoop, Hank spinning the boys' small rubber ball in his palm for Lucy until she grew bored with it and they watched the cars drive by instead, hypnotized by the shapes the headlights traced in the night sky. They sat in this way for several hours, not talking, waiting, until Lucy fell asleep, her bony skull cupped in the basket of his lap.

"What am I going to do with you?" Hank asked Lucy. She was as likely to answer asleep as she was awake.

Hank called Dawn three times and was sent to voicemail; he did not bother to call again. He knew she would not be coming. Instead, he carried Lucy to his truck and arranged her as carefully as he could on the bench seat, then slipped behind the wheel, pausing only a moment to watch the girl, the twitching of her eyelids, the ragged tug of her breath, before he pulled out of the carport. He turned the truck away from his home, away from all the things Stella and his boys had owned, had touched with their miraculous flesh, and he drove west.

IV

As it turns out, Lucy was a good traveler and an even better listener. The cadence of the truck's wheels on the highway seemed to relax her. She could ride for hours in the passenger seat without complaint, squirming only when she needed to use the restroom every few hours, a physical cue he'd learned to interpret after she'd pissed the seat, her urine pooling, warm and plentiful, under her thighs. She'd slapped her hands in it merrily, like a toddler exploring the rain.

At first, Hank told Lucy stories of growing up buck-wild in the woods of their hometown before the outsiders began buying up lakefront property for vacation homes in earnest; of shooting snakes out of the lake for target practice; of swimming with the bream and painted turtles on the beaches of the islands his father would take him to on the weekends he bothered to show up for his visitation time; of a black widow he once saw while picking blackberries in a field with his cousins, the way its hourglass marking glowed like a jewel in the midday sun; of how that field had been razed years ago, lakeview condos rising in its place.

Her silence encouraged Hank to continue until he found himself telling Lucy things he had never told anyone, such as how a pudgy girl from middle school, a greasy kid with buck teeth who wore a man's undershirt and a blue jean jacket covered in Guns N' Roses patches every day like a uniform, had once whispered into Hank's ear that she'd consulted her Ouija board about Hank's future, and the spirits had said he would die before his thirtieth birthday. Years later, a grown adult with a level head, Hank had hidden in the bathroom, sick with relief, the day he turned thirty, not yet understanding there were much worse things to suffer than his own death.

He told Lucy how lonely he'd been as an only child, how something inside his mother broke after his father left for good, how she didn't get out of bed for months—not to wash clothes, not to go to work, not to make a meal—until she finally rose from bed on a day with no perceptible significance. She'd emerged from her room in her Sunday heels and a red dress he'd seen her wearing in pictures from high school and wordlessly marched out the door, leaving Hank and his grandmother, who'd cared for him while his mother convalesced after the separation, sitting gape-mouthed and bewildered on the couch, microwave dinners in their laps, Robert Redford as Jeremiah Johnson in a suit of fur contemplating whether or not to pass through an Indian burial site to get to a stranded caravan of white settlers on the television screen. His mother spent the rest of Hank's boyhood pursuing a new husband with an impressive focus, succeeding three times before Hank left home, none of the husbands lasting longer than a year or two.

He told Lucy how he'd married Stella too young, eager to get out of his mother's home and not brave enough to do it on his own, how he'd loved Stella, but what he'd loved most about her was how she loved him. Though he sometimes felt burdened by it—her love, her idea of the man she thought he was or could be. And because of that, he'd punished her in small, cruel ways he knew hurt her most, such as not complimenting a nice dinner she made to surprise him, or working late on a night he'd promised to take her dancing, or casually mentioning how the baby seemed to prefer the way Hank rocked him to sleep.

He told Lucy how he'd dreamed of living in the Rockies after watching old westerns like *Jeremiah Johnson* and *The Man in the Wilderness* over and over again as a child, the landscape in the panoramic shots honest in its starkness, as if a man could attain a clear view of his intended path by staring into the vista. How he ended up living a mile from where he grew up, only crossing the state line once to take the kids to Disney World, a fact that made him so resentful he'd refused to ride the rides with the kids, and when they'd seemed to have fun without him, he'd made them leave the park early out of spite.

He told Lucy her mother was a wonderful and generous woman who, if anything, loved her too much, and if she had not gotten hooked on dope, she might have made more of herself. He told her drugs and alcohol were the worst kind of thieves, and though he knew this better than most people, he could not and would not give up his booze, not now, not even for her. He might die if he kept at it, but he would certainly die without it.

He told Lucy about the night he'd met her mother, about Stella's friend Helen, how she'd confessed to taking a boy from a park, and how he'd been so defeated, so numb, it hadn't even registered, how in his grief-mangled mind there had been no boys worth considering but his boys, but how, now he'd taken Lucy, he could understand Helen's desire to do right by doing wrong. How Lucy's mother, in her own way, had saved him that night, and in Lucy's own way, she'd saved him, too.

He told Lucy about sitting through the trial of the boy, William, of that perfect V on the nape of his neck, of the way the judge tapped the end of one index finger with her pen when she got bored, which was often. He told Lucy how his teachers had taken his class his senior year to that very courthouse to show him how justice worked, how Mrs. Moran, the Social Studies teacher, had walked the students through the adjacent county jail to show them their future if they made any of a host of wrong choices, and Hank had heard his name called out, a jovial, "Hey, Hank! Good to see you, man." How he'd turned to see Mick Campbell locked in a cell, an old Little League friend a year behind him in school who'd taken to crack the previous summer with stunning ferocity and fallen off the face of the Earth. How Hank had found out later that Mick was in jail for bashing in an elderly clerk's head with a tire pump at the 7-Eleven for no good reason at all other than he was high and needed money and didn't like the way she'd laughed at his ride, a kid's go-cart he'd stolen.

He told Lucy how awful he had thought Mick then, but how, now, when he thought about what Mick had done, when he thought about what Helen had done, when he thought about what William had done, when he thought about his father abandoning him at six, when he thought about his mother heading out that door in her red dress, when he thought about sitting in his truck at a work site and listening to wretched country dirges instead of going home to take his wife dancing, when he thought about Lucy's mother not coming home, he understood that decent people were capable of terrible things, that it was just a matter of time, and he wasn't sure if taking her with him was going to be the worst thing he had ever done or the only good thing he'd ever accomplish in this life.

Sometimes Lucy grinned at the sad parts of his stories and frowned or whimpered at the happier snippets, a mismatching Hank found disconcerting at first, and then, when he thought about it, revelatory. "You're right," he said from time to time. "It's all what we make of it."

What he did not tell Lucy: when he was a boy, a few years older than she was now, he and a couple of kids from the neighborhood stuffed a handful of Blackjacks down the mouth of a stray kitten they'd found, lit them, then shoved the cat in the mailbox of an old Black man who lived down the street. Hank didn't stay around to watch—he took off before the firecrackers blew—and when he thought back, it was his leaving, his inability to stay and witness the consequences, that shamed him the most.

What he did not tell Lucy: a few weeks after he and Stella first made love on the very bench seat on which she now sat, he'd done a small job for his dad laying some carpet in a sunroom in one of those big mansions on the lake, owned by the parents of a classmate he didn't know very well. No one was there but the mother. She spent most of the day sunbathing topless on the porch and sipping screwdrivers, catching his eye each time she found him staring, not bothering to cover herself when she did. When he went to collect the check, he'd tried to hide his erection behind his tool bag, but she knew, and she placed her hand there, and he let her, unsure of what came next. And then she dropped her hand and laughed, uproariously, as if his want was absurd, a thing for her amusement, and he'd never known he could feel such a helpless rage.

What he did not tell Lucy: what he saw in the drainage ditch the day the boy, William, mowed down his family.

What he did not tell Lucy: one morning not long before his family had been killed, he'd watched them through the sliding glass door as Stella prepared breakfast, the older boys shoving each other while fighting over that rubber ball, a plate skidding to the ground and breaking. Stella didn't even flinch at the commotion as she continued to strap Davey into his high chair. Her hair, still long even as all the other wives chopped theirs into sensible bobs, draped around her thin shoulders, a storm of curls, and Davey feathered it against his cheek. They were so beautiful, this family he had helped create, and while watching them Hank had been seized by a sense of dread— that he might somehow lose them, that he might never find a way to escape them.

V

They drove that first leg until night became day and then night again, the rolling, lush hills of Alabama and Arkansas giving way to the flat plains of Kansas, the late summer grasses, leached of their green, as pale as the exoskeletons of cicadas Hank used to scrape off telephone poles as a boy and crumble into dust in his hands.

He should have felt some trepidation—any sane man would—of what was to come, of leaving all he knew behind, of taking a girl who did not belong to him. But Lucy: her face pushed to the open truck window to catch the hot breeze, her red hair lashing her freckled cheeks, her mouth half opened, as if the words were right there, waiting to tumble out, if only the right person were willing to listen.

The need for sleep hit him like a punch outside of Vermillion, South Dakota, and they stopped at a Motel 8 that had seen better days. He peeled Lucy, already asleep, off the seat, filled out the paperwork in the front office with the girl draped on his shoulder, and then took off his boots and collapsed fully clothed into the king-sized bed in their room without turning down the comforter, Lucy a ball of heat at his back. Her hair smelled faintly of piss.

He slept hard, not waking until he heard someone beating on the door and yelling his full name. His first thought: Crystal had returned home and called the police and reported him for taking Lucy, and outside a ring of detectives waited, their guns raised and ready. He had no other choice but to open the door, and so he did, his head half turned in anticipation of a blow. A teenage girl in a Motel 8 uniform slouched in front of him, her metallic blue eye shadow hovering across her brow bones like a second pair of eyebrows. "There's something, like, wrong with your kid," she said. The parking lot behind her glistened with rain, the sky pinked by the new sun. A police cruiser idled in the fire lane, its lights throbbing but the siren off.

Hank looked at the bed where he and Lucy had slept; it was empty, the clothes Lucy had worn the day before in a pile on the floor beside his boots. "She's not here," Hank said, his words dumb and slow.

"That's what I am trying to tell you." The girl blinked languidly, as if it took great effort to heft the weight of her eyelids, then pointed toward the pool area adjacent to the parking lot.

He heard her before he saw her, a pained wail—purely elegiac—that sustained its pitch and intensity longer than Hank thought humanly possible, and in it he heard all that could not be said.

"Shit," Hank said. He took off running toward the pool.

Lucy stood on the diving board, her toes curled over the end, as if she were readying to jump. Her head was tossed back, her freckled skin slick with rain. She looked like a feral, wounded creature from the kind of macabre children's books from a century past. The cop stood a discreet distance away, his gaze fixed on his shoes. Hank got the impression Lucy's ululations unsettled the man more than her nakedness.

"She yours?" the officer asked when Hank approached.

Hank nodded, and the cop nodded back, barely lifting his eyes.

Hank was anxious the cop might ask more questions or demand identification, but he seemed disinclined to engage the situation any more than absolutely necessary. Before Hank had one foot on the diving board, the cop started drifting toward his cruiser.

Hank couldn't remember the last time he'd been on a diving board. He was surprised by its narrowness and spring. He poked his arms out for balance and scooted his bare feet across the nubby surface, the cloudy pool water beneath him a sickly green. The minute his hand touched Lucy's shoulder, her mouth hinged shut and she fell silent. She faced him, her tiny chest, all rib and skin, swollen with fury. She looked at him straight in the eye, something she rarely did, then punched him, her nails catching the delicate skin of his lips. He thought a barrage of blows might follow, but she just stood there, her eyes locked with his. Then her mouth began moving, a stream of nonsensical vowels and consonants spewing from her like the solitary language of an infant.

He knew she preferred not to be embraced, but he straddled the diving board and pulled her to his chest anyway, unable to offer her anything else. She stiffened but did not yank away. He held her for as long as she allowed, her babbling tapering into a sort of mewling.

"It's OK," he whispered, stroking her hair. "There aren't really words to explain most things that matter."

Over Lucy's shoulder, Hank could see the Motel 8 girl angling her cell phone for a good shot. He stood as quickly as he could without losing his balance, Lucy in his arms, and turned his back to shield her from the camera.

"Everything good here?" the officer called from his car, his door already swinging closed.

The Badlands came upon them like an apocalyptic dream, the earth erupting in bony-looking formations of Biblical proportions. The desolate landscape demanded a reverent silence, and Hank and Lucy obliged as they took the Loop Road through the national park, Hank chewing on a gas station tuna salad sandwich and Lucy nibbling the edge of a Pop-Tart, the sounds of their mouths' workings eerily loud. They pulled off at the first overlook, Big Badlands, and joined a travel-worn family—two little girls and their parents—on a great slab of gray stone overlooking the ravines stained crimson by the setting sun, which appeared to tumble from the sky in its daily descent. The cool wind pushed at their backs like an unseen hand. Hank held Lucy's arm firmly, not trusting her so close to a precipice. Lucy, awestruck by the scenery, barely resisted his grip. The family chittered, the little girls arguing about some transgression from earlier in the day, the mother fussing over a snapshot no one would smile for, the father, his eyes haggard, ignoring it all as he stared into the distance.

The park brochure said the ravines and canyons and pitted pinnacles were created by a process of deposition and erosion, a giving and a taking away, that had occurred over thousands of years and lifetimes; the place looked forsaken, a wasteland, and Hank was struck by the thought that if a landscape could mirror the terrain of a man's soul, this would be his.

Lucy, however, was enchanted. She gestured toward a bird circling above them Hank had yet to notice, a large bird of prey, perhaps a falcon, its massive wingspan a black gap in the sky. She flapped her free arm excitedly, which she sometimes did for no reason at all, but it seemed clear to Hank that she was mimicking the bird above them, the synapses in her brain firing new connections.

The two little girls, round-faced brunettes in frayed braids, giggled, their eyes darting to Lucy, then each other, and if Hank had been close enough to shove them into the gulch in that moment, he would have done it in a heartbeat.

Lucy didn't notice the girls making fun of her; her face lit with pleasure at the strangeness of the landscape, the proximity of the swooping falcon, and he supposed there was a lesson to be learned in Lucy's obliviousness to the derision of others. "Bird," he mouthed slowly, releasing her for a moment to thrash his own arms like wings. Lucy grinned at him, not past him, and without thinking, he bent and kissed the crown of her head; for a split second, Hank felt like a very lucky man.

That evening they drove for hours without stopping, the bulging Badlands yielding to the plains of eastern Montana, the vast oceans of grasses disorienting to Hank, who had spent most of his life under the sheltering canopy of trees. The open land and strong winds seemed menacing, as if nothing rooted him in space or time, as if the truck might veer off into nothingness at any moment. He was grateful when night fell and stars ruptured the dark sky, and Lucy, who had grown fussy, refusing to sit in her seat and banging her head against the dashboard, wore herself out and fell asleep on the floorboard, the caps of her knees tucked to her chin.

He pulled off at the Columbus rest stop outside Billings to stretch his legs, the cold bite in the night air shocking as he opened the truck door. He'd never known an early fall evening to offer the kind of relief he felt standing in that parking lot, popping the tired joints of his knees, wrecked after twenty years of slamming a knee kicker.

He left Lucy sleeping in the truck and got a Coke out of the vending machine in the rest stop lobby, then stood by the Chevy and sipped it down a few inches, watching a wobbly RV try to back into a parking spot. He told himself he wouldn't even as he dumped into the Coke a shot of bourbon from a pint he kept under the seat. He hadn't had a drink in more than a day, and his hands shook as he tipped the bottle to the can, the bourbon pooling on the aluminum top. It burned his chapped lips.

The truck had started coughing up black smoke just before they'd hit the Montana state line, its volume increasing with the altitude. He popped the hood to take a look, the pen flashlight on his keychain barely casting a glow. He intended to check the belts, the transmission, the oil, but the engine, which he'd built wire by wire with his father, looked as foreign to him as the guts of a time machine, a forgetting that terrified Hank as much as if he'd woken one day not knowing his name.

Hank shut the hood and fished his phone out of his shirt pocket and dialed his father's number, not knowing how he would explain his absence or calling in the middle of the night but needing to hear his voice. His father answered on the second ring, as if he'd been expecting the call, and when Ape said, "Hello," Hank responded only by exhaling.

"It's OK, son," Ape said. "We can just sit here on the phone for a while."

Hank could hear a re-broadcast of the local nightly news in the background, the drone of the weatherman's voice listing the towns—Alexander City, Prattville, Dudleyville, Eclectic—threatened by a coming storm later that week, places that already seemed to belong to another world. Hank fingered the little rubber ball in his pocket, pressed its seam against his thumb.

Hank stood like this—listening to his father breathing, the newscaster's list of the dismal news of the day—until his drink was empty, and his father, somehow knowing it was time to end the call, said, "The bugs are so loud tonight I can barely hear the damn TV." Then, "I'll deal with your mother and keep an eye on your house while you're gone. You go on and do what you need to do."

It came to Hank that what he needed, more than anything, was to stand at the edge of the kind of mountain stream he'd read about in Maclean's book as a boy, to see his reflection in the clear spring water. He held this image in his mind's eye throughout the night as he drove, the sun rising with the mountains, stony beasts lurking in the distance. They were exactly what Hank had imagined, yet somehow different, too, strangely less real, like the mythical beauty of a woman you love sleeping beside you in the morning light.

VI

Enchanted by Crystal's descriptions of the town, Hank had intended to settle on Flathead Lake near Glacier Park, but the truck gave up the ghost an hour past Missoula. There was no logic to the reasoning, considering how far they'd come, but that last leg to Flathead Lake—some fifty miles—seemed an impossible distance.

Missoula sat in the bowl of a valley that once cradled prehistoric Glacial Lake Missoula, its waters upwards of 900 feet deep, the icy skin of its surface tattooing the mountains, surrounding the town with unusual patterns like dense bread cut with a serrated knife. Missoula served as the hinge of five mountain ranges; late-nineteenth-century French traders had dubbed it "Hell Gate" because of the visible graveyard of bones at the narrow eastern entrance of the valley, where Native American tribes strategically ambushed settlers. Hank learned all of this from one of the brochures he found tucked into a display at the gas station while they waited on a tow. He didn't even know where they were, if where they were had a name, or if it was just a collection of scattered cabins and trailers on Highway 83, the scenic route to Flathead Lake he'd foolishly chosen on a whim. The gas station was familiar to Hank, the same kind of gas station found in the small outposts near his hometown, the store selling more groceries—canned foods and prepackaged sandwiches—than gas. A rack of leopard-print, fuzzy slippers was wedged by the bathroom door. A basket of homemade brownies sat on the checkout counter. Four mismatched chairs ringing a slightly concave card table were arranged in the back left-hand corner, and Hank knew that a group of old men gathered there in the morning to sip their coffee and hash out the news from the paper. Some things were the same no matter where you were.

He read every brochure in the display, from fly-fishing adventures to huckleberry-picking hikes to backcountry snow-shoeing trips, while Lucy sat in a red plastic chair by the ATM, shuffling an avalanche of Hank's discarded brochures in her lap. The cashier, a young man in a KISS T-shirt, glared at them from beneath a gibbous brow as he mopped the floor with excruciating slowness, the dirty head of the mop grinding on one square of tile for a good minute.

A petite, pretty woman, fortyish, with long black hair as sleek and shiny as an oil slick, breezed into the gas station, a pair of men's work gloves tucked into the pocket of her overalls, which were rolled at the cuffs. Black, scarred, steel-toed boots peeked from beneath the jean fabric. The outward corners of her eyes dipped low over her cheekbones, giving her a melancholy air, but she spoke brightly and quickly, as if she and the attendant were picking up an ongoing conversation.

"Hey, Darrell," she said to the man. "You working hard or hardly working?"

"Good to see you, Little Wing," Darrell replied. He smiled broadly, the heavy folds of his face surprisingly malleable.

"You call for a tow?" the woman asked Hank.

Hank gestured to the Chevy in the parking lot. Aside from the tow truck and a rusty Corolla with plastic wrap for a back window, there were no other vehicles to be seen. "She finally gave out on me," Hank said. He'd been unreasonably anxious ever since the truck had rolled to a stop, fortunately, in the gas station parking lot. He felt an attachment to that Chevy viscerally, the force of it disconcerting. Hank, of all people, knew better than to put too much stock in things, but he couldn't help himself.

"Nice truck, though nicer if it ran, I suppose." The woman extended her hand, and Hank shook it, her palm as hard as rubber. "Call me L.W.," the woman offered.

"Hank Yost." He smiled toward Lucy, who had yet to look up from the brochures. "This is Lucy." It was the first time he'd introduced her on his own, and it felt dishonest, the casual claiming of her, the protective surge he experienced as L.W. boldly assessed the girl, inventorying Lucy with a frankness Hank found both refreshing and invasive.

"Pretty girl," L.W. said.

"She looks like her mother."

"Lucky you, then," L.W. said, winking so quickly with one eye it looked like a nervous tic. There was nothing nervous about this woman. In fact, she had to be the most self-assured woman Hank had ever encountered, and he wondered if this were a regional thing, a necessary trait women developed in response to the rugged landscape. "You got a destination for that Chevy?"

"I was hoping you could suggest one."

"It's Sunday. Only one garage worth a damn around here, and Frank's won't be open 'til morning. Where you headed?"

"Here, I think," Hank said.

Darrell snorted, said, "Here blows."

"Darrell needs to put down his video games and drag his ass outside and take in the splendor of the world around him. Then maybe he'd have a better appreciation for his home," L.W. quipped, but she smiled gently at Darrell after she'd said it, and he smiled back with such adoration Hank made a show of looking at the snowshoeing adventure flier in his hand.

"I'll get your truck hitched up," L.W. said. "We can figure out the rest from there."

What they'd figured out—or rather, what L.W. decided—was she'd tow the Chevy to her place, and Hank and Lucy could stay in the guest cabin she used as a rental for fly fisherman and outdoors enthusiasts. The cabin was her paternal grandmother's childhood home, the actual place of her grandmother's birth.

"You can see the blood stain on the wood floor in front of the fireplace," L.W. said. "My great-grandmother was a demanding woman, and she wanted a cup of cream, had been screaming for one for hours, and no one had brought it, so she wrestled the midwife and got out of bed to fetch it herself. The walking must have loosened things up. She squatted in front of the fireplace and out came my granny."

"You're making that up," Hank snapped. He was surprised by the adamancy in his voice.

L.W. shrugged. "It's a good story."

Hank watched in awe at the towering fir trees lurching by as they moved north on 83, past Cordon and toward Swan Lake, the mountains on either side of them nothing more than a dark smudge, a giant thumbprint, in the night sky. Lucy sat between Hank and L.W. in the cab of the tow truck, her chest pitched forward, her eyes taking in the curves of the narrow road. Every few minutes, Hank turned around to make sure his truck was still there.

"Where you guys coming from?" L.W. asked. She hunched over the steering wheel, her elbows touching the dashboard, the way a roughneck slumps over a good plate of food.

"Alabama."

L.W. whistled low under her breath. "That's a long ways on the road with a kid that age." She leaned toward Lucy. "You like driving across country with your daddy?"

Lucy, being Lucy, ignored her. The girl kept her eyes on the road, the headlights of the tow truck illuminating only a few feet ahead. Every few seconds, the view shifted into something new.

"How old is she? Four or five?"

Hank, to be honest, wasn't quite sure. He couldn't remember if Lucy had turned four or five on her last birthday, though he remembered the party quite clearly, the pains Crystal had gone to, the house decorated with what seemed like a hundred helium balloons from the dollar store, the homemade chocolate cake in the shape of Lucy's Tonka truck. It had been a good day.

"Four," Hank answered, figuring the year would allow Lucy a little leeway in developmental expectations.

"So I guess she'll be starting school soon."

"I might teach her at home," Hank said, not knowing it was a possibility until he said it.

"That's a lot of work," L.W. said. "I loved being with my kids when they were little, but damn, nothing was sweeter than the sight of that yellow school bus rounding the corner come August."

"Lucy has some . . ." Hank paused, not knowing the right word. "Needs."

L.W. snorted. "Don't they all."

"Special needs," Hank added.

"She mute?" L.W. asked.

"Something like that."

"Philomela was mute. Until she became a nightingale. Then she had a song, at least."

"Who?"

"Philomela," she said. "Sorry, I did a few semesters in Missoula. I learned a bunch of neat and useless stuff." She rapped her knuckles on her skull and smiled. Hank, who was not yet sure the woman wasn't talking down to him, did not smile back.

They drove for another twenty minutes in silence until L.W. pulled off on a dirt road, and the trees parted and the hills flattened into a small meadow, a large A-frame log cabin nestled in its center, a smaller cabin a few hundred feet to its right, a barn to the right of it the color of driftwood in the moonlight.

"I smell snow," L.W. said, craning her neck to get a better view of the sky through the windshield. Hank didn't see a cloud in sight. The sky was the gray blue of an elephant hide, the moon engorged with light.

"The sky looks clear to me."

"The deer this morning in the backyard were skittish, held their ears low to their skulls," L.W. said.

Hank had assumed that Little Wing was Native American with a name like that, and they were on or near—Hank wasn't quite sure exactly where they were—the Flathead Reservation. He guessed reading the animals and the landscape was some kind of ancestral skill passed from generation to generation, so he gave what he hoped was a respectful nod.

L.W. let out a sharp hoot, slapped the gear shift as she parked the truck between the two houses. "You're too easy, Hank Yost. I watched the news before I came to get you and your girl. The first storm of the season is moving in."

Hank bristled, jerking open the cab door, ready to be done with this woman. A chorus of plaintive warbling echoed through the night, the sound so mournful his eyes stung with tears before he'd even completely registered it.

"The dogs talking," L.W. said as she unfolded from the truck. "Wolf hybrids. I breed them. The trustafarians in Missoula love to own a little piece of the wild." She pointed to a large kennel behind the main house Hank had not yet noticed. It was an impressive structure with a wooden building that opened to a twenty-foot fenced run. A whorl of large, wolf-like dogs paced the fence, their necks bunched with thick fur, their eyes reflecting the light of the moon in golden flashes.

"Is that legal, breeding hybrids?" Hank asked.

"You're in Montana now, Hank," L. W. said. "If you own the land, it's legal until the court says otherwise, and even then, the court doesn't always have the last word. Besides, they're mainly Husky—only a bit of wolf. Like most things, it's the idea people like. Very few people would want a true hybrid. They don't make good pets."

Lucy slipped out of the cab, avoiding Hank's outstretched arms, and immediately walked toward the kennel, stopping a few yards away to stare at the animals.

"Ahh, we have a wolf girl," L.W. said. She tossed Hank a set of keys without warning, and he was inordinately pleased with himself when he caught them. "Everything you need— soap, shampoo, towels, sheets, water, some canned food— should be in the cabin. Don't let my granny's spirit bother you. She generally doesn't cause any trouble."

"Spirit?" Hank said, but L.W. was already laughing from a deep place deep inside her chest, the sound clear and joyous, a complete contrast to the muddled cries of the mawkish dogs.

"Hank," L.W. said, still smiling. "I thought we already established that everyone loves a good story."

The cabin was rustic but charming, the couches and chairs in the small den a supple brown leather, each draped with a red-and-green flannel blanket. Hundreds of books lined the floor-to-ceiling bookcase that framed a large window on the south wall. A trio of stuffed beavers grinned from the broad fireplace mantel. Before he could retrieve their things from the Chevy, Hank had to lift Lucy no fewer than five times so she could caress the dentin stumps of all the beavers' orange teeth with her fingertips. Lucy grunted like a pig each time she touched a tooth, and Hank grunted back, the vibrations strangely pleasant against his cheeks. The stain, as promised, was there, a dark pooling on the wooden floors in front of the fireplace. Lucy traced its outlines with her fingers, too, as if she'd heard and comprehended the conversation in the truck. That was the thing with Lucy: sometimes he thought she understood more than anybody he knew, and perhaps the rest of the world was wired wrong and Lucy was the one who saw things as they were meant to be seen.

When she tired of the beavers, Hank took her to the smaller of the two bedrooms and dressed her in the only pajamas she had—a mismatched Hello Kitty top with bottoms sprinkled in fire trucks. She lifted her arms when he asked, balled her fists to punch her hands through the sleeves, and didn't fight him when he worked the neck of the shirt over her head, the webbing of her rib cage beneath her pale skin astonishingly delicate. He remembered making comments to relatives and friends about his sons' incredible smallness and fragility after they were born, how when Stella explained that the soft, shifting plates of a newborn's skull left patches of brain exposed, he hadn't believed it possible. If they were created by some all-knowing being, he'd thought, why in the world would God have chosen such a vulnerable design? But even with his own boys, Hank had never experienced the same titanic sense of responsibility he felt for Lucy now as he watched her chest flutter with the pressure of her beating heart.

He blew a raspberry on her belly button, the small intimacy too considered, too performed. Lucy, who sometimes shrank from his touch in a way that made him worry he'd hurt her, giggled, snatching up her shirt and offering the globe of her stomach to him. So he did it again, and then again, Lucy's giggles mixing with the warbling of the wolf dogs, a sound that, decades later, when Hank took his daily constitutional along Sixmile Trail, would rise around him like a sudden fog.

"What now?" he asked her. If she had an answer, she did not offer it.

The storm came fast and hard, dumping a half a foot of snow in a matter of hours. While Lucy slept, Hank sat in the dark on the leather couch in the den and watched, sipping his bourbon as judiciously as his need would allow, grateful he'd bought several pints at the gas station. The quiet of the snowstorm shocked Hank, who was used to the raucous, brash lightning storms of the South. Within an hour, the moon was extinguished by snow clouds, the tinder-dry grass replaced with a pristine canvas of white, the low-riding Chevy up to its footboard in snow, the entire transformation as hushed as a whisper.

Hank rolled the little rubber ball in his palms while he watched the snow fall throughout the night. L.W. emerged from her house every hour or two, her overalls covered by a cumbersome, knee-length coat. She'd trudge through the thickening snow to the kennel to check on the dogs, then wind her way to the barn, the warm glow of the barn light seeping through the wood planks of the walls. When she turned off the light, the night went black until his vision adjusted again, like the universe blinked its eye.

Hank had never seen snow. Not real snow anyway. The few snows they'd had back home had been nothing more than flurries, smatterings of snow and sleet that melted before hitting the ground, all the children in the neighborhood racing around with socks for mittens, bodies mummified in layers of sweaters and fleece jackets—no parents bothered to waste money on heavy winter coats—their tongues jutted out to catch a taste of the magic before it disappeared. It had tasted, Hank recalled, like nothing.

He must have fallen asleep that way, his face pressed to the windowpane. He woke with a crick in his neck and a tongue of sandpaper, his cheek a numb slab. Lucy had crawled onto the couch and was crouched next to him, a hum brewing in her throat, her eyes glued on the landscape.

"Snow," Hank said, enunciating carefully. He took Lucy's index finger and pressed it against the window. "Cold," he added, shivering to illustrate. Lucy snatched her hand away and lodged her finger into her mouth.

"Too much cold can burn," Hank warned, thinking of all those old westerns he'd read as a kid, men freezing in the mountains, sometimes stripping themselves bare when the hypothermia set in as if their flesh were on fire. "I know it doesn't make sense, but it's a fact. You want to open the door to take a peek?"

Lucy blinked, her finger still stuck in her mouth. She walked over to the front door and waited. When Hank opened the door, the frigid air poured into the cabin, the sensation so sharp his teeth contracted in their sockets. Lucy squealed, her hands flapping in front of her the way they did when she couldn't contain herself. The air smelled clean and woodsy. Hank took a deep draw of it, holding it in as long as he could before exhaling, the heat inside him exiting in the form of a rabbit or maybe squirrel. Lucy grabbed at the mist with both hands. They made a game of it, both of them huffing into the morning to see what secret shapes emerged from their lungs, until the cold became too much and Hank eased Lucy out of the doorframe and back into the warm cabin.

He was fishing in the kitchen pantry for breakfast when he heard a knock at the door. He opened it to two plates of foil-wrapped food resting on a man's wool coat and a backpack spilling a mess of little girls' winter clothes. L.W. was already halfway back to her house, her long black hair studded with snow.

"Hey, thanks," Hank yelled her way. "When can we head out?"

L.W. paused, twisting at the waist to face him. She squinted her eyes against the snow. "When the roads are plowed," she hollered back.

"When might that be?"

L.W. shrugged. "They plow them when they plow them."

One day turned to two and then three, the snow falling in great, random heaves before tapering into a slow but relentless sifting, the roads plugged like an old man's arteries. Lucy became restless stuck in the cabin, often opening the front door the minute Hank turned his back. He had not considered this, the danger of the freezing temperatures. Crystal had double-locked her doors to contain the constantly escaping Lucy, installing a chain lock on the top of each one well out of Lucy's reach. There was no way to get to a hardware store now, not with the roads the way they were and the Chevy dead, so Hank gave in, dressing Lucy in the clothes L.W. had given them, a faded, purple puffer coat two sizes too big and pink boots printed with yellow ducks.

They passed the days stomping through the woods, the landscape as foreign as if he'd been plucked up and set down in a new world, slash pines and blackjack oaks and cottonwoods replaced by towering firs and spruce and Ponderosa pine. Hank kept a notebook and a pencil in his jeans' pocket, and he pulled them out as he and Lucy learned the land, carefully sketching each new tree to compare with the guidebook he'd found on the bookshelf in the cabin. He had not expected the nostalgia he felt for the landscape of his home, the panicked want to know the names of the living things around him. When he crouched on his haunches to draw, Lucy paused patiently beside him, as if she understood the importance of his work, and in those quiet moments, he felt like they were explorers from another era on some grand expedition, though what they were in search of he couldn't say.

Lucy, however, gave herself over to the woods with unstudied abandon. She raced ahead of him as fast as she could in the deep snow, her tangle of a red braid, his first attempt at styling a girl's hair, bouncing from beneath her borrowed knit cap. Occasionally, she disappeared into a drift to spring from its depths a few seconds later in her purple coat like a brave, lone poppy. In the pocket of her coat he'd found the wishbone of a chicken, the rusted blade of a small pocket knife, a toad-shaped eraser with legs whittled from use, a butterfly barrette, a tube of half-used cherry ChapStick, and a page of a fashion magazine folded neatly into a small square so that just the face of the sloe-eyed model showed.

The styling of the coat was at least a decade or two old. The clothes obviously meant something to L.W. for her to have held on to them this long. He thought of his own boys, all their things in their closets back home exactly as they'd left them, how something as simple as a child's coat, the random objects collected in the pockets, could tell the history of a childhood long after it had passed. The idea, when he lingered with it, was a gut punch, the anguish so crushing he wanted to lay down in the snow and give himself over.

But Lucy did not allow much lingering with sorrow, and her laughter, which unfurled from her like a streamer as she slogged along, served as a tether, pulling him deeper and deeper into the woods each day until the burn of his face and toes made him turn back, often with a sleeping Lucy in his arms.

On the final day of that first snowstorm they walked for a very long time, much farther than they had before. Lucy grew bolder, racing through the trees ahead of him, at times hidden from his view by the snow-weighted branches. He would look for her footsteps, the stamp of her pink boots, and follow her path, his heart beating too fast until he caught a glimpse of the purple coat in the distance. Hank recalled a day many years ago, the summer before his senior year in high school, when he'd helped search for a missing woman—the same woman who'd taunted and humiliated him on her sunporch just months before—in the woods off an old dirt road where some of her clothing had been found. He'd hated that woman, the memory of standing there before her, his tool belt shifted over his crotch, the humiliation he'd felt when she'd laughed. He was glad she was gone, hoped she would never be found. But he'd searched all the same, whooping through the trees with his buddies, all of them eager to have their picture taken in the local paper. He couldn't have known then what it meant to lose someone, to have someone taken from you. They never found her, and now, all these years later, Hank couldn't even remember her name.

The memory, the guilt and grief it conjured, made Hank even more anxious, and he called out to Lucy, who'd disappeared in a clutch of spruce, to stop and wait for him to catch up. For several long minutes, he could not see her at all. There was only his breath, the crunch of the snow, the beating of his heart. When he finally spotted her, waiting as he'd asked, he tried not to frighten her with the intensity of his relief. He praised her, patting her head gently, the warmth she radiated a salve. And then he heard the faint burbling and realized she'd stopped only because she'd stumbled upon a wide creek, half frozen, the current of water beneath the patches of ice almost imperceptible.

They were at the creek for some time before he saw it, the dead elk caught in the ice and detritus a few feet upstream, its wide eyes staring skyward. Even dead, it was magnificent in its size and structure—nothing like the scrawny white-tailed deer back home that swarmed the country roads like packs of wild dogs—its rack the length of a short stepladder. Lucy noticed it, too, her sharp gaze studying the bulge of belly, the tender white of the flanks, the orangey bristle of its rump. And the eyes, as polished and round as river stones, staring so convincingly upward, that she, that he, could not help but follow its gaze. Above them: the sun, finally, burning a white-hot hole in the Montana sky.

VII

They plowed the roads the next day. By then, Hank and Lucy had settled into the guest cabin, which seemed as good a place as any to linger. The cabin was booked only sporadically in the winter, the vacationers who visited Glacier during the snow season tending to stay closer to the park. L.W. seemed elated at the prospect of drawing consistent rent for a few months. They settled on a fair rate, and Hank wrote her a check. Just like that he and Lucy had a ready-made home.

L.W. towed the Chevy to her mechanic. The news, as Hank had suspected, wasn't good. It would cost more to fix the engine than the truck was worth, and since its real value was more sentimental than material, and Hank needed a reliable vehicle in the Montana winter, Hank asked L.W. if he could tarp it and keep it on her property until he decided what to do with it, and she agreed. He paid her $200 to drive him and Lucy down to a dealership in Missoula. On his Visa he bought a used GMC Extended Cab with four-wheel drive. With the exception of the down payment on his house, it was the most he'd ever spent on one item, and the first personal purchase he'd made with the insurance money. He surprised himself by not getting upset about using the money. He didn't feel much but relief as he and Lucy drove off the lot, Lucy bouncing on the plush leather seat while she spun the dials on the stereo. His demands that she stop were of no more significance to her than the whistle of the icy wind as it wheezed through her cracked window, which he finally kept shut by utilizing the fancy child locks.

Hank had a job since he was fifteen, first pumping gas at the corner store, then, after he graduated high school, installing flooring for his father, the rhythms of work dictating when he ate, when he slept, when he fished, when he spent time with his family, when he made love with Stella. He'd assumed he'd take over the business from his father, doing the installs himself until his knees gave out and James could step in and handle most of the labor, and then Jake might join them, and eventually Davey, too. That version of the future had been so real for Hank he could see it in his mind's eye like a photo in a scrapbook.

Hank had never considered not working, could not even imagine a world in which it was not required of him. But he no longer needed the money, and he didn't want to leave Lucy—not now, not yet—and so he found himself without a purpose other than the girl. In this way, Lucy became Hank's job.

He bought a secondhand laptop at a pawn shop and then ordered a slew of preschool workbooks and any toy he could find with "learning" in the description. Five large boxes arrived at once, and Hank unpacked everything carefully, organizing the shape sorters and other manipulatives on one of the bookshelves he'd cleared. Most kids would have thought it the mother of all Christmases given the amount of toys and books that arrived. But Lucy, who could be dangerously curious sometimes and suspicious of anything new at other times, grew shy and agitated, peeking from behind one of the leather couches as he unpacked each box.

He introduced one new toy and book each morning, sitting on the floor with her as she played, pointing out colors and numbers and sounds. *Two green triangles, the dog is on the roof, five red circles, the dog is under the car, P is for pig, the dog is beside the bowl.* If anything sunk in, he couldn't be sure, but she didn't run from him or howl like she used to back home, and she even pointed to some of the drawings in the books at what seemed the appropriate time. *Where's the blue bird, Lucy? Can you point to the blue bird?* He worked with her until he couldn't stand the sound of his own voice anymore, until the words he strung together lost all meaning.

Then they had lunch, Lucy sitting across from him at the small dinette table wedged into the corner of the kitchen, watching him as they ate, usually a plate of raw vegetables, her look quizzical, as if she hadn't quite parsed the game he was playing. She lined up her carrots and celery like missiles before she'd eat them, one by one, the process so painfully methodical Hank fought the urge to sweep the food off the table or cram it down her throat. But she usually ate, and on the few occasions she did not, the times she herself pitched the food on the floor, then raged through the cabin, pulling all the new toys off the shelf, ripping L.W.'s books from the bookcase, he'd give in and let her have a sleeve of saltines, her relief so apparent when the package materialized from the kitchen cupboard, he'd felt terrible that he'd ever denied her.

After lunch, he put her down for a nap she refused to take, but they went through the motions anyway, Hank hauling her back to her bunk bed each time she wandered into the den. In the afternoons they hiked through the woods if the weather was nice enough, then worked their way back to L.W.'s to visit with the ancient and blind Appaloosa, the occupant of the barn, and the dogs, who clamored at the sight of Lucy, rubbing their flanks against the kennel fence. A new litter of pups had been whelped since their arrival, and when they were old enough to be handled, L.W. would take the runt—born with a bony nub in place of its right hind leg—into the main house for Lucy to nuzzle while L.W. and Hank talked over hot tea. Lucy hissed each time she held the runt, a reptilian slithering of her tongue, and because he thought it would amuse Lucy, Hank called the puppy Lizard, and Lucy sometimes giggled when he did. So the name stuck, and the dog stuck, too, often spending the nights with Lucy in her bed.

Hank and L.W.'s relationship had taken some time to define itself. In the beginning she brought over a few meals as she had that first morning, knocking at the door and leaving them on the step. Eventually, she lingered at the threshold, chatting about the weather and the animals before wishing him a good day and returning to her house. And then she was sitting at the table with Hank and Lucy as they ate, talking up a storm—the woman liked to talk—her good nature and sly wit softening Hank, who found himself, a few months after his arrival at Swan Lake, sipping coffee with L.W. in her living room each morning before Lucy woke and tea each afternoon to close the day.

She was an attractive woman, a few years older than him, yes, but slender and girlish, even in her men's work clothes. As brazen as she could be, she rarely pushed him for information he did not want to share, and if she had opinions about how he was raising Lucy—and L.W. had opinions about everything— she kept them to herself. If there had been a time in those first months when they were newly learning each other and the awkwardness of novelty might have been read as sexual tension, neither of them chose to test it, and the opportunity passed, providing another in its wake: that of a fiercely deep friendship.

Those afternoons, talking with L.W. in her house, Hank always chose to sit on the couch that faced the large picture window with the view of the Mission Range, the red of the sun exploding like a slow-motion mushroom cloud as it sunk. The sun held another kind of power here, it seemed, as if it could, if inclined, scour the earth clean of all the detritus, human and otherwise. Hank found the prospect reassuring.

At night, after he was certain Lucy was asleep, he pulled on a pair of his new thermal underwear, his warmest pants, a wool-lined shirt, a North Face jacket and gloves he'd ordered online, and went outside, the cold of the night and the moans of the dogs never failing to surprise him with their intensity. If a new snow had fallen, he'd take a small hand broom he kept on the porch and brush the soft layers off the tarped Chevy, then peel back the canvas carefully, folding it on itself like he was re-rolling wrapping paper. He'd climb into the driver's seat and sip his bourbon while he rubbed the boys' little rubber ball between his palms, replaying the day with Lucy.

Before Lucy, Hank had never considered that love of any kind might be a choice. He thought it descended upon you, willing or unwilling, a spirit like the one that inhabited the charismatics in the country churches back home who laid hands on each other and erupted in tongues. It lit itself inside you, and that was that. That's how it had been with Stella, with the boys. But now there was Lucy, and Hank was determined to give her as much of himself as he could, so he spent these nights chronicling their days together, what was accomplished, how he might do better by her.

If he drank too much or too fast, the bourbon unraveling his memories, he'd think of his own boys, what he could have done differently, and then of their mother, the first time he'd laid Stella down on that very bench seat—God, they'd been so young—the way she'd shocked him by opening her thighs eagerly when he raised her hem to her waist, how she sang a snippet of a song playing on the radio as he kissed her through her underwear, and then giggled, more embarrassed by her singing than her nakedness. It had been as awkward and brief as most first times, he guessed.

After a few hours sitting in the truck, he'd usually see L.W. standing in her picture window, likely concerned he'd pass out and freeze to death. He did not acknowledge her, and she did not gesture or try to get his attention, but it was nice, knowing she was there, that someone in the world marked his presence, his absence.

He did not like to burden her with worry, and a few minutes after she appeared, he always obediently exited the truck, rolled the tarp back down over the hood, and went inside to fall asleep on the couch, where he dreamt of atomic sunsets and Stella's cotton panties against her tan skin and Davey crying in the night and Robert Redford standing in silence in the center of a frozen Crow burial ground and Crystal laughing a plume of smoke into the summer sky and a navy stroller abandoned in a meadow and L.W. scrubbing the crimson stain in front of the fireplace, wondering aloud why the blood would never come out.

L.W. had a fondness for stories, particularly her own. She told it often and with a dramatic zeal, which allowed her to distance herself from her own history, so that sometimes Hank had difficulty discerning Little Wing the woman from Little Wing the character.

L.W., as it turned out, wasn't named Little Wing at all but rather Annie Picolli, a name that sounded decidedly un-Native American. When Hank told her as much, she'd laughed, taken a sip of the hot tea she kept in a thermos within hand's reach at all times, and said, "Well, fuck no it doesn't." L.W. was about as Native American as the plastic tomahawk—the last gift he'd received from his father as a child—Hank had dragged around the summer his father left for good, hacking at any poor plant unfortunate enough to expose its defenseless stem, each and every one of his mother's tulip beds massacred. L.W. had grown up in Missoula and had good enough parents as far as Hank could tell, school teachers and soft-core hippies who, according to L.W., were really pedestrian, middle-class suburbanites whose unconventionality began and ended with fringed vests and backyard chicken coops. To their dismay, she took to heart their lessons regarding personal freedom and expression and ran off to Seattle with a boyfriend twice her age when she was fifteen. The boyfriend dubbed Annie "Little Wing" on account of her hair, which did indeed look like the wing of a raven when it splayed against her back, and because she reminded him of the woman in the Jimi Hendrix song, a tune he strummed on his guitar for her often, which is how he got her into bed in the first place. After she'd told Hank that part of her past, he'd asked if he could call her Annie, and though she said no, he often did anyway.

"I was a crazy young thing," she confessed with her signature wink as she told her stories, and he didn't doubt it.

"I learned the hard way soon enough, though. I guess we all do eventually."

She kept the nickname because the vacationers who rented the cabin seemed to like it, thought it added to the romance of their western adventures, and when she guided women's horseback spiritual retreats in the summer months up in Glacier, the Californians delighted in the idea of an authentic Native American leading them on their journeys of awakening. She never claimed to be someone she wasn't, but she didn't disabuse them of their assumptions unless they asked directly; Little Wing made better tips than Annie Picolli.

"Doesn't that piss them off," Hank asked, "if they find out?"

Annie shrugged. "It embarrasses them mostly. That they saw what they wanted to see says more about them than me."

In fact, she made such good money leading tours during the summers and renting out the cabin and breeding her dogs— her house and tow truck were paid for clean and clear—she didn't have to do much more than a half dozen tows a week to live quite nicely. She spent most of her free time caring for the dogs and horse and visiting with Hank. In a few months' time Hank considered her the truest friend he'd ever had, in spite of the fact he did not tell her about Stella and the boys and Crystal. Or perhaps because of it.

Annie had married at seventeen and, by the time she was twenty, had two children with her ex-husband, her lover several lovers after the man who'd wooed her away from her parents. He was an aspiring novelist who earned a living as a plumber. She liked to joke he was good at both trades because he was full of shit, but Hank could tell by the way her jaw stiffened when she talked about him and the fact she never used his name that whatever had transpired between them had been uglier than she liked to admit. Her ex had moved her back to Montana for a gig maintaining the guest facilities at Glacier and eventually hooked up with a metal artist from Missoula who made installations from recycled eighteen-wheeler hubcaps. Annie hadn't heard a thing from him in close to fifteen years.

Her firstborn, a girl named Rose, lost her legs and a forearm to an IED in some desert in Afghanistan, and they'd shipped what was left of her home to Montana. Within a month Rose injected enough morphine to down a bear, and though it nearly killed Annie, she never begrudged her daughter's choice. A picture of Rose in uniform hung over Annie's mantel, the flag they draped over her coffin folded in a triangle and displayed in a wooden-edged glass box on the coffee table. Hank noticed that Annie touched the box often during their talks, not unlike Stella with the boys when they were babies. A reassuring brush of the palm, an anchoring.

When Annie spoke of her daughter, Hank didn't imagine Rose as she must have looked after her injury, or even as she looked before she was deployed—a pretty woman with hair like her mother's and serious blue eyes as clear as the water under ice down at the creek. Instead, he pictured her as a girl in the purple puffer coat he knew, without asking, she'd once owned, the kind of kid who collected both chicken bones and the faces of beautiful women from magazines, her future not yet converging into one narrow path.

Annie's youngest, Leif, a son barely twenty, cooked meth in an old Dutchman camper in Bigfork with his childhood buddy, both of them so ravaged and perpetually tweaked Annie said you could hear their bones rattling in their skin sacks. Every week, like a landlord collecting rent, Leif, a rangy, hoodied kid with greasy black hair and pocked skin and a graveyard of busted teeth, came over to Annie's in his beat-up Volvo station wagon. He went inside for no more than a few minutes, his childhood friend, Hudson, headbanging to some beat in the car, skeletal fingers slapping the dashboard. Leif generally tripped out of the house and down the steps with as many electronics as he could carry, the wires threading through his thighs. He'd dump them into the backseat of the Volvo and take off without ever looking back at his mother, who stood on the porch sipping tea from her thermos as he drove off, the only hint she was upset in the shaking of her hands. The next day, she'd drive over to Apache Pawn in Kalispell, where she had an understanding with the owner, and buy back her things. By Hank's calculations, she'd shelled out at least a few hundred bucks over the course of two months for a five-year-old Gameboy.

"You should call the cops on the little dipshit," Hank often advised, but Annie shut down that conversation fast.

"He could empty this place and I still wouldn't have paid him all I owe him," Annie said.

Leif had been a momma's boy, sickly and small, a late walker, a late talker, a clinger, a whiner, and in her second husband's eyes generally weak and sorry as stepsons went. Annie's husband had liked Rose well enough, a resilient girl who flashed a laid-back smile in the photos Annie had peppered around the house, a savvy kid who knew the best way to avoid trouble was to make yourself scarce. But Leif was an easy target, and his stepfather tended to be cruel to him, which Annie, who desperately wanted to make a home and stable family for her kids, overlooked for far longer than she should have. When Leif was sixteen her husband caught him swiping the keys to his truck, and before Annie could stop him, he'd beaten the boy so badly he put him in the hospital for a week. Before that, though, he'd taught Leif how to smoke meth using a light bulb and the ink tube of a pen.

"I love stupidly and blindly," Annie said when she talked about this part of her past, her tone grave, not playful like when she told her stories of youthful indiscretions. But it didn't take a genius to see there hadn't been much love between her and the men she'd married, and after he bathed Lucy and put her to bed and sat in his truck watching the wide Montana night, his boys' rubber ball warming in his palms, Hank thought about this sometimes, about how hope, no matter how carefully you tended it, could sometimes, in the end, be punishing.

Annie was a kind of Florence Nightingale for sick souls around Swan Lake, and every week or so a drunk or pop-pupiled stranger slept on her couch or tweaked in her sunroom. She rounded them up all over town, but she favored the Rocky Mountain Roadhouse north of the lake. She sometimes parked there at closing time, waiting to get a glimpse of Leif stumbling out of the bar with Hudson, though she never spoke to her son, who acted as if he did not see her. Occasionally she took pity on whatever poor fool lingered aimlessly by the bar door after all the trucks and SUVS had pitched out of the gravel parking lot to stagger down 83. More often than not, the stragglers were tourists or wanderers. If they had someplace to go, they were too wasted to know how to get there. Hank would find them in Annie's living room when he walked over for their morning coffee—apologetic, bleary-eyed drunks tucked under a quilt on Annie's couch, a glass of water and a bottle of ibuprofen on the side table. Most of them had no idea how they got there and were too embarrassed to ask; as a whole, they were exceedingly polite, funereal in tone, like they'd awoken to find themselves in the midst of a somber church service. The meth heads he rarely met. They usually bolted sometime in the night, often stealing anything they could readily find. Hank never could figure out how Annie corralled them into her SUV in the first place; it would have been easier herding cats. Hank and Lucy had driven up 83 more than once on their way to breakfast at Swan Lake Trading Post to discover a tweaker toe-walking along the side of the road, Annie's laptop or radio, even her blender, cradled in their arms like a wondrous newborn.

It was useless to warn Annie of the dangers of picking up strung-out strangers or to ask her to stop. So instead, he tried to keep an eye on her place, sometimes sitting up the entire night when he heard her truck pull in late, searching the shadowy windows of her home for any sign of distress. At first light, Lucy still asleep, he'd turn on the baby alarm he'd put in Lucy's room so he could hear if she stirred, then trudge over, using the key Annie'd given him to let himself in and start the coffee.

In this manner Hank met a host of people, some of them with impressive lives—a federal judge from Missoula with a chin like a bear trap who'd gone AWOL on a guided snowmobile sightseeing tour, a wealthy tech entrepreneur from San Diego who'd taken a sabbatical to finish her book of sonnets about the death of her beloved Wolfhound. But most led the small lives people generally lead: a bank clerk who'd lost her son in a custody dispute, an electrician whose wife left him for his best friend. All of them with their own tales of woe, which they seemed to feel the need to share by way of explanation—*this is how I got here*—when Hank sometimes drove them back, if Annie had a tow call, to wherever they had to go, Lucy strapped in her booster seat in the extended cab.

When Annie showed up at his cabin door early one morning in mid-March, Hank assumed she'd collected another random drunk from the Roadhouse who needed taking somewhere. He was surprised to see Leif standing in front of the barn, sucking a cigarette so aggressively Hank marveled it didn't launch down his throat.

"I found him passed out on the steps in middle of the night. He was too messed up to get his key in the door. He has no idea where his car is or how he got here. He's lucky the dogs made such a ruckus, or he'd have frozen to death. I asked him to stay, but he won't. I got a call down in Condon, a pregnant lady with a minivan full of kids, I can't get out of. You think you can get him home?"

A purple bruise ringed Annie's eye, her upper lip swollen and cut. Hank felt his own hands tighten into fists; there was no need to ask what happened, and if he tried, Annie would lie anyway. Hank looked over his shoulder at Lucy, who was sitting on the living room floor with a Hungry Hippo game in her lap. "Sure," he said. "I can get him home."

"He and Hudson had a fight. He won't tell me over what, but it must have been a doozy. Be prepared—he's in a foul mood."

"Is he ever in a good one?"

Annie's eyes tugged down even farther on the outer corners, her tic when irritated. "Just a ride, Hank. No lecturing. This is the most he's had to do with me in three years. I don't want to ruin it."

Leif, in Hank's estimation, had long passed ruination.

"He's my son, Hank," Annie added.

What else was there to say?

Leif didn't talk for the first five minutes. He climbed into the truck sans greeting and was overly particular and huffy about the giant black duffel bag he crammed under his feet in the floorboard. Hank assumed half of Annie's valuables were packed inside that bag, and she'd be driving over to Kalispell in the morning with most of her week's earnings to fetch her things back.

Without directions, Hank just turned north on 83 toward Bigfork. Annie's property was sandwiched by Swan Lake and Flathead National Forest, and there weren't many ancillary roads. Eventually, he would get Leif close enough to where he wanted to go.

When Leif did speak, he first addressed Lucy, who'd insisted on bringing along the Hungry Hippo game. She mashed the same hippo's mouth open repeatedly and seemed content doing it. Lizard lay next to her, his tongue furiously working the snowballs out of his paws. For a three-legged puppy, he managed to get around surprisingly well. Wherever he went, Lucy was not far behind.

"I had that game," Leif said. "The marbles always got stuck. Do your marbles get stuck?"

Lucy growled, something she'd picked up from the dogs, and Leif laughed. "That's about how I felt." He lit a cigarette. Hank let the smoking slide but rolled down the passenger window. When Leif drew his hands to his mouth to take a drag, Hank could see his fingernails were gnawed down past the quick, the fingertips pulpy.

"She's cute," Leif said. "Looks like that girl from that musical, with all the red hair. I always wanted red hair. Redheads, like, glow or something. Like they're lit from inside. Like a human ornament or a lighthouse. My hair, this black crap—it eats all the light. Sucks it all in and obliterates it." He popped a tip of a finger in his mouth and chewed hard.

Hank had no idea what Leif was saying. The kid grew animated as he spoke, his free hand twitching, ash from the cigarette powdering the dashboard, and Hank gathered it was important to Leif that Hank understood, so Hank said, "Yeah, man. I can see that." Leif actually smiled. Hank caught a glimpse of what he must have looked like before, and it made him heartsick for Annie, who surely saw that other son each time she laid eyes on Leif.

The lake's surface shimmied with the early morning light, the snow glittering on the top of the Mission Range. "When I was your age," Leif said to Lucy, gesturing dramatically toward the lake, "I used to imagine that on the other side of those mountains was a magical, tropical world with fan-fucking-fabulous coconuts the size of boulders, and monkeys hanging from these prehistoric-looking palm trees, and the sun so warm your skin felt like melted butter or some shit, you know?"

He turned to Lucy, who, Hank could see in the rearview mirror, had stopped torturing the hippo to stare at Leif. "That's the best part of being a little kid. You think up stuff like that, and it makes total sense. You ever think of stuff like that?"

Lucy blinked, then tugged her ear three times.

Leif looked at Lucy as if they'd made some kind of profound connection. "Exactly," he half sighed. "But you know what's over there? Another lake just like this one. Only bigger. Same thing is on that side that's on this side. There is an island in that lake, though, at least. An island of wild horses. That's the name. Wild Horse Island. So that's sort of magical, right? But then I got to thinking, what's the use of being a wild horse on an island? Where can you go when you only got a little acre of land? What good is that? You might as well be trapped on one of those rich fuckers' big-ass ranches. If it was big enough, you wouldn't even know you weren't wild, which is about the same thing as being wild, right? It's perception, kid, and the dude in charge of perception is in charge of it all."

Then, to Hank, "So you with my mom now? You the new one?" He leaned into Hank when he said it. He smelled of smoke and something rotten, like uncooked meat left in the garbage for a few days. His pupils: black disks floating in a sea of red. He was sweating buckets, his jeans so wet he looked like he'd pissed himself. Hank, who was slightly hungover himself, felt his stomach flop.

"It's not like that."

"It's always like that with her."

"You should cut your mom some slack."

Leif clutched his throat with one bony hand, imitated choking. He said, "That's such a big wad of shit to swallow, I almost choked on it."

Lizard starting barking at a man walking on the side of the road, and Lucy joined in merrily.

Leif turned to admire Lucy again, said, "I like your kid. You're all right, kid."

Hank thought of telling Leif about Stella and the boys—or maybe he'd change the story to just Stella, three dead sons too much for anyone, especially Leif, to handle—to remind this boy to appreciate his mother, the gift of life. But when people wanted to be pissed off and angry at the world, they generally resented anyone trying to persuade them not to be pissed off and angry at the world, and really, Hank didn't want to give this boy any part of his family, so instead he said, "Let's focus on getting you home instead of talking."

"Sure," Leif said. "Absolutely. Okey dokey."

The drive north of Swan Lake to town always unnerved Hank. Swan Lake, ten miles long, a mile wide at its broadest girth, and windy as an open prairie, loomed on the left. A stony bank towered on the right of the road, as if some giant hand had torn a path where none should exist. Logging trucks barreled south, their beds stacked with hardwoods, the drivers reckless and road-greedy. Expensive lake homes, even more opulent than the ones he had grown to loathe back home, nestled along the forested shoreline, their massive windows glinting in the sun. Hank thought of those movies he used to watch as a boy, of dirt-dusted scouts hiding in the hills with a scrap of glass or metal to signal to their men in the distance. Somehow, those images from old films seemed less fantastical than the behemoth stone-façade mansions.

"Did she tell you what she did to my father? How she ran him off? Or how she killed my sister?" Leif said. His silence had lasted less than two minutes, his fried neurons firing all kinds of uncontrollable connections. The boy, Hank estimated, would likely be dead within a year.

"An IED killed your sister," Hank said.

The truck was veering toward the water before Hank realized Leif had grabbed the steering wheel. There wasn't much room for error on the narrow road, and they were fully in the opposite lane before Hank whacked Leif hard enough in the jaw that the boy let go. Lucy howled in laughter from the backseat, her booted feet kicking the console.

"Fuck, man," Leif said. He clutched his face with his hands, his cigarette miraculously still fastened between two fingers. He looked genuinely dismayed that Hank had struck him.

"Just tell me when to turn," Hank said. They passed the Swan Lake Cabin Rentals, the highway boomeranging away from the water into heavily treed, level land. After Johnson Creek, Leif poked a fleshless finger to the right, and Hank pulled off onto a dirt road, the packed snow pushed to each side like a crude luge track. They'd had a few warmer days the past week, the road's icy crust thawing a little during the day to ice hard again in the night. The tires strained to grip the surface, spinning any time Hank accelerated too quickly. He drove at an old man's tempo, the road tapering as they moved closer to Forest Service land, the firs, heavy with spring snow, tunneling the road. It would have been a mystical fairyland if it weren't so nerve wracking to drive it; one agitated pump of the gas and they'd be lodged in a snowbank.

Finally, they came upon a large, log A-frame with a long drive shooting past it, which led, after much careful maneuvering on Hank's part, to Leif and Hudson's place: a rusted-out Dutchman teetering on cinder blocks in the heart of the forest. From what Annie said, the boys were essentially squatting, the owner visiting for only a week each summer. Hudson was taking in the spring sun in the front yard in a fold-out lounge chair sunk to the webbing in snow. His eyes darted from the sky to the road to the camper to the trees with such rapidity Hank thought they'd spin out of their sockets. He wore a sweatshirt, faded boxers, and unlaced hiking boots. His skin was tinged a strange blue, like he'd been dipped in watery ink.

Leif rocketed out of the truck, throwing his duffle bag to the ground, and pounced on Hudson, who went tipping over backwards in the snow. "You fucking fucker," Leif yelled. "Where is it?" He kept shoving his hands down Hudson's boxers and shirt, as if he were hiding his stash there in the flimsy cotton. Almost naked, Hudson was impossibly skinny; it looked as if he'd been turned inside out, his engorged liver a boulder jammed behind a claw of ribs, his spine a bony ladder to his neck, where it barely supported a head oversized for his malnourished body, as out of proportion as a baby's. Hank let them roll about in the snow to blow off steam and was about to get out of the truck to break things up when he realized the two boys were no longer fighting but rather laughing.

Lucy watched closely, as she watched all things, then clapped enthusiastically. "You hopeless optimist," Hank said, and she grinned at him as if she understood the complexity of the moment, the need for humor in the face of absurdity. Smiling like that, her Hungry Hippos in her lap, Lizard asleep beside her, she looked like she could be any regular kid, maybe even Hank's kid.

VIII

Hank was an hour into his nightly ritual in the truck when Annie pried open the frozen passenger-side door and climbed in beside him. They sat there for a long moment, staring straight ahead at the dogs, who thrashed each other in the moonlight, their plaintive, warbling cries reverberating inside the cab. That one wolfish plea summed up all Hank felt.

Annie sighed, hooked the heels of her steel-toed boots on the dashboard. She tilted her head back and studied the pitted roof.

"You should put in a skylight," she said, breaking the silence. "Maybe a sunroom in the truck bed. As much time as you spend in this thing, might as well turn it into a home."

"Hush for a minute, Annie," Hank said gently, and she did, sliding her small, warm hand into his. The boys' ball was gripped in his other hand. He didn't feel like explaining what it was or why he had it, so he tucked it into his coat pocket.

They sat for a while, their breath mingling in the cold air, their hands twined in commiseration. Hank wondered if he'd ever touch a woman again in a way that did not feel like an apology.

"The job was a beast," Annie said. "There was a wreck on the way down and it took two hours to clear 83, and then that pregnant lady blamed me, like it was my fault she had to sit in the cold for half a day, that she chose to patch her tire instead of buying a new one. I swear, the hormones cooked her brains. I don't remember being like that when I was pregnant with Rose and Leif, but then again, you always remember a better version of yourself." She leaned into Hank, rested her head on his shoulder. She was polite enough to divert her eyes from the bottle of Jack wedged between his thighs. "What was Lucy's mom like when she was pregnant?"

Hank thought of Crystal riding in a string of semis across the country, Lucy a little bean in her belly. "Brave," Hank said. "Really brave. Maybe a little impulsive, too."

"I'm sorry it didn't work out for you guys." Annie surprised him by plucking the fifth from between his legs and taking a long pull and then another, holding the bottle to the moonlight to admire the swirl of amber before handing it back to him. "You're a good dad to Lucy, though. She's changed a lot since you got here. She's a sweet kid. She's going to turn out as good as any of us."

"Oh God, I hope she fares better," Hank said, and they both laughed.

"My boy's really sick, isn't he?"

Hank tucked his chin over Annie's forehead. He could feel her shivering, could sense the tears she must have been crying for some time now.

"He is."

"He took it," Annie whispered.

"Took what?"

"It's not worth anything to anybody but me. He hates me that much. He was such a special little boy. But so needy, Hank. A bottomless pit. You never think about those things when you imagine your babies. How they might be broken, how you might break them."

"Took what, Annie?"

"I didn't feed the dogs today. That's why they're so fussy. I guess I should feed them."

"For God's sake, Annie."

"The flag. Leif took Rose's flag."

Hank needed to run.

He'd finished the Jack, and that hadn't helped. He'd tried sleeping, but the dogs were moaning at the moon. He couldn't think of anything to make it stop—the gnawing ache—except running, which he hadn't done in months, not since the day Crystal disappeared.

It took him an hour to find his running shoes, one of the few things he'd had in his truck the night they'd left Alabama. Lucy had shoved each one down a separate air vent in his bedroom, and he would have never found them if she had not tied the laces in decorative bows through the metal slats. The hour hunt helped sober him up, which was a good thing because the ice-packed driveway was as slick as goose grease. He was bulky in Carhartt pants and his coat, but he somehow felt lighter the faster he moved. Momentum kept him upright, and after a few strides, Hank glided down the drive to the gravel lane that led to the main road.

Hank had read once about young boys from some faraway country who ran as many as twenty miles a day, checking on the cattle in the pastures. He'd been enamored of the idea of running—all day, nonstop—lingering just long enough to check on what needed checking on, life measured, literally, by each step. Hank doubted he'd ever run twenty miles in a single day, but he felt good, the bitter cold wonderfully numbing, his feet almost levitating on the ice. He gave a little hoot, and the dogs moaned back, so he did it again—*hoot, moan, hoot, moan*—a guttural beat, his heart syncing to the rhythm.

And then he was facedown, the driveway rising to meet him with an icy fist, his nose exploding in a bloody plume. He lay there for a minute, pumping blood into the ice, the blood cooling and then freezing in ornate flourishes. The ice eased the pain in his nose. He gently pressed his face into the earth; it coughed his breath back at him in frosty gusts.

There was, he knew, nothing left to do but get the flag.

He drove slowly—he'd had too much to drink to be on the road—the lake a black hole beside them. He knew he shouldn't be driving Lucy in this state, but he couldn't take her over to

Annie's without Annie asking questions, and he worried if he left her behind she'd let herself out the cabin. And so there Lucy was, wide awake in her booster seat, her pointy little face lost in the collar of her purple coat. Lizard sat alert beside her, his tongue lapping at the overheated air. Lucy had woken without much of a fuss, and if she'd been alarmed by the condition of Hank's face, she didn't show it.

It was late, half past two. Nights were days, and days night, and the whole calendar a timeless loop for meth heads like Leif, and sure enough, the Dutchman was lit up like a Christmas tree, jarring metal music pounding its walls. Hank parked a few feet from the camper, cut the engine, checked Lucy's straps to make sure she was buckled in tight, then and told her and Lizard to stay put, that he wouldn't be more than five minutes.

Locks festooned the metal door, but the old RV was thin as a tin can, and one swift kick punched the door open. The smell—like dirty diapers and cat piss—nearly knocked Hank to his knees. They'd gutted the thing, pulling out the fold-out couch and the table and the cabinets, leaving only the stove. The floor was covered in fast food wrappers and Big Gulp cups and cold medicine boxes and stained coffee filters. Graffiti, math equations and nonsensical charts with columns of half moons and stars, mottled every wall. A gigantic, penned angel with fangs soared over Leif, who perched on the edge of a filthy recliner, intently staring at a TV playing an infomercial on juicers. Hudson, completely naked now, his pale body crusted in scabs, jittered in a corner, rearranging a stack of books, pausing every few seconds to jerk to the music. If hell existed, Hank was pretty certain this was what it looked like.

"Holy fuck," Leif yelled. "Why'd you do that to the door?"

Hank waded to the stereo and yanked the cord from the outlet. Hudson didn't seem to notice the music had stopped; he gyrated around the tower of books until some detail about their ordering upset him, and then he knocked them down to restack them.

"Where's the flag?"

"What flag?"

"Just give me the fucking flag."

Leif's eyes darted to a metal trash can sandwiched between a wall and a twin air mattress. Both of them leapt for the can at the same time, Hank easily besting Leif, who couldn't have weighed much more than a hundred pounds. "It's the dust of angels," Leif screamed. He hugged the bottom of the can like it held the key to the mysteries of the universe. Hank tried to grip an edge to peer inside.

"You burned Rose's flag?" The can contained nothing but a few inches of ash and soot.

"We had a funeral out back. A real one. Not some military, government-controlled bullshit. The angels played their trumpets." Leif trilled a mock horn, thumping his fingers against imaginary keys.

The mattress was half inflated, its give making it difficult to move, but Hank still managed to pin Leif in a matter of seconds, his legs straddling the boy's chest, his hand wrapped around Leif's ropy throat. Leif thrashed like a landed fish. He clawed at Hank's face. Hudson giggled from across the room. Hank tightened his grip, his fingers digging into what little flesh was there. It terrified him, how good it felt.

And then Leif went limp, his fight gone in the space of a breath. He stared at Hank, his pupils the size of saucers but his eyes wide and calm, their expression as trusting as a child's. "It's OK," Leif said. He closed his eyes as if bracing for a blow.

All Hank could think: Why his boys?

The anger was gone, and in its place a crippling wave of grief. Hank realized he was weeping, awful, ragged sobs. He released Leif's neck, cupped his face in both palms. Leif's beautiful face! It was wrecked, his cheeks cadaverous, his skin pitted and pocked, but there was something of the boy still there. Hank leaned over, pressed his lips to Leif's brow as he'd done with his own sons a thousand times.

Leif flinched. His eyes popped open. "What the fuck, man," he said, wiping at his brow.

Hank patted Leif on his cheek as if they'd finished a friendly wrestling match, then rose as nimbly as his knees and the mattress would allow. He was out the door before Leif could start hurling a string of curses and half in the truck when he noticed that the passenger door hung open, the backseat empty, Lucy and Lizard gone.

IX

Hank had lost Jake once in a Walmart. It was Davey's first Christmas, and Jake, who'd been the baby for a long time, was struggling with having a new brother in the house. He'd grown petulant and fitful, screaming at his mother for no reason, jabbing the baby with his fists when he thought Stella and Hank weren't watching. Of all the boys, Hank worried about Jake the most; he still wasn't reading well by the end of second grade, and nothing came as easily for him as it did for James, who breezed through school without cracking a book. Jake didn't have many friends other than his older brother. When Hank asked him once who he played with at school, he'd offered a long list of names Hank eventually recognized as characters from a cartoon. If he could have crawled back into his mother's belly and lived there until he was twenty, Hank suspected Jake would have gladly.

Hank was in a hurry at the Walmart that day, the lines outrageously long and Stella's shopping list for Christmas dinner even longer, and when Jake threw a fit over a Lego set Hank refused to buy, planting his butt in the middle of the toy aisle, Hank turned and started walking, assuming Jake, who was anxious in public, would follow.

He didn't. By the time Hank noticed Jake wasn't sulking behind him and retraced his steps to the toy section, his son was nowhere to be seen. Hank looked up and down the aisles, alarm swelling inside him as he called Jake's name, politely at first so as not to disturb other shoppers, and then, after fifteen or so minutes, like a crazy man, his fear metastasizing into a kind of frenzy he'd never experienced before, every nerve in his body alive with it.

He hadn't thought to ask Guest Services to call on the intercom—the first thing Stella would have done if in his shoes—until after he found Jake in front of the fish aquariums, enthralled by the flouncing, iridescent tails of the guppies. Hank didn't say a word. He hauled off and slapped his son with an open hand. He connected with Jake's cheek hard enough to snap his head back. Hank had spanked the boys, gentle swats on the rear end, but he'd never hit them, not like this.

Finally, Jake looked appropriately scared. He belted out a wail, and when he stopped crying, Hank told him to remember the fear, to hold it to him, because a good measure of fear served us well in this world. Hank bought his son a half dozen guppies and an aquarium they couldn't afford, and Jake, tear streaked and sleepy, hugged the plastic bag of fish to his chest like a hard-earned prize the entire ride home.

Hank would never forget it, the panic, the overwhelming awe at the sight of Jake in front of those aquariums. They'd been spared some calamitous fate that less fortunate families suffered. He'd been weak with it, the pure joy, as if someone had let the pressure out of his veins. He couldn't have known then how deceptive the feeling was. One moment looking away: the handful of seconds it took to bend over and retrieve a sippy cup from a sidewalk.

This time, with Lucy wandering somewhere in the forest, Schmidt Creek lacing its way into Flathead Park less than a hundred yards away from where Hank now stood, the fear was different. He understood that the possible outcomes—Lucy found safe, Lucy found facedown in the creek—depended little on him and more on chance, that all the choices he carefully considered—should he turn right or left after the giant cedar, go toward the creek or away from it?—were illusory mental acrobatics. This truth was the most terrifying thing of all.

He plowed on anyway, deeper and deeper into the forest, the weak light from the flashlight he kept in the truck barely patterning the snow. Every few minutes he pulled his phone from his pocket and dialed 911, but there'd been no reception in Leif's driveway when he'd first discovered Lucy missing, and he knew it was unlikely he'd find service further in the woods. Branches grabbed at his clothing and face as he moved, wet snow pelting him in soft punches. He tried tracking her, but every tree, every stump, every expanse of snow looked the same as the last. He gave up searching for her footprints and went by instinct instead, moving along the creek toward the Forest Service land. He called her name as he walked, his throat raw from yelling. But Lucy didn't respond to her name like a typical kid, couldn't or wouldn't register the urgency in his voice, the necessity of a reply.

How could he have left a little girl alone in a truck in the middle of a freezing night?

When the flashlight gave out, he sat down on a stump to remove and reinsert the batteries, hoping to coax more juice out of them. The bank along the other side of the creek rose high and sheer where Hank sat, and when he called Lucy's name this time, it threw his words back at him, the echo rippling in the quiet. He listened for several minutes, hoping to hear Lizard, but could make out only the snow falling from the trees. It had been almost an hour since he'd realized she was gone. He'd struggled to make his way through the dense woods; as little as she was, surely she'd be moving even more slowly. She couldn't have gone far. But a hundred yards might as well be a hundred miles; Hank wasn't going to find her.

Why not here? he thought. Here was as good a place as any. He eased down off the stump and smoothed a patch of snow. He lay on his back, the moon shifting behind the trees above him. The Montana sky looked like every sweeping, symbolic shot in the scores of movies he'd watched over the years. It was everything he'd imagined as a boy. He closed his eyes and crossed his hands on his chest and waited.

After a few minutes he felt foolish and a little drunk and cold. Cold-cold and not hot-cold like he told Lucy she might feel in situations like this. He sat up, shook the flashlight to life, and was bracing himself to stand when he saw her. Lucy, her red curls matted to her face, her purple coat dusted in snow, less than five feet away, Lizard beside her. A girl and her dog.

"Hey," Hank said softly.

He patted his thigh. She trudged over to him, slumping into his lap. She was shivering and wet but seemed to be more cold and tired than anything else. She burrowed her head into his chest, shoved her hands, her mittens soaked, into his coat pockets. They held each other for as long as Lucy would tolerate it, Hank singing a lullaby he pieced together from the fragments of lullabies he knew, Lizard calling to the elusive moon. Lucy howled, too, a perfect imitation, and then waited for her voice to answer back.

"C'mon," Hank said. "Let's get you home."

When she pulled her hands from his pockets, she took the boys' little rubber ball with her. She studied it in her palm for a split second before hurling it—it was a ball, after all—toward the creek. Hank watched its arc in the moonlight, the gentle plop as the snow absorbed it. There was no use, he knew, to look for it now. He made a mental note of where they stood: the bend of the creek, the shape of the towering bank. With any luck, Hank thought, he might find it after the thaw.

Jennifer S. Davis is the author of two previous collections of short stories, *Her Kind of Want*, winner of the Iowa Award for Short Fiction, and *Our Former Lives in Art*, a Barnes and Noble Discover Great New Writers selection. Originally from Alabama, she lived most of her adult life in the American West before settling in Baton Rouge, LA, where she lives with her husband and four sons and serves as Director of the Creative Writing Program at LSU.

ACKNOWLEDGMENTS

I would like to thank my husband, Eric Sorensen, for his steadfast encouragement and his commitment to making space for my writing in the midst of chaos, as well as my four sons, who have taken many, many Sunday drives with their father on River Road to give me a few hours to work. I am incredibly thankful for my parents, Joe and Lois Davis, who made this privileged life of writing and teaching possible and who taught me the most important lesson of all: to have faith. I am also immensely grateful to Pallavi Rastogi and Lara Glenum for their insightful comments during the editing process. These stories would not exist without the research support I received from LSU. And finally, I want to express my gratitude to Press 53 for giving my stories such a generous home.